Sap and Green People

By

Patricia L. Dick

They will still bring forth fruits in old age.
They are ever full of sap and green…
Psalm 92, RSV

© 2002 by Patricia L. Dick. All rights reserved.

No part of this book may be reproduced, stored in a retrieval system, or transmitted by any means, electronic, mechanical, photocopying, recording, or otherwise, without written permission from the author.

ISBN: 1-4033-7714-6 (e-book)
ISBN: 1-4033-7715-4 (Paperback)

Library of Congress Control Number: 2002095974

This book is printed on acid free paper.

Printed in the United States of America
Bloomington, IN

1stBooks – rev. 11/11/02

My special thanks to my husband, Fred, who, most importantly, set me up to feed my words into the computer and, all too often, got the computer to spit them back out. He also urged me on (and on and on!) and buoyed me up and critiqued my copy. Never could I have realized my dream of becoming an author and publishing a book had it not been for him.

Many thanks to my daughters for encouraging me,

> the Ragdale Foundation's community for hosting me while I edited,
>
> my friends Nita and Georgia for reading crude copy without flinching,
>
> Dorie and especially Jeanette for calling errors to my attention,
>
> Henry for providing ideas,
>
> Kathleen Finneran, a former student and author for setting an example,
>
> Kathleen, Carol, and Mike for recommending me to Ragdale,

and P.E.O. "sisters" who read my copy and cheered me on.

And my sincere thanks to anyone who afforded me readership by purchasing my book. I pray that it will please, touch, inform them.

THE CHARACTERS

<u>Independent-living residents</u>

Bill and Marg Davis, who recently move into the Haven at Oak Hill

Henry and Georgia Graham, their friends, also residents of the Haven

Norbert Blair, a former banker who becomes active in Haven affairs

Jack Clausen, a retired college professor who also becomes active

Rob Rymer, Jack Clausen's technician

Bud Walsh, another technician

<u>Convalescent-living residents</u>

While residents are given names,
those persons are representative
rather than instrumental to the plot

<u>Assisted-living resident</u>

Gloria Fields, a stroke victim

<u>Volunteer Ice Cream Parlor helpers</u>

Grace Kuhn, manager

Bill Davis

Dell White

Daisy Charlotte

Mike McGuire

Betty Mansfield

George Steiner

<u>Haven staff members</u>

Harry Wright, the Haven administrator

Pat Marsh, Haven nurse

<u>Members of "The Girls" group</u>

Bertha Brinkley

Essie Brinkley

Elaine Bruce

Eliose Brady

Joan Cutler

Myra Kelly

Marti Morton

Ruth Roberts
Gail Russell
Moira Sheer
Mary Spritzer

Sap and Green People

Dressed only in her underclothing, Margaret Davis stood in front of the full-length mirror that hung on her bathroom door and looked at herself ruefully. More particularly, she was studying her legs. "Ugly!" she said of them. "Positively ugly."

Wrong from the beginning, she'd decided when she was thirteen and old enough to realize that legs were important to girls and hers bent out just below the knee. And since then, they'd acquired knobs and indentations, bleachings and discolorations, scars and scales.

"But I don't care," she insisted. "I simply don't. They've held me up and walked me around for over seventy years, and there's no use being depressed by them at this point in time."

With the palms of her hands, Marg pressed in her tummy—as far as it would go. "I could do without this though," she lamented. "The legs I can stocking, but my stomach defies correction. Can't do anything about it now so I don't care about that either." In truth, though, the pouching tummy bothered the heck out of Marg.

With her left hand, Marg yanked up the left strap of her bra, and with the right, the right strap. "If I could keep 'em way up here," she muttered, "they'd pull out a roll around my middle, one of them anyway, which would substantially help my appearance. But my bustline would look ludicrous, artificial and ludicrous. Worse, my shoulders couldn't stand the pressure," and she let her breasts drop, putting considerable strain on her bra straps momentarily.

"Egads," she heard Bill say from behind her, "if I'd known what was going on in here, I'd have slipped in earlier. Wow!"

"Oh," Margaret moaned as she crossed to Bill and put her arms around him, "when did I get like this?"

"While I was acquiring this," he said as he patted his stomach, "and losing this," and he stroked the crown of his head where the hair tended towards sparse. "But we've still got each other and our family and our nice, little apartment," he reminded Marg, and

Sap and Green People

the two clung together as they marveled again at how fortunate they were to be happy, well, and alive.

Bill and Marg had worked through an up-and-down courtship; been separated by war, the second Bill was called upon to fight; moved away from their families to another part of the country; raised three children; pursued two careers and shared a third, and through it all, they'd given of themselves and served, served, served. Causes, movements, and persons. They'd done all that and more over the course of the fifty-one years they'd been married, while providing a peaceful home for their three children and seeing that they were suitably educated.

Glad they had done those things and now in their 'twilight' years, aware that their bodies where changing, that time was running out for them, Margaret and Bill limited their service commitments and gave a larger degree of their attention to 'fitness', family duties and doings, keeping in touch with friends, and living quietly in the Haven at Oak Hill, the seniors' community in St. Louis, Missouri, to which they'd moved two years previously.

Sensitive to the fact that Margaret might be feeling somewhat depressed, Bill asked, "Movie this afternoon, if you ever get dressed? Botanical Garden? Farmers' Market?"

"I'm okay," Margaret assured him, "and I've got things to do: iron, make up a shopping list, tend to correspondence with which you never help, make telephone calls, mend. A nice thing about living here is that you don't have maintenance responsibilities anymore while I have…"

"…less to do, also," Bill said matter-of-factly. "Considerably less than you used to have, and I'm glad of that." Kissing the top of Margaret's head, he turned away. "You get some of your jobs done and I'll pay bills," a subtle reminder of his major responsibility, one Margaret never helped with, a rub she picked up on immediately. "Then we'll take a little snooze and a walk and go over to Dave's or Susan's or Carrie's, whichever you choose. To see how everyone and the grandpets are doing."

Having loved each other and lived together for so many years, that was how Margaret and Bill Davis had

Sap and Green People

learned to accommodate each other, readily, sensitively, unselfishly. Not perfectly, to be sure, but very well.

Patricia Dick

The dentist was scheduled to spend the day in the Haven at Oak Hill clinic, so resident Henry Graham, a jovial, popular volunteer, was to do what he did every Wednesday: call for and deliver residents of the seniors' community who were scheduled to see the dentist and needed help getting there.

The dentist's office was located on the first floor of the Haven's Manor, the six-story building which housed offices; a large and small dining room; meeting rooms; a workshop, craft room, and library; other facilities; and the over three hundred persons who leased studio, one-room, and two-bedroom apartments.

Because Henry, who was compulsively punctual, arrived at the clinic a full twenty minutes early and found it deserted, he strolled over to a lounge in the adjacent Assisted Living Building to find someone to talk with for, say, the next eighteen minutes. Henry didn't see well, thanks to that scourge, macular degeneration, which relegates millions of older persons, fat or thin, nasty or pleasant, penniless or monied, to impaired vision. "Totally democratic, that macular," Henry would say of the disorder, and you

Sap and Green People

gotta give her credit for that," which always got a laugh. As well as being overly-prompt and somewhat-blind, Henry was trim, red-headed, popular, and humorous.

Spotting what looked like several persons across the lounge, Henry headed their way. Drawing close, he discerned that the group was comprised of Gertrude Magnus, a thin, bent, white-haired woman whose wheelchair was parked on one side of a round table; Mattie Faulkner, carefully blonde, also bent and as plump as Gertrude was thin, seated in a pull-in chair across from Gertrude; and Dora Woods, pink, pretty, and passive, who more than filled a second wheelchair parked several feet to the left of the table. Of the three, Henry knew Gertrude best because he pushed her to the beauty shop every Friday morning at 8:55 and returned her to her room at a little after 10:00.

"Gertrude, Dear," he said in his pleasing voice which was softened by a charming accent, testimony to his having been born and raised in Tennessee, "you look distressed," and indeed Gertrude did, for her shoulders were slumped, her mouth turned down, and her eyes completely closed, as if she were totally defeated. "What's the matter, Darlin'? Somethin' botherin' you?" Typically southern, Henry seldom put the g's on the ends of his words.

"Yes," Gertrude stated definitively, "I don't like her," and she opened her eyes to stare at whom she found offensive for no reason other than Gertrude's own senility: Dora Woods, who couldn't hear much of anything, even when she wore her hearing aids because she never turned them on.

"Good mornin'," Henry mouthed to Dora who hadn't heard Gertrude's comment, and he smiled and reached over to pat her fleshy arm. Turning back to Gertrude, he asked, "Would you like me to move you somewhere else. Away? Perhaps over by the window?" When Gertrude said she would, Henry released the wheelchair's brake and turned the chair away from the table.

Before he could begin the trek to the window however, Mary Washington, who smiled more often than she spoke and also suffered from senility, asserted

Sap and Green People

herself by saying, "I don't like her either," and the tone of her voice and set of her chin supported her claim.

"Hold on, Mary," Henry replied. "I'll be back," and he pushed Gertrude to the window, situated her to her satisfaction, set the chair's brake, returned for Mary, and repeated the process. Turning to the women then, he bowed slightly, smiled warmly, and asked, "I have to go on now. Do you ladies like each other well enough so you can sit together 'til someone comes to fetch you?" When they answered affirmatively, Henry left to determine whom he'd be taking to see Dr. Tory O'Brien, much-liked by his patients, according to the Haven's active grapevine.

"Bless 'em," Henry philosophized softly. "God's people, all of 'em. Like me and mine."

Patricia Dick

Life hadn't treated Gloria Fields as kindly as it had Bill and Margaret Davis. Not in recent years anyway, not since Gloria suffered a stroke twelve years previously.

Before the stroke, the story went, Gloria had been animated, athletic, and beautiful. In fact, people said she looked like the singer-actress Doris Day, her husband Grant, tall and dark-headed 'til the day he died, like Rock Hudson who often played opposite Day. Gloria and Grant were allegedly so attractive that people whom they passed stopped dead in their tracks to look back at them. Childless, monied, and socially connected, they shared what Gloria came to describe as 'a lovely, lovely life'.

Sadly, their life was less lovely after Gloria suffered the stroke one afternoon at her club following a game of tennis which she and her partner, Sue Shriner, typically won. After Sue and everyone else left the premises, Gloria collapsed and lay unconscious and undiscovered for over an hour, doctors surmised, which contributed to lasting impairment of her left side.

Sap and Green People

Grant quit his job as a stock broker, avocational anyway, and he and Gloria worked out a quiet, homebound lifestyle. Unfortunately, Grant died of a massive heart attack while running errands one day, and his death mandated that Gloria move into the Assisted Living Building of the Haven at Oak Hill where she was comfortable and well attended.

Slowly moving towards the library, her intended destination, one afternoon, Gloria steadied herself on the handrail running along the side of the hall. "Hello," she said out of the right side of her mouth as she approached Essie and Bertha Brinkley, sisters-in-law who were leaving the library, and she smiled her half-smile at them.

"Morning," the women answered.

"So sweet, so cheerful," Essie commented after she and her sister-in-law had moved beyond Gloria's range of hearing, the two adjectives people invariably used to characterize Gloria.

"Though one-sided and getting oldish,…"

"Not as old as we!"

"…she's still pretty. Always fastidiously groomed and smartly dressed," Bertha added, two other oft-used, descriptive phrases used relative to Gloria's appearance.

"If we had a girl come each morning to get us dressed, we'd look good too, Bert," Essie answered.

"No we wouldn't. We'd still look like us. And we wouldn't either one of us want to be the shape she's in to warrant having a girl-attendant."

"An attendant would clean out our dresser drawers, catch up our correspondence, straighten out and balance our bank accounts like hers does, I hear," Essie persisted, and the two giggled at the thought of the financial tangles their accounts represented.

"I'd like to have seen her husband," Bertha ventured. "Hear he was exceedingly handsome and very much the gentleman."

"No more handsome and gentlemanly than your George," Essie said.

"A better lover, though."

"Well, I wouldn't know a thing about that."

Sap and Green People

"You darned well better not," and by way of emphasizing what she'd said, Bertha stepped close to Essie and maneuvered to bump Essie with her left hip, a thing they'd done since they were little girls living next door to each other in their Iowa hometown. Anticipating Bertha's move, Essie stepped aside adroitly.

"Down, Girl," Essie commanded. "Sex comes up and you still get crazy."

"So?" Bertha answered.

"No husband, no sex."

"Yeah, I know," Bertha answered with an exaggerated sigh. "I can think about it though, by golly, and someday, just for the heck of it, I'm going to go around the big Manor dining room, table by table, and ask old women how often they still think about sex."

"Don't, Honey," Essie cautioned. "You might be surprised, one way or the other. Shocked or disappointed," and the women snickered as they crossed the bridge connecting Assisted Living to the

Manor where they lived in adjacent apartments on the east, backside of the second floor.

Sap and Green People

Norbert Blair, short of stature and small of girth, had been a banker in his hometown since a week after he graduated from the state university. He loved the job and he loved the town: keeping the bank 'sound' and busy; smoozing with customers as they paraded in and out of the facility; representing the bank on boards and commissions; contributing to the community.

At one point, however, Norbert almost lost his love for the bank: when as its president, he had to replace adding machines with computers which were then widely regarded as newfangled, darned-fool contraptions. What a rumpus the change caused!

"Shoot," exclaimed Guy Bellows who'd been employed by the bank for ten years before the mandated change, "I named my adding machine 'Sure thing', and that's what he is. I talk with him. Nurse him when he's sick. Revive him when he dies. Why would I want a computer?" Rather than change, two female tellers got pregnant and reverted to homemaking. Joe Spenser, a longtime bookkeeper, switched to sharpening knives and servicing small appliances to avoid becoming a 'a tech nut'.

Eventually, after all the kicking, screaming, and negativity, largely because of Norbert's persuasion, persistence, and patience, employees made the required adjustments.

Claiming computers were impersonal, subject to breakdown and error, customers also resisted the transition. "What's the world coming to? Computers indeed!" old Mrs. Tower, the town's wealthiest dowager, wondered aloud. "They'll boob everything up," Ray Morris insisted, and mean, mouthy Rex Garrison told everyone, "They better look out!" which coming from him sounded more like a threat to management than a prediction. After an uphill battle and given time, customers also gave up their protestations.

Despite the tests and challenges that came their way, things went well for Norbert and Mary Louise, his high school sweetheart whom he married in the fall of his twenty-second year. That is, they went well until Mary Louise died unexpectedly a year after Norbert retired, just when they were gearing up to do "everything we never took time to do when Norbert was so busy," as Mary Louise explained.

"I was so grieved," Norbert told several persons after moving into the Haven, "that I hid from people. Wouldn't answer the door or phone. Was splayed out on the sofa with the blinds shut and door locked day after day. Didn't sleep. Eat much. Lost thirty pounds, which was just as well 'cause there used to be a lot more of me than there is now," and he'd chuckle. "Cried and prayed, prayed and cried: that's 'bout all.

A time comes, though," he'd go on to say, "when you have to get going. When something moves you, tells you to get on with your life. I heard the message and recognized that since my daughter lives in Maine and my son in Idaho and I didn't want to depend on them, couldn't even if I did, I needed to find a nice place to spend my last years. There being no options in my hometown, I came to St. Louis, took a hotel room for a week, explored the city and looked at senior housing, applied for admission at the Haven, and moved in when a two-bedroom apartment in Building 707 opened up. Haven't been sorry since."

Patricia Dick

Norbert's background, his introducing the computers and acquiring computer knowledge, made him a natural for helping set up a computer lab in the Haven at Oak Hill, a lab designed for teaching residents computer-usage.

The first step was taken by Mr. Wright, the Haven's Administrator, who situated the lab in a small, well-lit meeting room on the first floor of the Manor, down the east hall from the dining rooms. Wright then purchased three Korean-made computers which Norbert checked out and loaded. The computers, which they named 'Huey', 'Duey', and 'Louie' after Walt Disney characters, were placed on L-shaped tables, with posture-friendly chairs poised at each. A sofa sat against a long wall; a square, oak table hosting computer magazines and manuals in a vacant corner, with folding chairs at its two open sides. The carpet was beige, likewise the walls upon which pictures of a seascape, swimming ducks, and a hilltop house hung. Overhead lighting illuminated the room, and though minimally furnished and muted in tone and color, the lab appeared functional, comfortable, and inviting.

Sap and Green People

Norbert proceeded by enlisting 'computer-literate volunteers' whom he designated as 'Mouseketeers' and introduced to the new machines. He and they then hosted an open house which was attended by residents who wanted to liven up a portion of their day, partake of refreshments, see what computers looked like, or enroll in the classes Norbert and the Mouseketeers would teach.

"We'll start classes soon on designated mornings," Norbert explained to open house attendees. "Offer them as often as demand requires. Additionally, we'll have the lab open most of the time. For anyone's use, with one of us," and he swept his arm around the room in reference to the Mouseketeers who were serving as hosts and hostesses, "on site to offer assistance."

"And to monitor the language used by beginners who are driven crazy?" someone asked.

"And dry tears?" someone else queried. "Or will classes be closed to women?" which got a big laugh from the men who overheard the question.

"Gentlemen, gentlemen," Norbert protested cheerfully, "those were sexist remarks and sexist laughter!"

"You're all duded up, Norb," someone commented.

"Thought you was a movie star for a minutes there."

"A 'seasoned', 'senior' star."

"Them's the best kind!"

"Very senior."

"You people have gone from sexist to mean," Norbert retorted, "and I want you to know that I'm both ashamed of you and offended."

"Me too," Bill Davis, a Mouseketeer, interjected as he stepped into the circle after overhearing what was being said. "Just for that, I'm going to sign Marg up for classes so she, female, can show you chicken-livered clowns up!"

"Man, that scares me," Jack Clausen said. "No classes for me."

"Me either!"

"Yup," and the group broke up.

Sap and Green People

"What a bunch," Norbert muttered affectionately as he moved across the room to welcome a couple who'd just stepped into the lab. "What a really great bunch."

Patricia Dick

A 'bunch' of older persons is a grouping of people who are, metaphorically speaking, over the hill, moving down its other side, and keenly aware of where they are in terms of their life expectancy. Take the people in the Haven's Apartment Building 709, for example, the building where Jack Clausen and the Davises lived.

Mary Teller also lived in Building 709, and on her birthday, December 8, her daughter and two grandsons served an ice cream cake, coffee, and punch to residents in the second floor 'parlor', the place where residents entertained. The room was festive, boasting as it did two trees strung with Christmas lights and ornaments, garlands swagged in appropriate spaces, centerpieces arranged on two buffets, and seasonal figurines clustered at the centers of the two oak tables generally used for eating and game-playing.

As residents arrived for the birthday celebration, they hugged and congratulated Mary, greeted her family members, seated themselves, and began chatting because most of them hadn't seen each other for a number of days. On cue, they sang *Happy*

Sap and Green People

Birthday, then ate and talked for the next hour and a half, first in mixed company, then man-to-man and woman-to-woman, the male components having moved their chairs to one end of the room and left the women the other.

In the men's circle, one man was asked about the vertigo he was suffering for the third time: it was better. Another about how the broken bone in his foot was mending: well. Pete was asked about the biopsy performed on him the previous afternoon: he'd get a report in the morning, but regardless of how it read, he'd be having surgery right after Christmas, which his friends regretted.

In their circle, the women were interested in the laser treatment Ellie received earlier in the day. The scar tissue clouding her vision disappeared instantly and painlessly, Ellie said, and she saw clearly again. Another modern-day miracle, everyone agreed. A ninety-one-year old beauty who'd blacked out in the beauty parlor the previous week, cause unknown, was feeling fine, she insisted. She was angry as blazes, though, because her car insurance had been canceled, or so her son claimed, rendering her dependent on others to a degree she wouldn't enjoy. Another dear woman was to have her lower dental plate relined the next day, an oft-repeated treatment for a problem of long duration.

Both groups lamented that Ernest couldn't be with them because he was suffering a sneak attack of stomach flu, and they rejoiced that Bob's knee replacement was coming along nicely and he'd be appearing at the next get-together. A number of jokes were exchanged in one circle, anecdotes in the other, complaints in both. At breaking-up time, everyone pledged to appear in the downstairs 'great room' for happy hour the following Monday, it being the first Monday of the month, and thanked the hostess and her sons for favors extended.

"Some older persons would sooner drink hemlock than give up their homes to move into a place like this," Jack Clausen said to the couple who lived in the apartment next to his as he and they rode the elevator up to the second floor. "Isn't that unfortunate? Misguided?"

Sap and Green People

His neighbors agreed, as would have the others who resided in the one-, two-, and three-bedroom apartments in Building 709, had they been polled. Because they were over the hill and coming down its other side, hand-in-hand, with pleasant, caring, supportive persons who were also in descent. Not for anything would they, having experienced very satisfactory, communal living, have chosen to make the journey alone.

Patricia Dick

Marg Davis woke up at 5:30 to a positively frigid bedroom, frigid because she'd turned the furnace off before going to bed and raised the window halfway, only to have the temperature drop seventeen degrees during the night. A frigid bedroom suited Marg fine. Was one of her fetishes, actually, but she knew Bill, who was more sensitive to the cold, would absolutely hate having to forego the warmth of his bed for the chill of the room.

With Bill's comfort in mind, Marg tucked the blanket and sheet around his shoulders and dashed to the thermostat which was mounted on a living room wall. Except for the light coming through the front windows, the room was dark, requiring that she squint and strain to determine which way to turn the thermostat, usually Bill's first, cold-morning task.

Failing to read the pointer, Marg shivered her way back to the bedroom. There, she grabbed up her glasses and shut the window which she hadn't taken the time to do when she'd first gotten up.

Two years previously, Marg's ophthalmologist had told her that she had the beginning of macular degeneration in her left eye, the visual disability that had plagued her mother and was afflicting Henry Graham. Fortunately, Marg's condition hadn't worsened, but the diagnosis had prompted Bill to insist that he and Marg move into a seniors' community, a place where Marg would receive whatever assistance she might require in the future.

At the thermostat a second time and with her glasses on, when she still couldn't read the control, Marg turned a lamp on and studied the face of the thermostat. She also blinked and rubbed her eyes to clear them, then curled her fingers to make a hollow fist which, when put to an eye, sometimes helped her make out images when she wasn't wearing her glasses. Only, none of those measures helped: she absolutely could not see what she needed to see to turn the heat on.

Panicking, Marg whimpered, "Oh no! No, no, no! Please no," and she ran to the bedroom again, this time to get the self-examination eye chart the ophthalmologist had given her so she could check periodically for deterioration.

Lamp-side in the living room, Marg held the chart in front of one eye, covered the other with her free hand, and studied the chart's dots and lines. They were decidedly irregular. Dim and blurry. Crazy!

Thoroughly shaken, her heart racing and head spinning, driven to tell Bill that she had, in fact, lost her vision, Marg dashed back to the bedroom and crouched beside the bed. As she did, in the light afforded by the living room lamp, she spotted a pair of glasses on the arm of her desk, her own. She'd picked up Bill's, she realized. Put them on. Was wearing them.

"Oh Bill," she wailed as she leaned over Bill's supine figure. "I thought I'd lost my eyesight during the night. Was really, really going blind. But I'd put your glasses on. Yours! What a nut I am! As dumb as that! I'm getting dumber and duncier all the time. What's going to happen to me?"

"Come here," Bill urged, and he sat up in bed and extended his arms. "You're shaking like a leaf. I'll warm you up," and gently, tenderly, he pulled Marg into bed, covered her, rolled her on her right side, her sleeping side, and pressed his body to her back. "There, there," he said as he held her close. "You're not dumb or a dunce. You're my wife, my Marg, and in a few minutes, I'll have you as warm as toast."

"Oh," Marg murmured, "how could I do without you?"

"Well enough if you have to," Bill answered matter-of-factly. "You'd come out all right, and the same's true of me. I keep telling you that we, the one of us who gets left behind, will make the adjustments required. The changes. Do what's necessary. You know we will. And you're not to dwell of the future, Lady, 'cause the past and the present are what we have left. Particularly the present," and he felt Marg relax. Heard her sigh as she settled into the curve of his arm.

Patricia Dick

There's a 'Laclede' this and a 'Laclede' that in St. Louis, the 'Laclede' harkening back to Pierre Laclede, a Frenchman who arrived in New Orleans in 1762 and later, boated up the Mississippi River to establish a trading post which he named after Louie, the King of France. One of those Laclede-named entities is Laclede Station Road which runs south from the center of the city.

At a point along Laclede Station Road, on its west side, the approximately sixty-acre Haven at Oak Hill nestles in a valley ringed with tall trees, many of them oaks. Originally a convent, the acreage is now home to almost eight hundred residents, all 'senior', who live in either 'independent' living, 'assisted' living, or 'convalescent' (nursing) quarters.

The fall had been long, warm, and beautiful. Prairie-spawned breezes blew in from the Southwest; petunias and chrysanthemum bloomed on and on and on; and maple, ash, and sassafras took on vibrant colors. Finally, in early December, temperatures plummeted, vegetation gave up the ghost, and Haven

Sap and Green People

residents looked ahead to Christmas. How they'd celebrate the season. To what extent.

"Celebrating together binds a family," Marg Davis told Bill after he suggested minimizing their Christmas observance one December afternoon. "The time will come when you won't want to bother with putting up a tree,..."

"Soon!"

"...and I won't feel like having a big family dinner at our place. It'll come, but not yet. You can still get the tree up,..."

"Barely!"

"...and I can still manage the dinner since the children live in town and all I have to do is feed them, rather than house and feed them both. I don't want to throw in the towel yet, Bill."

Bill grunted and shrugged his shoulders to indicate reluctant acquiescence, then set about opening the mail and assigning it to junk, business, or Christmas piles. Actually, Bill and Marg had the same discussion every year, for while Bill was inclined to minimize social endeavors, Marg tended to maximize them, especially

Christmas festivities. A cherished part of those festivities was hosting the grandchildren overnight on December 23, initiated when the older three were four, six, and nine years old.

On that occasion, Marg served what she called "a kid-friendly meal"; she, Bill, and the children made candy after dinner; and the next morning, Christmas Eve Day, they took the children to a Denny's restaurant for breakfast. Back at Marg and Bill's, the children helped get an early-afternoon Christmas dinner ready, one Marg had more or less pre-cooked. They then showered and dressed in their go-to-church best, welcomed their parents upon their arrival, and following dinner and a gift-exchange, the young families left to attend their respective church services, with Bill and Marg doing likewise.

While Christmas was always joyous for Bill and Marg, they were sensitive to the fact that it was not joyous for everyone living in the Haven.

"Gracie Owens, downstairs, is estranged from both of her children. Never hears from either of them. Not even at Christmas," Marg informed Bill.

Sap and Green People

"How'd that happen?"

"Harold just lost Melba," Marg mused, "and Ted's lost his…senses since last Christmas."

"His Joan's having a hard time of it, I hear."

"The Brofman's son: gone."

"Some families are dying out. Breaking up. Scattered to the ends of the earth."

"Friends move away. Across town or far away."

"Drift apart."

"We're lucky to have our family and friends," Marg said.

"Jack Clausen never did have anyone," Bill reported. "Told me in the ice cream parlor that he's got nobody, absolutely no family. Aunts, uncles, cousins, siblings: none. Said that for holiday meals, when he was a kid, three persons gathered around the family table. His mother, his father, and himself."

"That's pathetic," Marg said.

"Oh, he has a lot of friends here now," Bill assured her.

"Sure," Marg observed, "friends are easy to come by here. New associations. Networks. Families.

Patricia Dick

Can't help thinking about Christmases past," she went on to say. "Feeling sentimental. Remember that one time, Bill, on the 24th, when we and the grandkids were driving to Denny's for breakfast and they had that continuing discussion about when Jesus was born?"

"Of course," Bill answered. "One of the kids mentioned that it was Christmas Eve morning, and Max, who must have been four, heard the words 'Christmas Eve', said, 'Oh, that's when Jesus was born'."

"The other kids all said no. That Jesus was born Christmas night," Marg added as she picked up the retelling of the story.

"Max kept insisting that Jesus was born on Christmas Eve, the others, on Christmas night. Back and forth they went."

"To settle the argument finally, Lee, ten, said, 'I'll tell you how it went, Max. Mary's water broke on Christmas Eve, she had a long labor, and Jesus was finally born Christmas night'."

"Satisfied Max. Totally, and he said, 'Oh, that's how it was.' End of argument."

Sap and Green People

"Again, thank goodness for the kids and grandkids," Marg said.

"Don't thank 'goodness', Mary. 'We' had a heck of a lot to do with their being here."

"You're right," Marg conceded.

"Always am, and don't you forget it. I'm Mr. Right!."

"Except at Christmas, Sir, when you become Scrooge," and she smiled her certainty that they'd again set up a tree, entertain several small groupings of friends, host the grown-up grandhildren for the evening (only) of December 23, and otherwise celebrate the sacred season of joy and love.

"That Mary's as pretty as anyone in this whole, big place," Bertha Brinkman told her sister-in-law Essie one evening as they stood in the cafeteria serving line and noticed that Mary Spritzer, a relatively new resident, was a short distance behind them.

At the head of the line several minutes later, Bertha and Essie 'punched in' by flashing identification tags in front of an electronic monitor, picked up trays, filled them with food, and scanned the room to locate a table where they could sit. The far end of the dining room, which served all Haven 'independent-living' residents, those residing in The Manor, Apartment Buildings, and Patio Homes, was comprised of two-story high windows which overlooked a hillside, pond, and woods, the view making the window-fronting tables choice.

"No window tables left," Essie told Bertha, "but there's a table for six there," and with her elbow, she pointed to a mid-room location. "That okay?"

"Sure," Bertha answered, and the two walked to the table, off-loaded their food, and stacked their trays on a tray-holder. "The room and tables look nice. Very Christmassy. In fact, the whole campus looks…"

"Festive."

"Yes. Whatever else slips our aged, failing minds, given the trimmings that abound, we won't be forgetting what month this is, what season. And you're right about Mary," Bertha said as she and Essie watched Mary thread her way between tables as she looked for a place to sit.

Mary was thin, straight, and taller than most women her age, though because her silver hair was piled on the top of her head, she appeared taller than she measured. Her skin was pink and smooth, makeup just right, walk measured, posture regal, clothing distinctive. That night, Mary wore a short, gold sari with good ballet slippers.

"May I join you?" Mary asked when she reached Bertha and Essie's table.

"Please do," Essie answered, and as the women visited during the course of the meal, she and Bertha came to appreciate that while Mary's appearance set her apart, so did her intelligence and personality, for her memory was sharp, rejoinders quick, stories unusual.

Mary made a point of stating that she was a 'spinster' who had no family, and because she didn't further explain her background, Bertha and Essie and others who'd met her wondered about Mary's past and regarded her an enigma.

"What cut of beef do you think this is?" Essie asked as she cut into her meat.

"Beats me," Bertha answered. "It could be roast monkey for all I know. However, I suppose it's cow since the menu board says 'beef'."

"It's not monkey," Mary volunteered. "I had monkey once when I was in Africa. Wouldn't eat a full portion because monkeys were endangered even then, but I tasted a morsel and found it very distinctive.'

"What were you doing in Africa?" Essie asked.

"Lived there for three years," Mary answered, using a non-sequitur and tone of voice to end the monkey-Africa conversation then and there.

Sap and Green People

"Our husbands, brothers, died within six months of each other," Bertha said following an elongated silence. "So we helped each other get through painful periods. One of the things we did was travel. Our first long trip was to the Orient." Mary had also traveled in the Orient, so the three conversed about that region.

Bertha and Essie did not forget Mary's statement about Africa, and they repeated it to Moira Sheer, who brought up the subject when she met and sat next to Mary at dinner several nights later.

"Heard you lived in Africa, Mary. Quite unusual"

"I did," Mary answered, and immediately, as if drawing from a pool of topics reserved for referencing when she wished to change the course of a conversation, Mary said," I saw tapioca on the dessert table. Positively love tapioca, but while I've seen it processed, I've never cooked it myself. How did you make it, back when you were cooking for your families?" she asked. After the women discussed the topic to its death, Mary told a tapioca joke, to the amazement of her companions who'd never heard a tapioca joke in their lives.

Patricia Dick

Another evening, while being transported by a Haven bus to a theater, Mary mentioned having been a reader of *The London Times*, leading her seat mate, Ruth Roberts, to ask, "Where'd you read *The Times*?"

"In London when I lived there," Mary answered.

"And when was that?" Ruth persisted.

"A while ago," Mary said in a voice which precluded additional discussion.

Three weeks later, while she and others waited for an afternoon organ concert to begin in the beautiful, spacious Haven Chapel, a Catholic church back when the campus served as a convent, Mary spoke of having lived in Virginia, which prompted Rhonda Stevens, who went to college in Richmond, to exclaim, "Beautiful, beautiful Virginia!"

"It is a beautiful state," Mary agreed, and she pointedly turned her attention to reading her concert program.

The same night, in the course of dinner talk about the careers young women were choosing, Elaine Bruce said, "Mary, you look like a scholar and have the mind of one. Were you a librarian or…professor? A lawyer?"

"Fine careers," Mary answered, "but absolutely not."

Though Mary was very much liked and respected by the women who came to know her, there were others who 'disliked' her because she was more attractive than they, differently dressed, distant. Occasionally curt. "Really non-traditional," someone had said.

But as far as her new, closer associates were concerned, Mary was clever and immensely interesting, also so mysterious and intriguing that they started gleaning biographical information from conversations, bits and pieces of 'Mary-stuff', they called it, with the hope of eventually profiling Mary, a gleaning-game of sorts which the very bright and alert Mary Spritzer recognized and cooperated with fully.

Patricia Dick

"'Bye,'" Bill Davis called to Marg who was straining to read what was printed on the computer screen. "Going now. Yuk!"

"Bill," Mary called as she pushed back from the computer, "come here a minute, please." When Bill stepped in front of her, she stood, put her hands on his shoulders, and though he trained his eyes on the wall high above her head, she looked into his face and said, "I hate to see you going off like this, feeling so negative. After all," and her voice was too coy, too sanguine, to suit Bill at that moment, "the endorphins that supposedly come from volunteering are supposed to give you a high. Benefit you. Make you feel swell. Not glum and grumpy."

"Well, this volunteer is reaping anger and possibly ulcers and high blood pressure instead of swell feelings," Bill replied sourly.

"Ah, come on," Marg pleaded. "You're no bear, no grouch. Lighten up, Honey."

"I can't stand working with those ladies," Bill restated emphatically. "The guys are okay. Fine. But the women, some of them, not all, are so…unpleasant.

Sap and Green People

They're mean to each other. Criticizing and undercutting and correcting, and you know I can't stand that sort of thing. Poisons the atmosphere," and he gave Mary a fleeting kiss and left to do what he could hardly stand doing, working in the ice cream parlor, though had he the chance to do so when he'd been, say, fifteen, he'd have been tickled pink.

Back then, as a 'soda jerk', Bill would have worn a white apron and cap, taken orders for ice cream specialities, concocted them, accepted payment and made change, then stood around joshing with customers, especially pretty girl customers, until someone required his services, this for perhaps thirty-five cents an hour.

Instead, the present-day, seventy-six-year-old volunteer, dressed in khaki trousers and a maroon knit shirt with 'The Haven' monogrammed on its breast pocket, dipped balls of ice cream in the relatively new Haven ice cream parlor, put the balls in cones or containers, then handed the cones or containers to the female volunteer who'd relayed the order to him in the first place.

Patricia Dick

The parlor was located opposite the elevator on the second floor of the Convalescent Center, in what used to be a small storage room. Residents of the Haven and their guests could patronize the parlor on Tuesday and Sunday afternoons from 2:00 to 3:30 and either carry away what they bought or eat it at tables located in a large room next to the parlor.

The ice cream parlor was popular, especially with Convalescent and Assisted Living residents whose quarters were close by, and judging by the number of lined-up patrons and the patience with which they waited, an onlooker would surmise that everything was hunky-dory in Ice Cream Land. Such was not the case as far as Bill Davis was concerned, however.

"Heh," Mike McGuire, a jovial, round-tummied, short Irishman, also sporting a maroon, imprinted shirt, said as he and Bill arrived at their workplace within minutes of each other. "What you got to say for yourself today, Old Man?"

"Only that I hope the ladies are…nice today," Bill sputtered.

Sap and Green People

"They're okay, Man. Good to the customers," Mike said in their defense. "Patient with them. Helpful. Courteous. That's first, wouldn't you say?" and hoping to jolly Bill out of his mood, he popped Bill's shoulder lightly with a balled fist. "Lighten up, you grumpy, old guy, you."

"Okay, okay," Bill answered.

"Hi," Betty Mansfield, who was wiping off table tops in the 'eating room', called when she heard the men talking. Betty's face and arms were generously dimpled, and Bill wondered if she were dimpled all over, then felt ashamed for having engendered the thought and relieved that he'd never know. Working with Betty were two other volunteers, Daisy and Charlotte, their last names unknown, dressed like Betty in hairnets, white aprons, and pink rather than maroon shirts.

"My knees are bad today," Daisy complained to Charlotte as they wiped off tables and chairs, and she put on a long face. "I'll manage though. Somehow."

"Mine hurts too," the yellow-headed Charlotte answered cheerfully. "The left knee, that is," and her cheerfulness convinced Daisy that Charlotte's pain was not nearly as severe as her own.

"Why," Daisy asked, "is it that all 750 or so of us living in the Haven have bad knees and most of them hurt on the very same day?"

"A lot of us do have bad knees," Mike answered from inside the ice cream parlor where he was inventorying supplies while listening to the women's chatter, "but remember that a bunch of us arthritic guys also have prostate trouble, and you lucky ladies have been spared that."

"Ya, ya," Charlotte answered, "and you all gave birth to babies too, didn't you?" which quieted Mike and made Charlotte and Daisy laugh.

Just then, George Steiner, tall as a chimney and as roughly complexioned, popped out of the elevator. "That's the slowest damned elevator in the whole damned world," he complained loudly.

Grace Kuhn, the designated manager of the ice cream parlor and its cashier, also a volunteer, had ridden up with George, and she said quietly, "Watch your language, George, please."

Sap and Green People

Because George had waited until the maroon shirts had all been handed out to ask about being issued one, he'd been given a pink shirt instead of maroon one, and to contribute to keeping the atmosphere as light and congenial as it was at that moment, Bill quipped, "Doesn't George look sweet in pink?"

"The pink doesn't bother me one bit," George insisted. "Goes with my eyes," and he issued a toothy smile.

"Glad you feel that way," Grace said, "but People, we need to get down to business. Get ready for the onslaught," and she and her helpers crowded into the wee ice cream parlor to talk about preparations.

"I checked the freezers," Mike reported, "and we got vanilla and strawberry ice cream.

"Anyone look at the sign on the counter to see what our specials are today?" Bill asked.

"Cherry vanilla yogurt, lime sherbet, praline ice cream," George, proud of his recall, answered.

"We'll need to get those in the big, downstairs kitchen then," Bill said. "I checked our cone supply. We have regular and sugar cones in the cupboard but almost none of the waffle kind. We'll get some of those too."

"We have plenty of cherries and nuts," Grace said as she checked another cupboard.

"Bill and me will get the cart and make a kitchen-run for the ice cream and other stuff," Mike offered.

"Hi," tall, skinny, pink-shirted, breathless Dell White called as she joined the others and tucked her pocketbook away in a corner of a cupboard.

The organizing done, George, who'd stood blinking behind his shell-rimmed glasses as he'd struggled to keep up with what had gone on, commenced putting chairs around the tables in the eating room, his weekly assignment. "Meriwether Lewis never woulda' done this, pushing chairs around in a sissy, ice cream parlor," he grumbled just loud enough for his co-workers to hear, and they smiled at each other because they'd been waiting for George's first reference to Lewis and Clark, his long-ago heroes.

A spiffy, green-and-white-striped canopy circled the top of two half-doors and the counter which comprised the front of the ice cream parlor. From

Sap and Green People

inside the parlor, Grace opened the half-doors so she and her helpers could ready the counter for service.

They proceeded by setting out signage, spoons, and napkins on the counter; order pads, pencils, a calculator, syrups and other toppings on a surface behind the counter; cups, containers, and ice cream scoops on a shelf above the ice cream freezers; and malt and sundae recipes, toppings and chocolate syrup, measuring cups and required utensils next to the malted milk machines.

"1:41," a nervous Grace said. "Nineteen minutes to go."

"The guys'll be back right soon," George said to reassure her, and after the men's return, the volunteers put away the just-procured provisions. All was then ready for the customers who'd already formed a line in front of the serving counter and were happily visiting with each other.

The first customers were two nurses' aides. "Two dips of ice cream in cones. One strawberry, one praline," one said. Dell wrote the orders on separate forms, passed one to Mike who commenced dipping, the second to Bill who dipped when Mike finished and stepped away from the freezer which sat on the floor about five feet behind the counter. Dell walked the cones over to Grace who marked the charges on the twin slips, announced the amounts due, accepted payment, and filed the slips in a coffee-can receptacle. Money transacted, Dell handed the aides their cones and watched as they stepped away from the line.

Two women and a man whose wheelchairs had been pushed by Assisted Living attendants were next. Daisy wrote up orders for two malts, walked them over to Bill who put the required amounts of ice cream in stainless steel containers. Daisy took the containers on to George then, the malt-maker, who added ingredients, let the malt machines whip for three minutes, and gave them back to Daisy who oversaw the rest of the transaction, this while Dell processed a cone for the third customer. Their attendants then pushed the customers to a table in the eating room and stood by while they ate.

A winter wind pelted windows, the sky spit snow, the early-December grey cast an oppressive gloom.

Sap and Green People

Nonetheless, staff members who were hungry or restless, residents who loved ice cream or wanted to break up their afternoon, and guests who'd wearied of trying to converse with oldsters who'd lost their conversational skills flocked to the parlor, the Tuesday and Sunday weather usually having little to do with the demand for ice cream.

As for the volunteers, seniors themselves, as the afternoon progressed, the walls of the work areas shrank and the rooms overheated. Elevator doors thunked open and closed a thousand times. Malt machines whirred almost continuously. Feeble voices placed orders which had to be clarified and asked questions whose answers had to be shouted and repeated perhaps two, even three, times. Workers bumped shoulders and ran into each other. Spilled. Had to work to keep their tempers.

"You slop hot fudge all over everything!" Charlotte charged as Mike ladled fudge on sundaes because she was too busy to do so.

Patricia Dick

"I'll leave it to you then," Mike shot back. "Have at the hot fudge, and I'll stick to ice cream dipping only, no matter how far behind we get!"

"You step on my foot one more time," Daisy told Dell, "and I'll...I don't know what I'll do!"

Somewhat later, when Daisy and Dell met at the freezer, an out-of-sorts Dell 'whispered' what she may have wished heard: "Those guys don't hear well, you know, and they get flustered and mix up orders." Having heard, Bill sucked his breath through pinched-tight lips and settled in for a confrontation with Dell.

That time came when Dell handed him an order for two chocolate cones and said, "That's CHOCOLATE I want. CHOC-O-LATE. NICE ROUND CHOC-O-LATE ice cream servings, please."

"DELL," he answered in a falsely-sweet voice, "would you like to change jobs for a while? I'll even lend you the WRIST BRACE I wear on my dipping arm and give you the TYLENOL I take on Tuesdays about now. And I bet you won't get flustered or mix up orders like we guys do, will you?"

Sap and Green People

A little before 3:00, Barb, red-faced, dripping with sweat, her hands on her hips, seemingly less dimpled than earlier, entered the parlor's side door and said, "I've been working the tables alone all afternoon, and I'm pooped. Could any of you six people come help me?"

"I will," George volunteered. "Mike and Bill can cover the malts."

Promptly at 3:30, glad that no one was standing in the ordering line, Grace pulled in the things placed on the serving counter and closed the half doors, thus closing the parlor until the next Sunday afternoon when a second set of volunteers would serve the Haven's Ice Cream Eating Public. Silently, the workers worked through their closing-up routine, and as they did, they relaxed. Became conversational again. Parted on friendly or near-friendly terms.

Marg was still at the computer when Bill entered their apartment. Looking up, she asked, "Well, how was it today?"

"So-so. Pretty much the same," he answered. "Maybe a little better. I'm going to try harder next time. Leave the chip on my shoulder at home. After all, people's jes' people, myself included."

"Good. And remember, Dear Heart, that no one ever promised you a rose garden."

"You're absolutely right," Bill acknowledged. "Not a rose garden. An ice cream parlor. A gosh-darn ice cream parlor instead."

Sap and Green People

When she heard a light knock, Gloria Fields, dressed in soft white slacks and a matching cashmere sweater, her pageboyed hair shiny and silver-gold, made her step-slide, step-slide way across the room to open the door for her expected visitor.

"How are you, Mrs. Fields?" Pat Marsh, an Assisted Living nurse asked as she entered Gloria's apartment.

"Okay," Gloria Fields answered, "good," and she seated herself on a light green and white striped overstuffed chair after pushing its matching ottoman out of the way.

"You don't say that with much conviction," Pat commented while draping her sweater around the back of the caned-back chair she'd pulled over to where Gloria was sitting. Opening her medical bag, she set about placing instruments and paraphernalia on a lamp table situated beside Gloria's chair.

"It's a pleasure to step into your lovely place again," Pat said so she could engage with Gloria for a few minutes before checking her vital signs, and she looked around the room. "Your furnishings are lovely."

"I didn't buy a thing," Gloria explained. "Whittled down nine rooms of furniture to come up with what I have here and in my bedroom. I'm used to having more room, but this is adequate. Fine."

"Italian Provincial, isn't it?"

"If anyone asks, I always say, 'Italianate'."

"Warm, medium-brown wood, straight lines: my taste exactly. That mirror's simply exquisite," Pat exclaimed, and she walked over to examine an ornate mirror mounted above a sofa.

"I do prize that," Gloria said with more animation. "An antique my husband bought me in Florence. I like the gold band which sets off the border and the wreath of etched flowers running along the lower edge."

"And look at the books! Six long shelves of them!"

"I don't walk well, but I can read. Oh yes, I can! Don't know what I'd do if I didn't."

"When I was here before, I was so intent on getting acquainted with you that I hardly looked around," and

Sap and Green People

Pat bent over so she could take Gloria's blood pressure. "It's good," she reported. "140 over 89," and she peered into Gloria's eyes and looked down her throat. Took her pulse. Listened to her lungs and heart.

"Now let me see you walk," and with her left foot trailing the right, Gloria walked across the room and back without using her cane.

"Good," Pat commented, "but when I'm not here, here and in other places, you use that 'stick', Little Lady."

"Oh, I do, I do," Gloria assured her. "I guess I was just trying to show off," and she laughed a notably small laugh.

"Your color's good," Pat said, "and you're looking pretty as a picture. Only," and she sat down beside Gloria, "how about your frame of mind? You seem sort of glum. Worried? Depressed?"

"Maybe," Gloria answered.

"We should talk about depression then," and when Gloria remained silent, Pat talked quietly about the relationship of physical and mental health, then by way of encouraging Gloria, she expressed the respect she'd come to have for Gloria after only having visited her twice, the same respect other residents and staff members had for her, she'd been given to understand.

"Well," Gloria said haltingly, "I feel like…I'm in good health, considering my condition," and she smiled, "and…I don't want to complain because I'm thankful to be as well as I am and to be here. Otherwise, I don't know where I'd be since I do need help and have no one to help me.

But I'm restless. Restless and lonely and, strange as it may sound in light of my disability, I feel misplaced here in Assisted Living. So many of the persons are way older than I and…more limited in terms of general physical and mental capabilities, I guess I could say.

Granted my mouth is crooked, half of my face drawn, and my left arm and leg aren't much good, I nonetheless wish I had…more companionship and stimulation. Access to different kinds of people and activities.

Sap and Green People

Forgive me for running on, for pitying myself," Gloria added as she wiped away tears with the linen handkerchief she pulled from her sweater pocket.

"Maybe you should see about moving into an Independent Living Apartment," Pat answered. "In the Manor, perhaps, where everything's under one roof, and arrange with Home Services for any help you may require."

"I get that now. With my bath and hair."

"I know you do. From looking at your record here."

"When I moved in, I was still recovering from my stroke. Still taking physical therapy. And in shock, I guess, over my husband's death. So the measure of my independence wasn't accurate, I don't believe. I'm considerably better now. Surely you see that I'm in relatively good shape. Something more than a semi-invalid?"

"Oh, I do," Pat answered affirmatively. "I believe you can function quite independently. Can you dress and undress and get into bed by yourself?"

"I don't always but could," Gloria answered.

"I haven't been here long," Pat told her, "so I don't know exactly how such transfers work. Under what conditions they're granted. Do you want me to make inquiries? Ask Mr. Wright, the administrator? Or have a social worker come talk to you?"

"No," Gloria answered. "Having someone intervene would indicate that I am quite limited."

"Ah," Pat said approvingly.

Gloria made her way over to Pat who had turned her attention to writing up notes. Bending over, she put her hand on Pat's shoulder, an uncharacteristic gesture, the touching of another persons, for her to make. "Thank you, oh thank you for listening to me! For suggesting the moving possibility. If only I could get into the Manor. Take advantage of what's there. Associate with other people!"

"Don't get too excited," Pat cautioned. "Moving might not happen and certainly not quickly. So don't expect too much or be too hopeful, Gloria. But by all means get working on the thing. Try! Before you lose your resolve."

"I will," Gloria promised, "and I might even sic my lawyer on the deciders, whoever they are, if I have trouble. He's a regular little bulldog, that man."

"By the way, has anyone ever told you that you look like the movie star, Doris Day? I watched one of her old movies the other night and found the resemblance striking."

"One or two," Gloria answered, a gross understatement. "People who knew me before my stroke. Maybe saw only the right side of my body," and Gloria's answer brought tears to Pat's eyes, a thing she could usually avoid.

"See you soon," she told Gloria, and as she hurried to her car, she wondered if she'd planted false hope and consequently done Gloria a disfavor. "Dear God," she agonized, "what may I have done to that poor, sweet lady? Led her astray?" and she shut her car door behind her with a car-rocking wham.

Patricia Dick

Some years previous, Bill and Marg Davis and Henry and Georgia Graham had lived in the same neighborhood and attended the same church. Henry's transfer to another part of the country put an end to that association, however, and thirty-five years later, after both couples moved into the Haven at Oak Hill, their paths crossed again. Having renewed their friendship, they frequently met in the Manor dining room where persons living independently ate their meals.

On one such occasion, as Bill and Marg approached the Manor, they spotted the Grahams laughing over a piece of paper they were reading as they stood in front of their car which was parked near the Manor's front entrance.

"What's up?" Bill asked as he and Marg drew abreast.

"The darnest thing," and Henry shook his head. "I live right here in the Manor and I'm classified as a handicapped driver, as noted by my license plates. We took the car to get its earl changed…"

"It's what?" Bill asked.

Sap and Green People

"To get the oil changed," Georgia explained in her quiet voice. "Remember, Henry grew up in Tennessee."

"It took longer than expected and we didn't want to be late meetin' you, so I didn't drive round back to my garage stall. Instead, I parked right here where the sign reads, 'Disabled Parkin', we went inside to wash our hands, came back, and found this under the windshield wiper." Henry handed the paper to Bill and Marg.

Written with a shaky hand, the note read *Shame on you, shame on you. By parking in this place, you deprived a 86 year old senior citizen of a parking space. I had you paged but you wouldn't answer, and I waited a half hour. Shame on you! Shame on you!*

"Well Henry," Bill said, "all you have to do to determine whose nose you should punch is find someone who doesn't know what handicapped license plates look like, has a shaky hand, and is 86."

"Woman or man?"

"Woman," Henry insisted.

Patricia Dick

"Just how do you know that?" Georgia asked contentiously.

"'Cause I can just picture her," Henry answered. "Hooked nose. Coke bottle glasses. Hair in a bun. Humped back. Flowered, belted dress. Lace-up, black shoes."

"You're being mean, Man, and I'm ashamed of you," Bill said as he and Marg preceded the Grahams through the Manor doors and down the carpeted stairs to the dining room.

Ever so slowly, the four friends followed an elderly couple, one halt and one lame, through the serving line, a test of their patience. Having finally been able to select their salads and entrees, they passed up a plethora of desserts, seated themselves, ordered beverages from a pert waitress whose hair was colored orange, and returned to discussing the note left on Henry's car.

"Parking is something of a problem," Georgia pointed out in an effort to placate Henry. "The writer was frustrated at not being able to park and he…"

"She"

Sap and Green People

"...failed to see your handicapped plates."

"All of us who eat here are supposed to be 'independent'," Henry protested, "so unless people have broken legs or not enough time to put their cars in their garages, they should be able to walk a little ways without getting all bent out of shape. Or they should leave their cars home and catch a ride on the shuttle that circles the campus all day."

"But they do have the right to drive and park if they choose," Georgia persisted, which stopped the discussion cold.

Marg commenced it again after an interval by saying, "Old people do get worked up over trivialities, don't they?"

"Their worlds have gotten smaller and smaller," Georgia observed. "They have less and less to occupy them, to enjoy."

"We, the four of us, get off campus a lot and have our children and grandchildren around to extend our worlds," Marg said, "but some of the residents live very circumspect lives."

Patricia Dick

"We're glad we're here, and, in fact, I told Marg a couple of days ago that I'd given her the best possible gift by insisting that we move in when we were given the chance. But nothing's perfect and living here's not either."

"Meaning'?" Henry asked.

"Well, seeing so many walkers and canes depresses me sometimes. Makes me impatient, like in the serving line tonight. Feel sorry for those people and like about everyone I've met, but things get to me."

"We'll eventually get used to them," Marg ventured.

"After all, we're going to be old/old ourselves before long."

"Cracked voices grate on my nerves."

"People yelling' back and forth because they can't hear."

"Easy there! They'd be yelling at me if I didn't have my hearing aids," Bill reminded his table mates.

"But you do use them. Recognized your need."

"The complaining."

Sap and Green People

"Not exclusive to this place. 'Member those griping, bitching people we had to work with before we retired, Henry?"

"Did I tell you that a couple of weeks ago, when I called for a nursing home lady to take her to the beauty parlor, she told me to come in, and lo'n behold, she shuffled out of her bathroom shackled by her slacks which were down around her ankles. Not the least bit embarrassed, she asked me to help her get 'em pulled up. Thanked me, and we went on our way."

"How'd you feel about that?" Marg asked.

"Didn't bother me a bit. The lady needed help."

"How many funerals and what precipitated them you heard about lately?"

"About how many doctors, operations, medications?"

"You mean 'meds', don't you? As of 'I have to take eleven meds every day'."

"I'm floor leader, and the complaints I get…," Henry lamented. 'Someone left a chair in the hall, Henry.' 'I always have to clean the lint out of the dryer.' 'The washin' machine's makin' a funny noise.' 'Too hot.' 'Always cold.' Cripes!"

"But Henry steps up to every complaint with charm, wit, and grace," Georgia said of her husband.

"Hopefully, there'll always be a Henry to handle complaints."

"We could continue griping," Bill, who'd started the conversation, said, "but what the heck?"

"We do pity people who need pity and care about them and help them. We can give ourselves credit for that, but what we need to remember when we get plaintive is that most of the people, certainly most of those we live with, are fit. Pretty fit."

"Sharp, active, informed, cheerful."

"Actually, most pitiful are the disabled or lonely who are toughing things out in their 'own' homes, as they call them. Worrying about their safety, roofs, and yards. What's going to happen to what they've accumulated over the course of a lifetime. Isolated."

"Having to depend on their kids—if they have kids who live nearby and are willing and not too busy to help them."

Sap and Green People

"There's so much to do here. Dumb stuff but swell stuff too. Social things. Recreation."

"Learning things. Service things."

"Excursions out the ying yang."

"Out the what?" which induced a round of laughter.

"What are we doing? Trying to talk ourselves into being happy here?"

"No, no!" Bill insisted. "We're happy. We're just trying to keep things in perspective. "Measure frustrations against benefits derived. Know what we need?"

"Sundaes!" Georgia answered. "Speaking for myself, I need a butterscotch sundae."

"I'm shocked at your suggestion," Marg claimed, "cute, trim, disciplined little you."

"We could put your car in your garage and I'll drive us over to Ted Drewes for some of that famous ice cream," Bill offered. "Or we can order sundaes here, custom-made by our pretty, orange-headed waitress. What's your pleasure?"

"Getting the earl changed and the trauma of gettin' that note has exhausted me," Henry answered. "Let's sundae here."

"Too, we want to give the hook-nosed, eighty-six year old woman time to discover that your car's still in place and write another message," Bill said as he raised his hand to summon the waitress who would customize their sundaes, the pert girl whose hair might be colored apple green or Mediterranean blue the next time the Davises and Grahams met for dinner in the Manor dining room.

Sap and Green People

"I wonder if they're ever going to clean the carpet," the tall, white-headed, smartly dressed, and often caustic Eloise Brady said to the women whom she joined at a table in the dining room. "It's stained to the point of being disgusting. There's absolutely no excuse for that. Makes me half-way sick," she further complained.

"Sounds like you're in a swell mood this evening," one of her table mates said.

"You've got a big, black Cadillac," another reminded Eloise. "If the carpet's disturbing you, why don't you drive to the Plaza, only four blocks away, and eat in one of the restaurants there? One with sparkling-clean carpeting."

"Because it would cost more?"

"Absolutely not," and Eloise glowered. "I just think the carpets shouldn't be stained like that. Perverts the whole room. Why aren't other people complaining? Insist the carpet be cleaned?"

"Maybe," Marti Morton, who was usually meek and mild, answered, "because they're not that concerned."

"Don't even notice or if they do, don't let a few spills bother them."

"Know they'll be cleaned up in due time."

"When feasible."

"Since you feel so strongly, you should voice a complaint, whether others do or not."

"Why me? I always have to. Why always me?" Eloise shot back.

"Because you like to," Marti responded, and she, Eloise, and the Brinkley sisters gave every appearance of not wanting to discuss the subject further.

Finally, Bertha Brinkley said, "Most of us here eat far too much, don't we? Especially in light of how inactive we are. Relatively inactive, that is."

"Food's comforting," her sister-in-law Essie suggested.

"And eating's social which is conducive to overeating," Marti added. "People around. Dressed up a little. Talking and laughing and being congenial."

"This is social? Congenial? That's what we're being?" Bertha asked as she looked directly at Eloise and smiled to take the edge off her remark.

"Sure," Eloise answered defensively. "Being sociable. We're with friends and expressing ourselves and engaging in kindly discussions."

"When I left the computer room at 3:45 this afternoon," Essie said to move the conversation along, "I walked past the dining room, and there were nine people already waiting for the 4:30 dinner serving to begin. All sitting along the wall where the chairs are, a few talking but most just sitting with their hands on their canes or walkers if they had them. All seemingly ready to push up and claim a place at the head of the serving line."

"In addition to the people in chairs, there were probably a half-dozen standing in back of the chair line."

"They greedy and piggish or what?"

"None of the above: Dinner's the highlight of their day."

"Hungry, too, most likely."

"What do you think about diners carrying food away from their tables when Management keeps asking us not to? Now, those people are piggish, and they make me angry."

"One lady supposedly brings Ziplocs so she can spirit stuff away. Rolls, bread, meat, desserts."

"One wonders if she is able to fix the meals not served as per her contract, the ones she, herself, must prepare."

"If not, she shouldn't be in independent living."

'Maybe she can't get to the store to shop…"

"There's the bus!"

"…or she's hard up financially."

"The high-level reason for getting on such people is, I've been told, that they sometimes leave the stuff they take in their cupboards or refrigerators until it becomes stale and moldy, which is wasteful and unsanitary."

"It could make them really sick."

"Or other people if the food is passed along."

"You better believe that their taking food ups our monthly fee."

"You know Bill and Marg Davis?" Essie asked. "They used to be Tour Planners, and Marg said they

Sap and Green People

had a rich client who owned a huge, profitable farm, plus vacation homes and rental properties and a big collection of antique farm machinery. Was a world traveler. And when they were in restaurants during the course of tours, the rich man and his wife filled their pockets and her purse with sugar, catsup, mustard, salt, pepper, coffee, and tea packets, rolls, and whatever."

"Why, for gosh sakes?"

"Maybe they were scarred by having lived through the Great Depression…"

"Which wasn't great. I'll testify to that."

"Some compulsion. Who knows what."

"Management has to offer refreshments to get residents to come to the health lectures it arranges for their own benefit."

"Verifying how important food is to people. For it, they'll sit through a health lecture!"

"The branch bank here in the Manor had an open house to inform people about its services. Well, though people our age need bank accounts but not many bank services, apparently a real crowd showed

Patricia Dick

up because the bank had promised to serve hors d'oeuvres."

"Only, the bank felt compelled to call them 'snacks', someone said, so people wouldn't come expecting to be served alcoholic drinks."

"The word 'hor d'oeuvres' infers them, apparently."

"Heard people say that they weren't interested in learning how to use computers but went to the Computer Lab open house some weeks ago because they expected something to eat. At least punch…"

"…and the organizers didn't serve anything because they wanted to 'protect the computers from crumbs and spills', which really disappointed some attendees."

"Overeating isn't limited to just old people."

"Watch the parade when you're at the mall."

"Hardly go there anymore."

"Myself, I shop by catalogue."

"Half the people you see there are tubs."

"Least half, young, middle-aged, and old."

Sap and Green People

"Getting back to here, I say that senility accounts for a lot of the gluttony."

"You said the dreaded word!"

"The most dreaded disease used to be 'the Big C'."

"Now is senility. Shiver, shiver!"

"God spare us senility," Essie Brinkley said, and she and her friends finished their desserts and coffee, excused themselves, and returned to their apartments to read or sit in front of their televisions until bedtime, having willed themselves not to give further thought to the demoralizing, absolutely devastating possibility of becoming a victim of senility, senile dementia, or worse yet, their terrible kin, Alzheimer's.

"Refresh my memory," Pat Marsh, until recently an Assisted Living nurse, asked Gloria Field. "How long ago was it that you asked to be transferred to Independent Living quarters? Having been transferred myself to another division, I've lost track of where you are, and that's why I stopped in: to catch up on your news."

"Seven months ago," Gloria answered.

"See if I have this straight, Gloria," Pat continued. "You asked if you could transfer from Assisted Living to a Manor apartment and were told, 'Perhaps'."

"Correct. My doctor then certified that, for all practical purposes, I'm capable of caring for myself. With that, 'perhaps' became 'okay', and I'm waiting for an apartment to open up."

"Do you believe you're being dealt with fairly?"

"Absolutely. There's a long wait for admittance, but I'll probably get in with another four to six months."

"Discouraged?"

"No. If I get in that soon, I'll count myself lucky. Besides, I need time to get ready."

"How so?"

"Well, to go through my things. I was in such a state when I moved into Assisted Living that I didn't even know what I brought with me. I'm weeding out things and doing a little mending."

"Have to do that myself," Pat confessed.

"Also, I'm learning to walk better. I started walking indoors. Progressed to moving into other parts of the building. Then I took on stairs. Walked outdoors next. Around the parking lot and along the sidewalk as far as the front of the Ad Building. Now I get to the bench in the Memorial Garden in front of the Ad Building where I rest before I start back. I'm not sure how far I'll ever be able to walk," Gloria confessed, "but I have to be able to manage a grocery store if I'm going to live independently. Also Walgreens and Lord and Taylor's," and she laughed at herself. "I even dream about driving a car again. Maybe a specially-equipped car, though if I don't get to, I'll hire a taxi or driver like several women around here do."

"Or use the Haven's bus. I can see that just the prospect of living independently has changed you," Pat told Gloria. "You're optimistic and full of plans. Have set goals."

"Oh, I am and have, and you're the one who got me started," Gloria answered. "How can I ever thank you?"

"Don't even try," and Pat picked up her briefcase.

"Don't go already," Gloria said, and the right side of her face registered disappointment.

"I have to get back to the Convalescent section. To my new job which I like," Pat answered. "Things were unusually quiet so I took a break, and it's time to return."

After Pat's departure, Gloria pulled on a bulky sweater; snapped a visor across her forehead, a visor because her left hand couldn't contribute to scarf-tying and her hats were too wintery, she decided; gripped her cane; and walked to an exit.

The prematurely warm April day was typically early May. Tulips and late-blooming jonquils bobbed their heavy heads when the breeze gusted. Lilacs smiled as busy robins, recent returnees, stopped-and-started their way across the greening-up turf. Paired, resident hawks circled high in the cloudless sky.

Step drag, step drag, step drag Gloria went as she advanced toward the Memorial Garden. Because treetops screened out a still-tepid sun, she stopped to button her sweater. All too conscious of her gait, she pictured how she used to look when she walked, and reflexively, she compressed her compromised body and pulled her shoulders forward, as if to diminish herself. Make herself less conspicuous.

Grant's image came to her, Grant who was strong, athletic, and physically perfect. Who loved her unconditionally. Kissed and caressed her body, in both its unaltered and altered state. Stroked her cheeks. Smoothed her hair.

More existential than traditionally Christian, Gloria wondered why she, who had taken good care of herself and been a moral person, had been so unfortunate as to be disabled. Childless. Widowed so young. Forgotten by friends. Her life was bare. Bleak. Black.

"Good morning," someone whom she'd neither seen or heard approach, called.

"Hello," Gloria answered, and she ducked her head to avoid direct encounter. Recognizing her response for what it was, an inversion, thanks to the counsel of the psychologist whom she was seeing, she willed herself to pull up her chin and look at the tiny, tennis-shoed, overly-bundled-up woman who came to a stop in front of her. Gloria smiled a half-smile and said, "A lovely day."

"Have to feel good on a day like this, don't we?" the round little lady answered as she looked Gloria square in the face without flinching.

"Indeed we do."

"Have a nice walk and goodbye," the woman said. "Hope to see you again," and she continued along the sidewalk.

Twenty paces closer to her destination, Gloria said aloud, "That's why I have to move. So I'll get out more. See more people. Have a bigger world. It's fine where I am, but I'm…stuck. At a dead end."

Sap and Green People

After walking to the end of the Memorial Garden path and as she prepared to cross the street, another voice greeted her, a male voice this time, and the man who'd spoken approached from her left.

"Good morning," Gloria heard herself say, and stopping to face the speaker, she said, "We have to feel good on a day like this, don't we?" The man agreed, smiled, and doffed his tweed hat which sported a smart, turned-down, two-inch brim.

"Indeed we do," he answered with more certainty than she'd answered the little woman who'd greeted her. "I don't believe we've met before. I'm Jack Clausen. Are you new to the Haven?"

"No," Gloria answered without ducking her head or turning her body away. "I'm Gloria Fields," and she extended her hand. "I've been here a while," she explained. "I haven't been very…social, though, so haven't met many people," and her laugh was self-conscious.

"Well then, I hope you meet more soon. Nice seeing you. Perhaps our paths will cross again on another fine day," and the man nodded and motioned for Gloria to cross the street before he proceeded, which she did without looking back.

My goodness, Gloria thought. I've met two people. On the same day! Today is indeed a fine day. A very fine day. Actually, the finest day in my recent history, and she grinned all the way back to the Assisted Living building.

Sap and Green People

"Georgia," Marg Davis said to Georgia Graham after the two women and their husbands sat down at a six-person table in the Manor dining room to eat dinner, "when I look at the little bit of food you have on your plate and compare it to what I have on mine, I'm embarrassed and feel like a pig."

"No-o-o-o," Georgia answered. "Don't feel that way."

"You and Henry have kept your weights down while Bill's gained a few pounds…"

"Few?" Bill interjected.

"…and I've gained five since we've been here, even with our walking and working out in the exercise room."

"The cooks are more concerned with taste than calories, I'm afraid," Georgia suggested graciously.

"What'd you do today, Friend Henry?" Bill asked, the weight subject having been exhausted.

"The usual," Henry replied. "Pushin' wheelchairs here and there mostly. Also talkin' to people who have complaints they want me to pass along."

"Serious complaints?" Bill wanted to know.

"Absolutely. The green bean casserole's too salty. Meetin' room's so hot that the card-players get sweaty. Someone left a folding chair in the hallway."

"Man, them's serious."

"Oh yes," Henry said. "Forgot one thing I did today. I picked up toenails."

"You what?"

"I often help the doctors change over," Henry explained. "You know: help the dermatologist put things away at the end of the half-day she spends in the clinic every three weeks. Then, shove clinic furniture around for, say, the psychiatrist who follows her and uses an entirely different room arrangement. And so forth.

Well today, Dr. Gray, the podiatrist, had to leave in a hurry to get to his main office. Was running behind. So I told him to go on, that I wasn't in a hurry and would pick up the toenail clippings that always shoot all over. Told him my eyes weren't good enough to see 'em but I'd get down on my knees where I could feel 'em and have them gone before the next doctor

Sap and Green People

arrived. He promised to bring a Dustbuster next time, which would do a real good toenail pick-up job."

"How many doctors use the clinic?" Bill asked.

"Never counted them, but an internist, dentist, psychiatrist, urologist who's also a gynecologist, ophthalmologist. Hearing specialists. Dermatologist and podiatrist and cardiologist. Probably missed a few. All connected to the same hospital system."

"For gosh sakes," Bill said. "I had no idea we had coverage like that," and just then, Bill looked up in time to see George Steiner grope his way around tables as he looked for a place to sit. Standing, Bill waved George an invitation to join him, Marg, and the Grahams.

"You've met my wife," Bill said after George had off-loaded his tray and seated himself. George, obviously confused, looked from Marg to Georgia and back, trying to determine which was Bill's wife.

"In the Ice Cream Parlor, some weeks ago now," Marg said to help resolve his quandary.

"Sure, sure," George mumbled.

"You know Henry?" Bill asked.

"Seen him around," George answered, "pushing wheelchairs."

"Never mind," laughed Henry, "that I'm a husband, father, engineer, reformed golfer, political independent, Methodist, and Confederate! What I've become and what I'm known as is a chair-pusher!" which set off a round of laughter and made George, who was not socially adept, relax.

"Well," George explained by way of characterizing himself, "I'm the male Ice Cream Parlor volunteer who wears a pink shirt 'stead of a maroon one like the other guys do," and he laboriously explained how he'd come to be known as 'the pink-shirted Ice Cream Parlor male volunteer'."

George also explained where he'd come from, Montana, one of the first pieces of information Haven residents exchanged when they met for the first time. "I worked on a railroad. Loved working outdoors and traveling. Moved to St. Louis after my wife died to be near my son. All the family I have, and five years ago, he died too. Boy," and he shook his head, "Esther had cancer fer six years so I was kind of prepared fer her going, but when Billy died, thought I'd die myself. Talked about heading back to Montana, but Billy's wife's a good girl, and she and their two boys wanted me to stay. So I did and came here."

"Good place to be," Henry said, and the occupants of the table agreed.

"The turkey fillets are tasty," Georgia, who generally opted for something other than red meat, commented.

"I shot a lotta turkeys in Montana," George told his companions. "William Clark liked turkey. Turkey and squirrel, and Meriwether Louis preferred rabbit. Or was it the other way around? Can't remember. You know?" and he looked around the table at first one, then another of his companions, who each answered negatively.

"I've heard you talk about Lewis and Clark in the Ice Cream Parlor a couple of times, George. You really dig those guys, don't you?"

"I do," George answered. "Great guys."

"Long time ago, I read that Lewis suffered from depression and migraine headaches," Henry said.

"They were army buddies. I remember that much."

"Lewis was Thomas Jefferson's secretary."

"'At's something!" George allowed. "That you know things about those guys. Lotta people don't know nothing about them."

"You must like living in St. Louis, what with Lewis and Clark being so tied to the city's history."

"I do, I do," George insisted. "Go to the history museum almost every week. My car's eleven years old, but it still goes and I still drive. So we get there often. Used to help down there, volunteered, though not much any more," and the conversation turned to the city's attractions, the art museum, botanical garden, butterfly house, zoo, parks, music, sports, and theater, a broad enough subject to take up the rest of the meal.

"Thanks for inviting me to sit with you," George said after he finished his walnut cake and stood to leave.

"Any time," Bill assured him. "Enjoyed your company."

Sap and Green People

"Our pleasure," Henry added as he stood to shake George's hand. "Glad to make your acquaintance, you old, pink-shirted son-of-a-gun, you."

"Interesting old man," Marg said as George walked away.

"Kind of pathetic."

"Yeh."

"Endearingly weird," Georgia said.

"God help him," Marg said, "God and we and his daughter-in-law and everyone else."

"You bet and amen!"

Patricia Dick

"House-watching and pet-sitting are a lot easier than taking care of the grandkids when they were little and their parents out of town," Marg Davis commented as she and Bill drove to their daughter's house.

"I can't really speak to that," Bill answered, "seeing as how you're the one who handled the grandkids while I took the coward's way out and spent the day back at our condo."

"Not always," Marg reminded him. "Sometimes we took them to the condo with us."

"Yeah, but I'd still retreat to our condo office and leave the kids to you."

"You had to tend our business, and where else other than from our office?" Marg asked which excused her husband as she so often did. "And I was glad to get the kids. They were so cute, so sweet.

Remember the time Susan and Tom went to Hawaii and got sick en route and the kids got sick back home?" Marg asked.

"You bet I do. 'Cause Tim threw up all over me and I got the bug too," Bill answered.

"Fortunately, I stayed well and could take care of the four of you."

"That was fifteen years ago, I'd guess."

"And remember when Dave and Glennie went skiing, Mandy had an ear ache for three of the days they were gone, and understandably, she wanted her mother? Poor little kid. And two years ago when Susan's family was gone and we sat with Toby and he started barking like crazy one night? I'm always half-scared at that house, and I thought we were about to be burglarized."

"Yah, yah."

"You got up, looked out, didn't see anything, and came back to bed until the doorbell rang," Marg recounted. "Expecting the knock was a ploy, I begged you not to answer. To hide in the bed with me until whoever was there went away."

"Fortunately, I looked out the window and reported that some kid was standing on the porch, someone who looked a lot like Bobby."

"And I sat bolt upright and said…"

"Yelled…"

"...yelled, 'It is! Bob's 'sposed to get home from skiing tonight at about 1:30!'"

"We'd kept him waiting on the porch in sub-zero weather. Must have frozen his tush off, but he didn't complain. Just laughed and hugged us and went on to bed.

The 'good old days'. Don't think about them for too long, Marg, or you'll get mellow on me."

"Already am," Marg answered as Bill turned into the circular drive which fronted their daughter's three story, modified-Colonial house.

Their arrival was anticipated, they found, for Toby, their ninety-five pound, Labrador retriever granddog, had heard them turn into the long cul-de-sac which the family and its two neighbors shared. Barking joyously at the prospect of company, a potty-break, and supper, Toby watched them approach from a foyer window, barking a welcome while his tail cut figure-eights.

The dog shot out of the door as Bill opened it, and before Bill could dig his penlight out, turn it on, locate the appropriate switch from among the many in the hallway, and snap on a light so he could see to punch

Sap and Green People

numbers into the burglar alarm, Toby was back at the door demanding admission. Focusing on his second need, he barked Bill and Marg into the laundry room where they fed him and gave him fresh water.

"Want to go for a ride, Toby?" Marg asked. Toby smiled and wagged his hindquarters. "Gotta go back to our apartment for awhile. You can go with us if you promise not to shed hair all over the place." Toby promised.

"We won't stay there long," Bill promised while activating the alarm, switching off the lights, pulling the door shut, and locking it behind him. "Get back here because Grandpa and Grandma may want to get into your hot tub." At the car, Bill coaxed Toby into the back seat, and after explaining the destination a second time and assuring Toby that he'd be comfortable where he was, Bill took his place behind the wheel.

Bill guided the car over to the Interstate and nosed it toward the Haven, approximately twelve miles away. After being passed by who-knew-how-many monstrous, hissy eighteen-wheelers, a trembling Toby hurled himself across the car's console and clambered onto Marg's lap.

"You idiot!" Marg exclaimed affectionately. "You can't sit here. There's not enough room," and she helped Toby get situated in her lap, which meant she no longer could see out the front window. Thus accommodated, Toby commenced pawing Bill's right wrist.

"Oh," Bill observed, "he wants me to hold his foot like Susan does when he's riding with her. I'm telling you, I always feel like a damned fool when I do this," and he took hold of and clasped Toby's extended paw.

"Toby," Marg said to the dog, "you like it at Grandma and Grandpa's place, don't you?" Toby yipped that he did. "I'll take you down the hall to see Joe. You remember Joe, don't you?" Toby remembered Joe. "And we'll call on Mickey who often asks about you."

"Toby," Bill went on to say, "a nurse at the Haven brings her dog to work so the dog can spend the day visiting residents. You'd like that too, wouldn't you?" Toby nodded. "And you'd like the cages full of

Sap and Green People

jabbering birds in the Convalescent center. No pussy cats, though." Toby relaxed his ears and barked his relief.

Bill dropped Toby's paw as he turned into the Haven, made the right turn which took the car past the Patio Homes, turned left to cross the bridge spanning the creek, and parked in front of Apartment Building 709. "We won't be long, Old Boy. An hour or so to do some telephoning and check on things. Then Grandma and I'll get back to your mom and dad's hot tub. Good idea, don't you think?" and Toby barked happily.

Patricia Dick

Mary Spritzer was alone when she boarded the Haven bus which would take her and twenty-one other persons to Powell Hall, home to the acclaimed St. Louis Symphony Orchestra. Mary didn't mind attending functions alone, but she was pleased to spot Joan Cutler, with whom she often ate dinner and whose company she enjoyed, already seated alone near the front of the bus.

"Hello, hello," Mary said to Joan as she drew abreast.

"Hello yourself. Had I known you were coming, I'd have planned to meet and board with you. Please join me unless you're committed to someone back there," and she looked over her shoulder to indicate whom she meant. Since Mary wasn't, Joan moved over a seat to make room for her.

"I never ask around about who's going to these things," Mary explained. "In making plans, too often someone gets left out and planning with people can get terribly complicated. So it's a lovely surprise to find you here," and the two settled themselves for the half-hour ride in the green-and-white, attractive but bumpy, rattly Haven bus.

Except in the case of cosmetically-colored heads, the hair of most Haven residents, male and female, was grey, and Mary's and Joan's hair was no exception. Characteristically formed into sausage curls anchored on top of her head by invisible means, Mary's hair was a silver-grey while Joan's grey was unique in that it glinted in the light, most particularly in sunlight, as if comprised of steel threads. Full-bodied, wavy, short enough to be 'mannish', it showcased Joan's well-appointed face and tiny ears.

The two women appeared almost paired, sister-like, for besides being grey-headed and tall, both were thin which distinguished them from many other women of their age. Because she was less approachable, people didn't comment to Mary about her slimness, but they did to Joan, and she'd answer modestly with, "I can't take credit: I just never plumped up." Dressed informally or formally, the two commanded second glances.

Mary was dressed for the concert in a mannishly-tailored, pin-striped, navy blue suit; Joan, in a loose black coat which came down to her ankles, brown linen slacks, and a soft, brown and white striped blouse.

"In the dining room, at meetings, in the halls, elsewhere, we keep running across each other. But we've never been solely in each other's company before, and I'm glad for this chance to get better acquainted with you," Mary said. "I'm afraid I'm regarded as being formidable," she added. "Are you worried that I'll confront you in some blatant way or gobble you up or worse?"

Taken back by Mary's directness, Joan looked Mary straight in the eyes and said, "You're kidding, aren't you? Being absurd?"

"Of course I am," Mary conceded.

"We dine-togethers are an interesting bunch," Joan said.

"Interesting, yes. Varied, inquisitive, and interesting," Mary answered, the 'inquisitive' a reference to the guessing game played regarding Mary's background, Joan felt sure.

"Does our 'inquisitive' make a problem for you?" Joan asked.

Mary tipped her head back, laughed, and said, "Absolutely no. I used the word 'interesting' very deliberately and last, if you noticed, to suggest that we're having fun, that the vying makes our time together more interesting than it would be otherwise."

"Are you always as mysterious as you seem to be with us?" Joan asked.

"Mysterious?" Mary answered. "I appear mysterious? Oh, I think not."

"Well, that's how you come across to us," Joan said.

"What I think happened," Mary suggested, "is our dining room relationship just sort of happened when some remark was made, can't remember exactly what, I came up with a 'smarty', evasive answer, and there it was, the pattern," Mary said. "I hope I have the energy and adroitness to sustain it."

"Oh do," Joan answered, "because it's fun. Also sets you apart. Assigns you to a special place in our circle."

"I hadn't expected or wanted that," Mary said.

"Why not?" Joan countered. "There's too much sameness at this point in our lives and around here. We love your being different. And for my part, I'll never tell our friends that the whole thing was unintended. That it just happened."

"Please don't," Mary said, "for it would spoil the fun of it and remove a challenge."

"I promise," Joan said, and she gave the raised-finger, Girl Scout promise-sign to back her pledge. When Mary appeared not to recognize the sign, Joan explained its significance and kidded Mary about her lack of what Joan called 'real-life' experience.

"Do the Girl Scouts still make promises," Mary asked, "or do they just sell cookies?"

"Are they even called 'Girl Scouts'?" Joan mused, and as the bus traveled along a street running north and south along the west side of St. Louis University, one Joan had traveled hundreds of times during her active

Sap and Green People

years, when her job and personal commitments had her driving from one end of the city to the other, she and Mary watched out the window.

"How it's all changed," Joan said.

"For the better?" Mary asked. "A newcomer, I've never been along here."

"Absolutely. The neighborhood had become really dog-eared. Dingy and dangerous. But it's turning around nicely now, thanks to the influence of the University."

"Believe it or not, I've never been to Powell Hall," Mary confessed.

"'My dear'," Joan answered in a voice imitative of Mary's, "'I've lived in so many exciting places that until now, I've just not had occasion to hang out in sleepy, old St. Louis'. Right?"

"Exactly," Mary said as she extended her left, upturned palm so she could tap it with the fingers of her right hand and consequently applaud Joan's performance. "How did you know?"

That said, Mary and Joan watched the bus turn right, drive a short distance, wait out a red light, and pull up at the north side of Powell Hall. Having clambering down the bus' three steps and walked two dozen more steps, they, who'd struck a bargain, entered the venerated symphony hall to share a most-pleasant symphonic interlude.

Sap and Green People

"I'm home," Bill Davis called to Marg as he opened the door to their apartment, stepped into the diminutive dining room, and snapped on the light. The four opaque globes in the ceiling fixture flooded the room with light which Bill compromised by turning a dimmer.

The dimmed light illuminated the round oak table planted beneath it, also what hung on the two dining room walls: pictures of the couple's three children when they were young; a print, prized by at least three generations of Marg's family, depicting a child-member of England's Stuart family; a triangular arrangement of three small plaques; and two glass platters framed against black velvet in a shadowbox, one plate marked '1876', commemorative of the country's first centennial and a wedding present given to Marg's great-grandparents who were married that year; the other, identical except for a 1976 marking, ordered from the Fostoria company, denoting the bicentennial. Bill crossed the living room to look out the deck door.

"How'd things go in the computer lab today?" Marg asked as she joined Bill in studying the purple crocuses bordering walkways, greening-up expanses, and budding-out trees.

"Good," Bill answered. "Old Tom came in today again. He's progressing well because when the computer room's open and tutorials aren't scheduled, he practices his head off."

"What about that sweet, smiley lady who thanks you for helping her every time she sees us in the dining room?"

"Doing okay though as I've told you, she has a tremor which makes it hard for her to control the mouse. She has two advantages, though. She takes everything I tell her down in shorthand, then uses the information when she practices, and she was an executive secretary and hence an expert typist to begin with."

"She your best student?"

"I guess so," Bill answered typically, for Bill almost never answered a question with a straight-out, decisive yes or no. "Students have different goals.

Sap and Green People

Many want to learn to use e-mail so they can communicate with their kids, grandkids, and friends who may live anywhere in the world. Some want to play games, probably solitaire or golf. Others, to get their financial data organized and recorded. When people accomplish their first goal, some continue on, which is gratifying.

Take Tom Springer whom I introduced you to last week. He wanted to learn to use e-mail and did. His kids are bikers and live away. They were to visit him and wanted to ride in Forest Park while they were here. So I helped Tom get information about the park from the net, and he was tickled pink to have something to give them. Now, he's always looking up some topic or another.

Not everyone can learn, though. Some lack motor skills. Shake. Senile. We feel bad about them. And there are the mean ones," and characteristically, he slipped off his shoes.

"Many of them?"

"Not really. The worst was the 'Battling Battleaxe'. She blasted into the lab on her motorized wheelchair one day, the chair with which she'd supposedly already run down two persons. She handed me her password and her granddaughter's e-mail address, written on a scrap of paper, and demanded that I help her send the girl an e-mail.

Well, I couldn't get the computer to accept the password so I tried to by-pass it and proceed other ways, without success. Frustrated the dickens out of me and made her madder and shriller by the minute. Good old Norbert, who's in charge of the lab, of course, and who'd worked with her previously, picked up on what was happening and came over. 'You must not have the right password,' he told the lady in a very understanding voice.

'I do,' she insisted. Virtually screamed at us. 'Look at this if you don't believe me. Look at it and you'll see that it's your handwriting. You wrote this password down yourself,' and she waved the paper in Norbert's face. Instead of arguing, Norb walked to the file cabinet where records of each tutorial are kept and pulled out a folder.

Sap and Green People

'You'll see!' the screechy woman kept screaming as he looked through the folder, and her face got all red. 'I'm right!' and her eyes were wide with defiance.

'Madam,' Norbert said after a few minutes, 'I gave you another piece of paper, a bigger piece. One with this written on it,' and he handed over his copy of what he'd written on the previous occasion.

'There is-s-s something else back in my room,' the woman answered reluctantly. But not apologetically or with contrition. 'On top of my television.'

'We have time left before the lab closes,' Norbert told her. 'Why don't you get that piece of paper?' which prompted the woman to throttle up and speed away. Norbert and I expected her to claim a third victim en route, and we told each other that we wished she were riding a broom instead of her chair.

She returned with the other paper which had the right address on it. I typed the letter she dictated, explained that actually we taught residents to use the computer rather than use it for them, and I shouldn't type another for her. That we'd be glad to work with her though, teach her, and Dottie works with her sometimes now on Tuesday mornings.

We gave her the benefit of the doubt, Norbert and I. Attributed her meanness to senility. That's what we do."

"One does wonder about mean old people," Marg answered. "If they were always mean or if senility has made them that way."

"Well, Dear, I can tell you that you have nothing to worry about. Absolutely nothing. Because I'll always remain my sweet, accommodating, communicative, affectionate, unselfish self. Right to my very end."

"Oh no!" Marg exclaimed. "Unaccustomed as I am to such behavior and treatment, I won't know how to live with that. Absolutely not!"

Sap and Green People

Having completed its eight assigned discussions, the Great Decisions group had disbanded until the following January. Consequently, its leader, Jack Clausen, who was considerably less active in off-campus activities and affairs than when he moved into the Haven at Oak Hill, found that for the first time in his life, he had time on his hands.

Had that been the case five, even three years earlier, Clausen would have picked a topic having to do with world affairs; spent months studying the subject; written a monograph or book about it; then continued researching, writing, and giving speeches until he had either exhausted his material or grown cold on the subject.

If he'd not chosen to follow the study route, Jack would have taken off for a place of his choice: New York, London, or Rome which he knew well, or Lima, Cape Town, or Port of Spain which he did not. He'd travel alone which didn't both him in the least, visit libraries and museums, read and look, in that order, his modus operandi.

These days, however, Jack was tiring of worrying about long-ago circumstances, unsolvable problems, unattainable causes. What had come from his learning, proclamations, and endeavors? What good had they done? I've not accomplished much, if anything, he'd come to believe, and I'm tired of weighty matters and gargantuan causes. Of being weighted down by raw information. Not quite hopeless, I'm almost totally joyless and lonely.

Why didn't I marry, he asked himself. Because I disliked women? Couldn't love, risk, change, compromise? Assume responsibility for another person? Was I closed-hearted? Selfish? Afraid?

Lovely Julia would have married me, he reminded himself. Likewise Charlotte. Gioia actually asked that I marry her. What excuse did I give? And though he could name the members of Teddy Roosevelt's cabinet, try as he would, he couldn't remember what he'd told Gioia to terminate their relationship. Couldn't remember because he'd chosen to forget, he knew.

Sap and Green People

Joyless, lonely, and regretful about many of his life choices and thoroughly depressed, Jack commenced looking around for a new endeavor.

What I'll do, he finally decided, is study, and he laughed at himself. Only, he resolved, rather than studying for my own edification, I'll study to find a campus need which I can address.

To identify that need, Jack queried the Haven's Administrator, Harry Wright, other staff members, and residents. He investigated activities and programs offered at other senior residences, read what gerontologists had to say, and brainstormed.

And what he determined was that while Haven residents were transported to restaurants, concerts, plays, and other attractions off campus and offered musical presentations, parties, fashion shows, pancake breakfasts, and chili dinners on campus, with the exception of Bible study, health lectures, and Great Decisions meetings, there was a shortage of what he regarded as educational offerings included in the Haven's on-site program.

Jack further determined that to help rectify that shortage, he'd prepare a series of multi-media presentations that met his criteria and suited the tastes of persons residing in the Haven. More particularly, the presentations would be approximately forty-five minutes long, the length of time older people could be expected to concentrate, as suggested by several gerontologists.

"Subjects will be contemporary personalities, both male and female. I'll introduce them with brief remarks, then follow up with videos I somehow put together, using cuttings from film, television, recorded music, and radio," he explained to Administrator Harry Wright who was most receptive and supportive of the idea. Jack planned to use his savings and an inheritance he'd never touched to bankroll the endeavor, at least initially.

Jack knew nothing about how to make videos. He had a computer which he used in his writing, but he didn't know how to use its capabilities in the course of video-making. He therefore hired a junior college computer student, Rob, and also a media student, Bud, to help him with his enterprise.

"We'll make use of libraries, local media companies, and other community resources," he told Rob and Bud. "I don't know what they are or how to utilize them, but hopefully you do—or will—which is one way you'll assist me.

Jack selected six subjects for his first series of videos: Fidel Castro, Mahalia Jackson, Arthur Ashe, Beverly Sills, George Orwell ('not quite contemporary but close enough', Jack declared), and Lady Bird Johnson. He and his team purchased and rented videomaking equipment; Jack researched the first subject, Castro; the three worked out an introduction to the subject which would shape the video's development; and Rob and Bud selected excerpts from print, film, recordings, and photo files, their use having been cleared or purchased, Rob's primary assignment. Preliminaries completed, Jack wrote the scenario.

And so the making of the video proceeded, slowly, well, badly, unevenly, and satisfactorily by turn, and some months later, the little company presented its first offering which was entitled 'Fidel Castro: God, Guru, or Ghoul?'

"Ladies and Gentleman," Jack addressed his audience of about sixty-five persons on the night of the showing, "what we've put together for your edification," and he regretted his word choice, "for your entertainment, that is, is admittedly imperfect. That notwithstanding, we hope you'll enjoy what you see and return in the future for the rest of the series. That's our aim, and we thank you for coming." The show was warmly received.

"A great idea, well executed," one gentleman told Jack over a cup of Caribbean punch served, along with nuts, fruits, and coconut macaroons, after the showing. "Thanks to the three of you."

"Excellent, excellent," Norbert Blair proclaimed.

"Super!"

"Great production."

"We knew you could do what you were doing," Joan Cutler said, "but we didn't know what it was," which induced laughter.

"Congratulations on a job well done."

Sap and Green People

"Gonna do a program on Lewis and Clark?" George Steiner, whom Jack hadn't met previously, asked.

"They're not on our list, but possibly," Bud answered.

"Maybe later," Jack added.

"Should. Great guys," George said as he stared off into the distance, looking very much as if he were entranced by a vision of the two explorers. "Better do it sooner than that, though, 'cause when it comes right down to it, none of us got too long a future."

Jack laughed and thanked George for his suggestions before excusing himself and Bud so they could get to the packing up of their equipment, and only after it was packed did he let himself acknowledge how pleased he was with that he'd done. How certain he felt that his life had taken a turn for the better. How hopeful he was about his immediate future.

"Right on!" he shouted as he raised a clenched fist, a most uncharacteristic behavior for Jack Clausen, a

117

Patricia Dick

decidedly brilliant, inhibited, ultra-formal, heretofore stuffed-shirt sort of a guy.

Sap and Green People

"My sunglasses enhance the color red, but they diminish green, which is a good thing," Marg Davis told Bill as they took their almost-daily walk around the campus. "Because this spring's green is simply dazzling. So dazzling, it might mess up my eyes."

"There you go again," Bill told her. "Exaggerating."

"Not true," Marg insisted. "I may be hyperbolic, but I don't exaggerate," and Bill reacted to her statement with a high-pitched laugh as they paused to look at the hillside, woods, and lake which stretched out ahead of them. "Beautiful," Marg commented. "Simply beautiful."

"Tulips, jonquils, iris are gone already," Bill observed.

"Wasting-away blooms don't make the jonquils and iris look particularly bad, but the tulips look simply awful when they're dying back."

"Hyperbole again," Bill said. "They don't look that bad. No one ever threw up at the sight of wilting tulips, I'd be willing to bet."

"Well, if you'll wait a minute, I probably can. Just thinking about how they look will do it," Mary insisted. "I'm glad you didn't use the word 'puke'."

"Why?"

"'Cause it's such a…pukey word," and they set out to cover the last third of their route.

Pansies, they noticed, turned their faces to the sun, violets bobbed in the breeze, phlox hugged rocks and hillsides. Turf, tall and thick, begged to be mown. April rains had cascaded into the lake, stirring it up and leaving it high and mud-brown. Dogwoods and redbuds colored the woods, Bradford pears bowed under heavy, pink blossoms, and tomorrow would be Easter.

"Spring's about renewal, isn't it?" Marg said just before the wind plucked the straw hat from her head and sent it cartwheeling across the street. Bill retrieved it for her.

"Got any warm memories of childhood Easters?" she asked.

"Naw-w-w," Bill answered.

Sap and Green People

"No Easter egg hunts? Baskets? Family gatherings?"

"None."

"Did your family go to church on Easter?"

"No."

"How'd you feel about that?"

"Didn't give it a thought."

"No memories at all?"

"None."

"Mostly," Marg said, "I remember getting up at 4:30 or 5:00 when I was in junior high and high school. To go to the Sunrise Service held at the top of a windy dune out at chilly Lake Michigan. Getting up that early and in the dark was a strain, and by the time I'd faced that cold, maybe even snow and ice, I'd pretty much lost the religious fervor I'd worked up prior to Easter," and with that, Marg left off citing Easter memories because Bill had none to share.

She consequently didn't tell Bill how the service held in the church sanctuary several hours after the Sunrise Service always moved her to tears. How being with fervent, joyous worshipers thrilled and inspired her. How her father's pulpit performance, his clear, expressive, persuasive voice and well-crafted, provocative sermon made her proud. How her heart swelled at the hymn-singing and choir music and organ's swell.

Neither did she tell Bill that while her mother never had Easter clothes herself, she always saw that Marg had an Easter outfit or special article of clothing. That one Easter when Marg had wanted a double-breasted spring coat and she and her mother couldn't find one that was affordable, her mother bought the single-breasted coat of their choice and sets of identical buttons, lapped the front of the coat over somewhat, sewed one set of bottoms to the left front and the other to the right front, thus making it 'double-breasted'.

That when she was fourteen and worked in a grocery store, a loutish, older boy with whom she worked gave her a heart-shaped box of chocolates as she left work on the night before Easter, the first box of candy she'd been given. The box contained forty-six chocolates, and though she didn't particularly like its donor, at approximately 9:00 for the next forty-six evenings, she'd ceremoniously eaten one piece, just one.

All that remembering made Marg wish with all her being that her own children were small again, she shopping for Easter basket stuffings, readying Easter garments, planning Easter delights.

"Slice the rib roast thin tomorrow, Dear," she said to Bill.

"Worried we won't have enough?"

"No. The meat will look and taste better if it's sliced thin."

"You still staging the art show?"

"Got all the children's and grandchildren's drawings, greeting cards, letters, poems, reports, and stories set out. Other art projects too. I'm ready.

"How you going to work it?"

"Scotch-tape most of the things to the backs of doors, woodwork, mirrors, television screens, picture frames, and such. In all the rooms. Tell everyone when they arrive that we're having an art show. That everyone must look at every single thing I've put up while I get dinner on the table."

"Use masking tape. It'll peel off easier afterwards."

"Bill, I hope you have a nice day tomorrow. At church, with the wonderful music and lovely lilies and nice people. Then, with our children and grandchildren."

"Of course I will," Bill answered, his voice registering surprise at what Marg had just said.

"You don't always. Sometimes you just sit back, withhold yourself, maybe even glower. Because I'm having to work to get people fed or because there's noise and confusion. Our routine's interrupted. I'm not really sure why. I have fun, and the kids have fun, but sometimes you don't. Or appear not to, anyway. Which makes me feel so, so sad. 'Cause of what you miss and of what the family misses. I hope you…engage. Have at least a somewhat memorable time."

"I will, I will," a sobered Bill pledged, Bill who was by nature solitary and rational rather than communal and sentimental. "I promise," and he put his arm around Marg's shoulders. "From the time the family arrives to when the leftovers are in the fridge, dishes in the dishwasher, and you and I in bed for an Easter nap."

Bill Davis, handicapped to a degree by what his doctor called 'plantar fascia' (a very sore heel), limped up the street towards the Administration Building, the core of the campus, where the ice cream parlor was situated on the second floor. Because two of his children had suffered the plantar abomination recently, when people inquired about his limp, Bill explained that it was attributable to "one of those maladies one inherits from his children, like headaches and poverty."

For some years, the Haven at Oak Hill property had belonged to a Catholic religious order. The order had constructed an administration building which also housed members of the order and a church, fittingly adorned with stained glass windows, the Stations of the Cross, a pipe organ, and a bell tower topped with an iron cross.

After the property was purchased by a Protestant denomination, the denomination added a Convalescent Center to the Administration Building and modified the church so it appeared more ecumenical. Over a period of the next twenty-five years, it also added the six-story Manor; an Assisted Living facility which was

Sap and Green People

linked to the Ad Building by an enclosed bridge; Patio Homes; and three two-story Apartment Buildings. The Davises lived in the middle Apartment Building, Building 709.

The volunteers who worked in the ice cream parlor had become used to working with each other and smoothed out operations and procedures. Bill was consequently comfortable with what he'd earlier regarded as an abominable duty. In fact, after entering the Ad Building, he took the steps to the second floor two at a time (and on his tiptoes, due to his facia).

"Hey there, you nasty old Irishman," he said to Mike McGuire as he clapped Mike on the shoulder. "Good afternoon Grace, Daisy, Dell."

"Today's specials are pineapple sherbet, cookies 'n cream ice cream, and raspberry yogurt," Grace told her cadre of workers after they'd assembled and executed their start-up chores. "I saw you gentlemen…"

"Who?" George quipped. "Where?" and he looked around for the 'gentlemen' Grace had referenced.

"…taking inventory of what we need from the downstairs kitchen, so while you go there, we'll finish here." George and Bill pushed a food cart toward the elevator and Mike, Daisy, and Dell headed in three directions to do what needed doing.

"Today's my lucky day," Bill said to George. "I get to go to the kitchen with you instead of with Mike."

"I still say this is the slowest damned elevator in the world," George insisted as he and Bill stepped aboard the slow, rattly contrivance.

"You don't need to persuade us of that," Bill responded. "When Grace called you up short for saying 'damned' that time, she didn't disagree. She just thought that you shouldn't use that terrible word 'damn' in public."

"She damned sure didn't." George answered somewhat bitterly.

"Maybe her deceased husband didn't use that sort of language," Bill said facetiously.

"Damned shame. He might a' lived longer. Say," George continued, "remember when I said at dinner that Meriwether Lewis liked to eat rabbit?"

"I do," Bill answered.

Sap and Green People

"Well, it was turkey he liked," and Bill thanked him for the information. "I had two hound dogs fer a long while. One named Lewis, the other Clark. Still miss those buggers."

Though ice cream traffic was heavy again when the parlor opened and two helpers failed to appear, serving went smoothly until a beefy, red-faced, wheelchair-bound man arrived, one of a small group of handicapped persons whom two attendants were shepherding.

"Outta' my way," the man bellowed to the woman in the wheelchair ahead of him, and he rammed his chair into hers. The surprised woman emitted a scream, then expressed her indignation.

"John," an attendant said to the errant man, "you promised to be nice if we brought you down. Remember?" and she stepped in back of John's chair and took over its operation.

"This is your second cone this afternoon," Dell said as she handed a cone to the tiny little, eye-blinking customer whose chair John had rammed.

"I just lov-v-v-e ice cream," the woman explained rather tenuously, and she scooted her wheelchair out of the way with her empty hand and beat a hasty retreat.

Next up, John ordered a strawberry malt topped with whipped cream and a cherry.

"That will be $1.75," Dell informed him.

"To hell you say," John raged. "It's free."

"No," Dell explained. "A cone or dish of ice cream is free. Extra, like a malt, the whipped cream, and cherry, cost extra. $1.75."

"John," his aide said, "we talked about the extra charge before we came down."

"Didn't," John insisted.

"Yes we did."

"Well," John's answer boomed, "I don't have any money on me."

"You told me you had money in your pocket."

"Did not."

"Oh-h-h yes."

"Charge it," John commanded.

"We'll charge it to your room," Dell told him.

Sap and Green People

"I got a charge card," and John commenced digging furiously in his pocket. "Five of 'em. Somewhere!"

"It's not a matter of having credit cards," Dell explained. "We'll just charge it to your room. What's your room number?"

"What kind of a place is this?" John bellowed.

"Shish," his attendant kept saying.

"Never mind," said Dell, whose voice was becoming quivery. "That's okay."

"It better be!"

"I'll pay," the attendant offered.

"No," Grace said in her managerial voice after stepping to the counter to resolve the fracas. "Forget it please," and to expedite John's departure, George, the malt-maker, rushed over with the malt in question.

"Here 'tis," he reported breathlessly, "and thank you very much, Sir."

"I'm very angry with you," the attendant told John as she turned his chair away from the serving counter.

At that moment, a pretty gentlewoman who'd placed a friend's wheelchair in the ice cream line and witnessed the whole incident stepped up to John and said in an indignant, yet controlled, voice, "Sir, you really should mind your manners. Everyone around here is trying to be helpful, and you're being very unpleasant and rude."

"Out of the way, Bitch," John growled, and his elbow shot out at the woman, missing her but leaving her shaken and embarrassed.

"Our 'incident of the day'," Grace announced cheerfully, and the serving continued, one customer, one group after another. Without respite. Cheerful until the woman who'd earlier declared her love for ice cream returned, that is. For her third strawberry cone. "You do love ice cream," Grace said. "Strawberry ice cream anyway,' and her comment coincided exactly with the arrival of a breathless aide who was in pursuit of the women. "She can't have ice cream," the aide explained to Grace and the other volunteers who were within hearing distance. "She's diabetic. Hopefully, you'll recognize her when she shows up again," and as the volunteers studied the woman in an effort to

Sap and Green People

memorize her face, she reluctantly surrendered her cone to the aide who returned it to Dell.

"That's it!" a weary Grace declared as she slammed shut the Dutch doors which closed off the counter at 3:25, five minutes prior to close-up time. "All I can stand today," and she sighed. "Seems like you're damned if you do and damned if you don't!" and her use of 'damn' left George Steiner positively bug-eyed.

Max, the Davises' nine-year-old grandson, was spending a June Friday with Bill and Marg. Since Bill was volunteering in the Computer Lab that morning, Marg and Max decided to hike parts of the campus before the warm day became hot.

Setting out on a mulch-covered trail running through the woods behind the Davises' apartment building, Marg and Max watched for signs of squirrels, rabbits, and racoons. Not successful in those regards, they did see and hear birds galore, especially sassy, raucous crows.

"Ever notice that crows don't stay put?" Max asked.

"No," Marg confessed. "Hadn't."

"They keep moving from one bunch of trees to another. Moving and talking back and forth. Do that in the woods behind our house too."

After emerging from a wooded stretch, the trail gave way to a sidewalk which took the hikers across the wide, oak-shaded front acreage in front of the Administration Building. Cutting east, then north, the two advanced to the shore of the Haven lake and a

Sap and Green People

bench where they sat down to eat and drink what they'd carried with them in a little cooler.

From the bench, the pair looked for waterfowl and the muskrat which supposedly lived under the lake's southeast bank. While they didn't see it, they did see dozens, maybe hundreds, of goldfish of varying sizes feeding at the east end of the lake.

"Where do you think they came from?" Max asked.

"Beats me," Marg answered. "I've never seen them before. Got any theories?"

"No."

"Well, the only thing I can think of is that someone dumped them in the lake. A while back, judging from how big and how many there now are. Maybe a resident was about to leave for vacation and hadn't made fish-sitter arrangements so resorted to dumping."

"Naw-w-w," Max insisted.

"Well, I have to confess that I did something like that once," Marg countered, and she told Max that she'd poured her children's two goldfish into the toilet and flushed them away because she'd forgotten to make provisions for them before the family went on an extended vacation.

"I can't help wonder," she went on to say, "how those goldfish have survived winters in that shallow lake, since some of our winters are severe."

"Ask Grandpa," Max suggested. "He's sure to know."

From their bench which faced the back of the Manor, Marg and Max watched aproned persons step out from a Manor back door, walk across a high loading dock, and look down into an open dumpster which abutted the side of the dock. After those persons returned to where they came from, the kitchen adjacent to the Manor dining room, Marg felt sure, they were replaced by others who also came to look.

Unexpectedly, as Marg and Max watched the scenario play through a half-dozen times and puzzled over what was happening, they saw two creatures dash away from the dumpster and disappear into lakeside underbrush.

"Racoons!" Marg exclaimed.

Sap and Green People

"Couldn't be," Max answered. "It's daytime and racoons are nocturnal."

"Well, I guess not then," Marg conceded, and she and Max watched as a pair of walkers approached the bench where there were sitting.

"Did you see the 'coons?" the man asked.

"Oh-h-h, they were racoons," Max said.

"Racoons," the smiling woman affirmed. "We were standing at the corner of the Manor, and they streaked by right in front of us, and we got a good look at them. We think they'd been eating out of the dumpster and the kitchen help frightened them away."

"The help could have been cleaning out refrigerators," the man said, "and the odors attracted the little fellows." With that suggestion, the couple resumed walking, as did Marg and Max.

"Where now?"

"Let's follow the path passing through the jungle behind our apartment," Marg suggested. "Complete the loop we started."

The 'jungle', which was not quite that, was comprised of trees of many sorts, scrub timber, and a tangle of vines, weeds, and underbrush, all so tightly entwined that in some places, the sun couldn't peek through. Decayed logs, pine needles, and rotting leaves rendered its floor rank and spongy, and when the grey-blonde grandmother and her white-headed grandson picked their way over it, they spotted a broad, fallen tree about fifteen yards to the right of the path. Rough-barked and perhaps twenty feet long, the tree spanned a gully measuring four to five feet.

"Dare you to walk that fallen tree," Marg said. "To the other side of the gully."

"Why don't you?" Max was quick to ask.

"Can't," Marg answered. "Bad knees and I don't dare fall. Old people should avoid falls, see, because their bones break easily. Yours wouldn't and the ground's soft anyway, but mine very well might. Otherwise, I'd do it in a minute. Always used to do things like that."

"Okay-y-y," Max replied, and he and Marg made their way over to the tree's break-off point.

Standing on the tree-become-log, Max extended his arms out to his sides, straight out, for balance,

Sap and Green People

concentrating on positioning his feet, first the right with its toes pointed straight ahead. Testing and balancing, he slid the foot back and forth, then planted the left foot squarely behind the right. Satisfied with their placement, he drew the toes of his left foot up to the right heel, then moved the right foot forward. Right forward, left likewise, he slowly, cautiously inched along the log, seesawing his arms for balance. Right, left, forward. Right, left, forward. Forward, forward, forward.

Why'd I suggest this, a panicky Marg wondered as she watched the boy's progress. He might fall. Hit a stone. Wham his head on the log. Scrape his leg. Hurt his stomach. Back. Slit flesh with a protrusion left when a branch broke off. Poke an eye out, and she commenced sweating. Fought the compulsion to cover her eyes or call a warning. Wondered if she should jump into the gully. Position herself to break a fall. Prepare to catch her grandson. Dear God, she gasped, help! Please, please, please! Save him.

"I did it! I did it," Max shouted as he giant-stepped off the far end of the log. "How'd you like that?"

"Swell!" Marg proclaimed. "Swell," and she scrambled over to the boy. "You're my sweetie pie," she said as she hugged him, "like I've told you so many times," all the while remembering the giving of hugs to other small, precious bodies. "You did so well that you'll be rewarded with two Popsicles when we get back."

"Want to go to the dumpster," Max stated. "See if the racoons came back."

But they found no gawking kitchen workers or rummaging racoons at the loading dock.

"Boost me up, please," Max asked. Doing so required all of Marg's strength, but boost she did. High enough so Max could grab the dock's sun-heated, pipe railing and pull himself up onto the dock. And when he looked down into the container, Max's face broke into a smile, his brow shot up, and he motioned for Marg to join him.

"Can't," Marg called. "Can't scale the wall."

Max squatted to look down into the dumpster, and after doing so, he waved wildly, as if to indicate that what he was seeing was amazing, spectacular,

Sap and Green People

confounding. Straightening, he walked to where Marg waited and jumped down beside her.

"One racoon's in there, Grandma," he reported in a hushed voice. "In the container. On its back. Sound asleep. With his fat tummy heaving up and down," and he mimicked the stomach's movement. "Looked like it'd eaten so much he couldn't move and fell asleep, 'n I decided not to waken him. And get this: He's got an empty peach can over his face. Big peach can. Covers everything 'cept his eyes," and Max doubled over with restrained laughter.

Not to aid or guide him but to communicate her love, Marg took the hand of her youngest grandchild and walked with him to her apartment, where the two Popcicles she awarded him dripped all over the dominos they'd left on the dining room table.

Thus ending a morning that Marg Davis would treasure forever and ever, one she hoped never to forget, regardless of what might intervene.

Patricia Dick

Even when summer days had sizzled, Gloria Fields practice-walked, the term she used when referring to her twice-a-day walks, one short, one longer. Up and down halls and walkways she went, a part of the regimen she'd worked out to strengthen her stroke-compromised body.

Despite her efforts, Gloria's left, atrophied leg failed to improve perceivably, her left arm either. Her perseverance paid off in other regards though, for it strengthened her right leg, increased her endurance, improved her respiration, and reinforced her determination to become as physically ready as possible for moving into Independent Living quarters.

As Gloria approached the exterior doors of the elongated, one-story Assisted Living facility one October day, she said to the receptionist, "I'm going as far as the top of the Manor hill this afternoon. So I can see the lake. I've never gotten that far before."

"Where I come from, Wisconsin, we call a shallow, puny body of water like our lake a pond, so don't expect too much. And don't be too ambitious because

Sap and Green People

you shouldn't overdo. Love the pink ribbon around your hair and your pink outfit," she added.

"It's a stretchy headband I can get on easily," Gloria explained. "If I'm not back in a half-hour, send a rescue dog," and she smiled her endearing, lopsided smile.

"One with a flask around its neck?" the receptionist asked.

Many Missourians regard fall as the best of the seasons, and that fall had almost outdone itself. Autumnal winds were pleasing and far more beneficent than hot summer winds which dried out the skin and blew dust into the eyes. The air was clear, fresh, light, and less humid. The sun, kind. Just-right conditions had turned trees vivid, especially oaks (maroon and red) and poplars (lemon-yellow).

As she passed Assisted Living co-residents in front of the building, Gloria nodded and spoke to each, also part of her self-prescribed improvement endeavor, and with the exception of one poor soul who was obviously vacuous, the walkers responded cordially. After several years of obscurity, Gloria, often identified only as 'that sweet, pretty lady with the bad leg and arm', had made herself known.

Walking the length of the sidewalk, Gloria stepped down from the curb with her right foot, worked the left foot down and placed it beside its reliable partner, then commenced walking along the side of the street. Had she crossed the street, she'd have had access to a sidewalk, but crossing would have added to the number of steps she'd be taking, and she needed to minimize those.

"Hello," another walker called.

"Good morning," Gloria answered. "Pretty morning," and as carefully as if she were walking on ice, she started down the block-long decline in front of her.

Crossing a street at the end of the decline, she continued past the last of the three Haven's Apartment Buildings. Pots of begonias, pansies, and petunias and baskets of red geraniums and multi-colored impatiens adorned decks and porches; petunias, purple and white, marked its entrance. Just beyond the building, she'd been told, was a stone grotto containing a bench where she could rest, and rest was her immediate concern.

The three blocks she'd just covered represented the longest stretch she'd walked since her stroke, and as she faced the get-to-the-bench part of her journey, the realization of how far she'd have to walk to return, memory of the receptionist's warning against venturing too far, and concern about the wisdom of what she was attempting made her uncertain and nervous. Spotting the bench, she threw caution to the wind and cut across the grass to get to it as fast as she could, and in doing so, stepped into a hole and fell. With a thump. Onto her knees. So quickly that she didn't have time to use her right arm to break the fall.

"No, no, no!" she exclaimed as pain radiated up and down from her right knee.

Rolling onto her back, Gloria looked around, only to find that no one was in sight. Without the help of someone or the cane she'd left in her room because she hadn't thought she'd need it, she was unable to get up. Angry at herself and nearly overcome by pain, she struggled to control the panic that was beginning to envelop her.

With her right hand, Gloria pushed herself into a sitting position and extended her legs, a position she knew she couldn't sustain for long, what with her left side useless and her back unsupported. There she sat, hurting and befuddled, helpless and vanquished.

When she couldn't hold to that posture any longer, she rolled to her right side, a position more sustainable but also more painful, which convinced her that her right knee had sustained serious injury. The realization made her cry.

Looking about, Gloria caught sight of her goal, the lake, which she'd momentarily forgotten. Transfixed, she watched mallards swim, submerge their heads in the water, and turn their bottoms up. Feeding, she supposed. A Great White Heron fished along the far shoreline, a Little Blue Heron further along. Something circled just below the surface of the water, sending rings spiraling outward, and she wondered if it was the Haven muskrat. At that point, her pain and hopelessness washed over her, she flopped over on her

Sap and Green People

back, and though she was crying again, she saw that the sky was pure blue and totally cloudless.

Two women walkers spotted Gloria when they rounded the side of the Manor. Stopping, they stared at her, sprawled-out as she was with her right arm thrown over her face. As they then drew near, Gloria withdrew her arm and, using the phrase that had been directed to her six months earlier by the little woman wearing tennis shoes, she said, "You have to feel good on a day like this, don't you? Only, I've fallen and am hurt. I'm Gloria Fields and I live in Assisted Living because…I'm…crippled. I've fallen, and I do need help," she said through her tears.

While the women identified themselves and hovered over her, Gloria wondered if her right leg would now also be disabled. If henceforth, she'd have no leg use whatsoever. If she'd be able to pursue the independent life she so much wanted.

The women, Claire and Joyce, conferred about whether they should call an ambulance.

"No," Gloria protested, and between shudderings and gaspings and stiffenings, she said, "just help me to the clinic in the Manor. There's almost always a doctor there."

"I'd feel better if we got an ambulance," one of the women answered, "but the decision should be yours," and she and her companion got Gloria into a standing position, placed her arms around their shoulders, and bearing all her weight, transported her the short distance to the Manor's back door.

"Good thing you're strong," Gloria said as the women struggled to get her over the threshold, down the hall, and into the clinic. "Thank you, thank you," she managed. "How can I ever thank you?"

Gloria was tended by a family practitioner who was seeing patients in the clinic that afternoon. After telling her that what had happened was most likely repairable, the doctor expressed the opinion that rather than having a fracture, she'd probably torn something in her knee. He put a splint on the leg, issued painkillers, arranged for x-rays to be taken at a nearby hospital early the following morning, and procured a wheelchair for Gloria's immediate use. Claire and Joyce committed themselves to driving Gloria to the

Sap and Green People

hospital the next day, and they wheeled her to the Assisted Living sector where a nurse helped her into bed.

"I kept waiting for the dog to come," Gloria told the receptionist who stopped by Gloria's room after finishing her shift.

"The dogs never go where we tell them to," the woman answered. "They just wander around in the woods, sniffing their casks and looking for rabbits."

While agonizing with pain, flipping and flopping, clenching and unclenching her teeth; regretting that she'd let herself fall and wishing she'd been more cautious; feeling thankful that she'd been helped and had made the acquaintance of two kindly women, Gloria cried herself to sleep. She cried and she dreamed about her dead husband who had loved her and cared for her and would never have left her to fend for herself, had he been given a choice.

"Girls," Essie Brinkman said as she and friends moved away from the serving line in the dining room with loaded supper trays, "we're going to have to graduate to two tables. At least sometimes. Because often, like tonight, there're more than six of us and the biggest tables only seat six. Are we a big bunch or what?"

"A what," Bertha Brinkman answered. "We're what."

"Always a smart answer," Essie complained, and she led her sister-in-law Bertha and the first four women in the group to a choice table, choice because it fronted the windows overlooking the lake, dam, and woods. The remaining women claimed a table somewhat to their left.

Leaning close to Bertha and the others as they off-loaded their trays onto their table, Essie dropped her voice to say, "I said 'always a smart answer' back there because I dared not use the word 'smart-ass' in reference to Bertha in a place where I might be overheard. But that's what she is, Girls, a smart-ass."

"I am not," Bertha answered. "I'm not but she calls me that six times a day anyway. What do you think of that?"

"No comment," someone answered, and everyone seated herself.

Sap and Green People

Essie said to Gail Russell who'd moved into the Manor three days earlier, "Though it may not appear that way, we're very close, my sister-in-law and I. Always have been. We have separate apartments, which is just as well, but Bertha is so much older than I that I suppose I'll have to give up my place some day and share hers so I can take care of her."

"Is your sister really younger?" Gail asked Bertha innocently. "It's none of my business, of course, but she brought the subject up, and it's piqued my curiosity."

"My guess," Mary Spritzer volunteered, "is that Essie is several years older than Bertha."

"Several?" Moina Sheer ventured.

"Ha!"

"Well, there is a difference of two years," Essie answered.

"Which way?"

"I'm two years older," Bertha admitted, "but people find that hard to believe."

"I don't."

"I do," and the conversation lapsed while the woman busied themselves giving beverage orders and sampling their food.

"Gail's moved here from Chicago. To be near her daughter who lives in Des Peres," Essie explained. "She lives up on the fourth floor, and I've been asked to be her big sister."

"Well, I hope you treat her better than you do your younger sister Bertha," Ruth said.

"I'm sure Gail's lovely and kind," Essie answered. "Not a smarty like Bertha and mean like some of you. So of course I'll be nice to her," and she told Gail the names of the women at the table because Gail hadn't met them before.

There followed a spirited discussion about Chicago, for all the diners had been to The Windy City and formed opinions about it and what it had to offer.

"Was it hard to leave there?" Joan asked.

"Frankly, I didn't think I could. I'd had a condo a block from Lake Michigan and near Lincoln Park. I lived in it for twenty-three years, my husband and I, that is. He died seven years ago. We were near

Sap and Green People

everything which we appreciated because we were goers and doers. I continued to go and do after he died and was relatively happy. Had a lot of friends. But my only child, my daughter, and her family are in St. Louis and will be forever, so I told myself I'd better get here too."

"Think you're going to like it?"

"Of course," Gail answered. "I've burned my bridges, and I'm going to be content. The facility's beautiful, my apartment's comfortable, and everyone has been cordial and helpful."

"Great attitude!" Essie said. "That's what it takes," and she turned to Mary. "Mary, I've admitted to being older than Bertha: that's pretty significant information. And Gail's told us about herself. Seems only fair that you share something. Like, how come you were in Mexico? In one of our group discussions, you mentioned that you were, and I've been meaning to ask you about that ever since."

"I said I was where?" Mary asked.

"In Mexico. You told everyone you'd seen environmental damage caused by big manufacturers when you were in Mexico."

"You did," Joan agreed.

When Mary ignored what had been asked and said and persisted with her eating, Essie further pursued the subject. "Were you vacationing in Mexico or working there?"

"Neither," Mary finally said. "Passing through."

"Only once?"

"No, a number of times."

"Stay long?"

"Usually one or two weeks," and Mary delicately forked her split lemon cake into her mouth and alternated bites of cake with swallows of decaffed coffee.

While Essie was trying to decide whether to 'thank' Essie for providing 'so much information' about herself, Mary did what she'd done several times before: switched the conversation adroitly by introducing another subject, one almost guaranteed to catch fire immediately.

"Did you read the new pronouncement by the American Gynecological Society about whether older women should be tested for cervical cancer?" she asked.

"No."

"Didn't read that."

"Missed it," and Mary repeated the information.

"Swell table talk, Mary," Moira commented when they'd finished discussing the matter.

"Been a long time since I've talked female anatomy. Personally, I thought it was great."

"And I, on the other hand, favor tabling it forever."

"Thanks for giving me something to worry about, Mary. Cancer. I've been worry-free for the last four hours," Moira said.

"In that case, I'll be glad to share my worries with you."

"Mine are too awful. You couldn't handle them."

"You ladies are fun," Gail said. "Thanks for including me."

"You're going to like it here," Ruth assured her. "Go on some of the excursions planned by the

Activities office and you'll get acquainted with people and the city."

"I've visited my daughter and family a number of times so know it's an interesting place."

"Do you have a car?" Joan asked.

"Yes," Gail answered, "and after Chicago, I'm not afraid to drive here."

"We have cars and will ask you to go places with us."

"You're too kind," Gail replied.

"That's true."

"We are."

"Haven't been able to overcome it."

"Terrible malady."

"Gail," Essie felt compelled to say, "there are cliques here. Also divisions. But things are relatively open. Feel free to assert yourself. Step up to anyone and introduce yourself and join any circle. Pull into any table."

"If you're rebuffed, forget about it."

"'N try again."

"Don't join anything you don't want to join."

"As much as possible, avoid people who bore you."

"Or are mean."

"Chew with their mouths open."

"Have dirty hair."

"Are bad bridge players."

"I don't play bridge," Gail said.

"Good for you," and advice, some helpful and some not, abounded.

"Well-l-l-l," Bertha said, "one thing you can do with us is play a little game with Mary here, because Mary's got us just real curious about her background which she never reveals. Consequently, when you're in her company, listen for little tidbits of personal information. Little clues. Because one of these days, we're going to put them together and come up with a Mary -profile."

"Do you suspect…criminal behavior," Gail asked.

"No, no, no," Joan answered. "We just have to have something to do. And it's fun, isn't it, Mary? Good, clean fun."

"My Dears," Mary answered, "I don't have the slightest idea what you're talking about."

"Neither do we," Essie said. "That's why we're playing the game." and as the women left the dining room, Gail shook hands with each one, expressed pleasure at meeting everyone, and promised to henceforth be a conscientious Mary-observer, -listener, and -inquisitor.

As Marg Davis drove to a restaurant where she was to meet friends for lunch, the wind coursed through her car's open sunroof, whipping her hair to the point where it relaxed the curl she'd worked hard to impose that morning. She could have closed the sunroof of course, but it was an open-roof day: freshened by a steady, all-night rain; enlivened by a strong, south wind that blew almost incessantly but not unkindly; tinted green, yellow, and blue; brightened to the point that made sunglasses imperative. Like a prime Florida day, Marg thought, when palms wave and whip, the air has been cleansed, and the sky's as blue as a newborn's pussy-cat eyes. Driving in light to medium traffic was exhilarating, which it sometimes was not, a thirty-five minute, Interstate, half-circle drive taking her around part of the west and north sectors of the city. The furthest removed from the restaurant, she was first to arrive, which she didn't mind because the wait granted her time to freshen her lipstick, tidy her hair, and relax.

"Hello."

"Hi-i-i-i."

"Hello."

"Hello there," rang out as her friends arrived, all dressed in pastel, light-weight pants and shirts, and wearing open-toed shoes. Back when they were at-home mothers and working wives, when they did not know each other well because they could get together only occasionally, they didn't embrace when they met. Now, however, coming together was noisy and joyous because they'd become very dear to each other. Of course they had, for collectively speaking, what hadn't they experienced and suffered and shared during the years?

After ordering light lunches and heavy desserts, the women became their usual loquacious selves.

"Bobby got admitted to Marquette University."

"Jerry's going to the junior college, and I can't tell you how thankful we are that he got admitted there!"

"Our granddaughter Collette may be pregnant and is not married, as you all know, and our hearts are broken, simply broken."

"Dear God no!" was the first reaction, "I can't believe it!" the next, "So sorry" after that.

Ola was counted cross-stitching again, she reported.

Carolyn was quilting. "Dave hogs the TV and I have to do something," she explained.

"Don't you have two sets, for goodness sakes?"

"Yes, but one set's in the basement," Carolyn explained, and she broke off the conversation to thank the waitress for her coke.

"Forget going way down into the basement. We couldn't have that."

"Nothing on television's worth going that far anyway."

"My daughter Flo's so busy that she said she wished she were clerking in a dime store."

"There aren't any of them any more."

"If there were, remind her, she'd be paid peanuts, and it's all about standard of living these days, isn't it?"

Jane told about an overnight trip she and her husband had taken, elongating her account with a plethora of details. No one objected because traditionally, everyone's stories were generously detailed.

Kay told about her son-in-law's mother's funeral, Ola about her daughter's new teaching job, Marg about the minor accident her son had while driving his own daughter's car.

"Got a cute e-mail today," Lida said. "The top ten things only women understand—or something like that. Anyone else get it?" No one had.

"Like, what were they?"

"One was, 'Cat facial expressions.' Another, 'Cutting your bangs to make them grow.' 'Fat clothes.' I'll send them to you if you'd like." Everyone wanted a copy.

"Better than 'Ten ways to know you have PMS' which I got. Anyone get that?" Several had.

"Not funny."

"Definitely not!"

"Don't you wish people refrained from talking about all that stuff publicly? Like in the old days?"

"And they didn't advertise underwear and 'personal hygiene' products on TV either?"

"Absolutely!"

"Stand-up comics are so terribly terrible now!"

"They ought to be flogged—in some gross way!"

Entrees arrived at that point, and conversation was sporadic while the women ate. When they were nearly finished, Kay said, "It appears that things are going swimmingly well for the six of us."

"Relatively speaking, yes."

"Yup."

"Right, only I forgot to tell you about Bob," Lida said.

"Is he family?" Jane asked. "We're only doing family today."

"He is. Jay's brother-in-law."

"Okay then."

"His wife, Jay's sister, died last year, and since then, Bob's gone down, down, down 'til he simply has to get into a nursing home. He's not that old, and we and his doctor thought he was in pretty good shape. But he's not, we're now told. Needs round-the-clock care."

"That can be temporary," Marg, the only one of the six who lived in a senior's complex, suggested. "Happens out at our place all the time. They come, get better, go home," and she took a deep breath and squared her shoulders because she knew that the conversation would swing around again to the pros and cons of living in a community such as the one where she and Bill lived.

"I dunno, Marg," Carolyn said. "Dave and I have been talking, and we just can't make up our minds," and her table mates knew what she and Dave had been talking about—senior housing.

"Well again," Marg said, "you know what prompted our decision: my macular degeneration which hasn't progressed in the last several years. And

I'll say again that moving into a complex is a trade-off. You get and you give up," and she tucked a piece of peanut butter pie into her mouth before continuing. "What you get are services and a community, new faces and lots of acquaintances. What you give up is your home and subdivision or neighborhood, neighbors and perhaps proximity to longtime friends, as was our case. I keep telling people that we still have our privacy even though we share a roof with other people, and privacy's something people worry about. Living in a complex costs money, but you receive a number of services, and the house-maintenance costs, property taxes, and most utility bills are included in monthly payments."

"I'm afraid Dave would go crazy if he didn't have the house and yard to fuss over. He's a fusser. No getting around that."

"Well, Bill's not. He figured he'd acquire new interests and the responsibilities he chose to assume, and that's the way it's worked out."

"I lov-v-v-ve my house," Kay said.

Sap and Green People

"I've had three houses," Marg replied. "They were fine, especially the condo, but I didn't lov-v-v-ve any of them. So I didn't have that problem."

"Your apartment's small, Marg."

"Limited space does require adjustment," Marg answered. "I'll attest to that. But we were at the point in our lives where we wanted to divest ourselves of the things we didn't need."

"Such a job, getting rid of all the stuff."

"Can't even think about it!"

"Granted," Marg said. "It's just short of terrible. But what a relief to have it done!"

"How 'bout living with only old people?" Lida asked.

"Ah!" Marg answered. "There's a rub because while there are a number of people as active and young as we, relatively active and young, that is, most are older, and some of those, though 'independent', are visually handicapped, deaf, becoming vague, hooked up to oxygen. We're not exposed a lot to the hard-core cases, I'll call them," Marg went on to say. "Such persons live in separate quarters, but we do see them.

Actually, we still live pretty much like we lived before, going and coming a lot, the difference being that we leave and return to a different place, a decidedly different neighborhood.

And not to sound self-righteous, Girls, I'll tell you that we feel that maybe what we're supposed to do for the rest of our active lives is help older, less-able people. In fact, Bill feels he's a better man for living where we live, that he's a more compassionate, more giving person."

"Maybe it's the smart thing to do, but I can't make myself do it, at least not now," Kay, a widow, said, "but I'm happy that you're happy."

"I am," Marg answered. "We made our decision and are relieved to be situated for the rest of our lives. To know we'll not have to depend upon our children to take care of us.

But heh! That's us. None of you has to make the move. End of subject," she said emphatically and to her friends' relief, she suspected. With that dismissal, conversation turned familial again.

Sap and Green People

Ola's granddaughter had bought a condo, Carolyn's daughter a piano. Jane's nephew was changing his college major, from geology to music, a significant change, everyone agreed. Betty, who'd characteristically said almost nothing during the meal, announced that her husband had a bad case of shingles, her Siamese cat arthritis. And Hollywood was brought to the fore, of course, this time with a report that Burt Reynolds might at long last have come up with a hit, that Cher might be on the verge of matrimony.

"You're my buddies," Marg told her friends on the restaurant's parking lot when they kissed each other goodbye.

"Best buddies ever!"

"Ever and ever."

"Love you, love you," Kay called as she slammed the car door.

"To the bitter end," was the last thing Marg heard as she pulled out of the parking lot.

The day was no less lovely, she found, so she opened the sunroof again. Less sunny, perhaps, because cumulus clouds, about which she'd learned

Patricia Dick

from Bill, the long-ago, wartime navigator, were layering up, if that's what they were doing, in the western sky. Having punched the "seek" button on the instrument panel, classical music flooded her sporty, little car, empowering her to have the courage to wiggle her way over to a middle, southbound lane of the Interstate.

"You're happy," Kay had said, and I am, Marg told herself, but should I have told my friends that I am still embarrassed when I tell people that I live in a seniors' community? Because living in such a place is a public declaration that Bill and I are old, and who wants to publicize that? Because someone might think we couldn't manage by ourselves anymore. That we've chickened out. Aren't fighting the good fight to its very end. Have turned our backs on the 'real world'."

Should I have told them that we do associate with stooped, gaunt John who's suffering from Parkinson's disease? Doesn't tremble but chokes, gags, and has to spit in his handkerchief?

Sap and Green People

About Jane who lives at the end of our hall, bitter, withdrawn, weird, also a victim of Parkinson's, whose everything shakes all the time, making her repugnant?

About Jerry, a former nuclear chemist, stiff and skinny as a stick, silent but forever smiling, a victim of Alzheimer's who's still able to live with his wife in one of the apartments but is very dependent upon her?

Tall, handsome Richard who more and more often forgets where he is?

Elsie whose right eye is temporarily sewn shut in the interest of saving the vision in her left eye?

The humped-back ladies (and men) so bent they eat in the dining room with their faces at the level of their dinner plates?

Poor, poor things. Pitiful, valiant people! We see them, Bill and I. Can't avoid them. Couldn't. Shouldn't. Can't ignore, look beyond, or hide from them whose appearance and deportment are unpleasant, the degree dependent upon one's state of mind, experience, and level of tolerance. Should I have told my friends about having to be with them?

Thank you for this good place, Marg prayed as she neared the Haven. Thank you, and bless us all. May we be good to each other, good, tolerant, and caring. Come to each other's aid. And specifically, watch over those of us living in Apartment Building 709, she asked as she backed into her assigned parking space, and she checked the other assigned spaces to see who were in, who out. Watch over us, every one of us, Bill and me included, and may he and I be together for as long as possible, she asked as she waited for the elevator. Amen, amen.

"I'm home," she called to Bill as she stepped through the door of their apartment.

"Good," Bill answered. "'Bout time. I'm reading. On the bed. Waiting for you 'cause it's way past nap time. Way-y-y-y past."

Sap and Green People

"Not right," Marg Davis told herself in regards to the worn-soft khaki pants and printed shirt she'd just put on. "They just don't represent how I feel today," and she peeled them off, slung them onto her bed, and replaced the pants and shirt with a denim jumper and white knit shirt. "That's not it either," she said as she looked at herself in the full-length mirror, and she hung up the two outfits, then donned the white cotton pants she'd previously worn for a half-day and a lavender top. "Naw-w-w," she decided, and she traded the lavender for a pink, short-sleeved, cotton sweater.

"I'm ready. Need help picking out something to wear?" she called to Bill.

"You've got to be kidding! Go through what you do to get dressed? Thanks anyway. I've been dressed for fifteen minutes," and the couple made their way to their car, drove to the east entrance of the Manor, and picked up the Grahams who'd elected to go to Ted Drewes with them.

Drewes frozen custard stands, situated in two south St. Louis neighborhoods, are St. Louis traditions. Unassuming in appearance, they're constructed of white siding; sport overhanging, pitched, shingled roofs; and are fronted with serving windows, more than a dozen in the case of the Watson Road location where the Davises and Grahams were headed. The stands open in March and close in November, and from then through Christmas, Mr. Drewes sells Christmas trees on the sites, trees he raised on his Nova Scotia property.

A Ted Drewes custard treat is more than container-plus-custard, flavoring-and-topping. It's an experience, one often shared with the family dog and entailing the finding of a parking place when not enough are available; standing in one of many lines which often extend as far as the street; talking to people who are also standing in line; stepping out of the way after being served; and eating the treat while talking to acquaintances or total strangers, whether it's blistering hot, raining like crazy, or downright cold.

"Look at all the people," Henry said. "The number always amazes me."

Sap and Green People

"Young and old, fat and skinny, courteous and otherwise, two-footed and four-footed, all wolfing down some form of frozen custard," Marg said.

"We were down here once," Bill reported, "when firemen were returning from a run. The driver parked the truck right here," and he pointed to the no-parking zone in front of the stand, "and while the other firemen got in line to place their orders, he stayed with the truck and sat little kids in the driver's seat, put a fireman's hat on their heads, and let them rotate the steering wheel and ring the bell."

"Let's go over there," Marg suggested after the two couples were served. "Out of the way," and she led the foursome to the curb lining Watson Road where, with groans and lamentations as to how they'd never be able to get up again, they sat down.

"Anything interesting happen in the line of duty lately, Henry?" Bill asked.

"Well, I got asked to be an officer of the Women's Auxiliary," Henry answered. "Guess that's interestin'."

"You what?" Bill asked. "The Auxiliary is for women, isn't it?"

"Yes, but a woman I know called me and said, 'Henry, you know how hard it is to get people to take responsibility around here,' and before I could say yes or no, she rushed on with, 'and you're volunteer-minded, so we wondered if you'd serve on the Auxiliary Board next year.' I asked if there were any men in the Auxiliary, and she said, 'No, but there would be if you're on it. Of course,' she'd cautioned, 'it might cause a little fuss and you might not get elected,' so I backed out right then and there. After we talked about it a couple of times more, though, I said I would."

After commenting on Henry's new responsibility, Bill said, "I know what I've been meaning to tell you. One day, when three of our computer students came to the computer lab to check for e-mail, they each found an e-mail message reading, 'Will you have sex with me?'"

"My word!" Georgia said.

"Were they offended?" Henry asked.

Sap and Green People

"No," Bill answered, "they took it in stride. It'll make a good story to tell friends, but I hope the story won't discourage anyone from learning to use computers."

"Might swell the ranks," Marg commented as she spooned another bite of her junior hot fudge sundae into her mouth. "Going to get a teramazoo next time," she stated. "They're still my favorite."

"Teramazoo?"

"Ice cream, caramel syrup, pistachio nuts. Sundae-style or whipped into a concrete, meaning as thick as wet cement."

"What else you got to share, Henry?" Bill asked.

"Well, had a couple of minutes to kill early one mornin' before I was to call for my first wheelchair lady, so I stopped in the beauty parlor to talk to the operators. Someone else had brought in an old woman…"

"What other kind is there?" Bill asked.

"Thanks!" Georgia said.

"Bill calls me 'Old Lady' half the time," Marg said. "Term of endearment rather than fact, of course."

"...who was the first appointment that morning. Needed a perm. They got the curlers in her hair, wrapped her hair with one of those plastic bags they use, put her under the dryer, and, poor thing, she began rockin' back and forth and mumblin' 'blah, blah, blah' and clappin' her hands. Blah, blah, blah, clap. Blah, blah, blah, clap. Over and over. Finally, a customer who I knew motioned for me to come over, and she said, 'Henry, get her the hell out of here!'"

"What'd you do?" Marg asked.

"Patted the complainer's hand and said, 'Not yet, Dear. Give her a break.'"

"Sad."

"You bet."

"Marg," Georgia said, "look at the three little girls sitting on the tailgate of the black van in back of us. So sweet," and Henry and Bill also looked over their shoulders at the trio.

"They may be sweet," Bill ventured, "but I'll bet they're sticky and all gummed up."

"Think you're right," Marg said. "They now have chocolate hair," and the Davises and Grahams returned

Sap and Green People

to watching the traffic, savoring their custard, and making small talk.

"We were in the hall the other day," Georgia said, "and met a neighbor who had a friend with her. When she introduced us to the guest, the neighbor said, 'This is Georgia and Mr. Georgia. They're two of the normal people around here'."

"Think we'd qualify as 'normal'?" Marg asked Bill.

"Not sure," he answered.

"One of the ladies I push regularly," Henry shared, "told me that I wasn't as mean as another wheelchair pusher she'd had, and I told her, 'Of course not. I'm not mean. I'm a lover,' which she thought very funny."

"Me too," Georgia commented. "Several women have told me they've seen my husband some place or another 'hugging up the ladies'. I told them, 'It does him a lot of good.' Also, when a lady who works with Henry on different things finds us together and thinks she needs to speak to Henry, she asks, 'May I ask your husband a question?' or 'May I talk to your husband?' As if I might shoot her if she didn't ask permission."

"Personally, I'm against shootin'."

"Absolutely!"

"Glad you took that Auxiliary job, Henry," Bill said as he struggled to get to his feet. "With time, you may get to be president."

"Wouldn't want that," Henry answered. "Look at all the trouble Bill Clinton got into during his presidency."

"Never heard of him," Bill answered, and the foursome returned to the Davises' sporty little car and drove back to their apartments in the nearby Haven, home to normal and not-so-normal, older folks.

Sap and Green People

"That pretty little lady, thin, real-blonde hair, with the bad arm and leg? She was planning to move into Independent Living and walked to get herself ready for that, and she fell and really buggered herself up. Two women found her on the ground, and they got help. Name's Gloria Fields." That's approximately the story that made the rounds of the campus relative to Gloria's fall. "Before her stroke," was sometimes added, "she played tennis and golf. Was a volunteer swimming coach at a community center. Jogged and worked out. Too bad she's so wrecked up, but she's doing well, I hear."

Gloria was relatively cheerful immediately after the fall. She talked matter-of-factly with the doctor who tended her in the Haven clinic, appeared to be relatively comfortable as she was wheeled from the clinic to the Assisted Living facility, joshed a bit with the receptionist as she returned to her room.

Later, however, despite having been treated and medicated, the pain in her right knee caused her to twist and turn and cry out all night, according to the Assisted Living night nurse. Sure that the doctor who'd treated her in the clinic would be up by 7:00 the next morning, Gloria called the number on his business card and talked to his answering service.

"I've suffered pain before," she told the doctor when he called back, "but this pain is terrible, just terrible."

"I'll call the Haven people and have them get an ambulance to take you to the hospital," the doctor promised, and a Haven representative called Gloria within minutes. Gloria asked that Claire and Joyce, her rescuers whose last names she didn't know, be called, for they expected to drive her to the hospital later that morning, and mercifully, a security man and nurse arrived at Gloria's apartment, almost simultaneously with the ambulance. Gloria cried softly while two strong, young attendants carried her to the ambulance and loaded her ever so carefully.

Her vision blurring, head buzzing, stomach churning, and knee pounding, Gloria remembered little about the ambulance ride. Nor did she remember being checked, x-rayed, and settled into a hospital bed. When an admitting doctor came to the room to question her, she could only answer, "I'm sorry," to whatever he asked and turn her head from side to side, as if trying to shake free of pain. Nor was she any more aware by the time she was given a shot which put her asleep at long last.

When she woke, Moss Gray, her lawyer, and Pat Marsh, the Haven nurse who'd befriended her some months earlier, were seated beside her, watching for her to wake up.

"Oh," Gloria mumbled when she saw them, "I do have allies," and she commenced crying again. "I'm so alone," she lamented. "I'm hurt, but worse, I'm all alone."

"You have us. You can count on me and this handsome gentleman here," Pat said with forced gaiety.

Pat called a nurse into the room, and when Gloria was more relaxed and composed, Moss Gray, seemingly genuinely interested in serving Gloria's best interests, bent close to explain in a kindly voice, "You twisted your knee, Gloria, and in the process, tore what's called the anterior cruciate ligament. The injury is serious and may require grafting a new ligament to the knee surgically. An orthopedic surgeon will come in shortly, and he'll explain what he can do for you. He'll ask you to sign consent forms, and once you've signed, he'll operate. Sometime this afternoon. Would you like me to stay until he comes and finishes talking to you?"

Dazed by the news, tearful, and morose, Gloria nodded. As Moss excused himself to make telephone calls, he asked Gloria if she'd like him to bring her a cup of Starbuck's coffee. Gloria declined, and Pat pulled up to Gloria and plumped up her pillows. Taking Gloria's hand in her own, she announced that she'd stay at least until Moss returned. With that, Gloria surrendered to sleep.

A graft was performed, and the following days were difficult, their only virtue being that they brought Pat to Gloria's bedside often, Moss periodically, and her rescuers, Claire whose last name was Campbell and Joyce, last-named Williams, frequently. The two women bathed her face, smoothed her hair, helped her with her meals, summoned nurses, even performed

Sap and Green People

nursing functions themselves if required. Whenever Claire and Joyce spoke encouraging words, pledged their friendship, or read poetry and short scripture passages, Gloria's introduction to the Bible, their generosity moved Gloria to copious tears once more.

Seemingly almost without respite, Gloria was subjected to physical therapy, to leg-lifts, assisted sit-ups, leg extensions, weight training, and other exercises; to heat treatments and massages; and all too soon, to walking on crutches. The therapy was painful, but the physical pain was not as devastating as the regret, hopelessness, self-pity, and dread of the future that plagued Gloria, causing continued periods of weeping and depression.

"She may be having the equivalent of a nervous breakdown," a psychologist suggested. "Perhaps because she never let herself mourn the twin facts that her person had been radically altered and her husband, upon whom she depended, taken unexpectedly."

"Her philosophical base and societal skills may be lacking," a social worker theorized, "rendering her incapable of dealing with what's happened."

The opinions sometimes made Pat Marsh, Claire Campbell, and Joyce Williams giggle, for they regarded Gloria as, more simply, an ill, pained, disappointed, lonely woman who was understandably concerned about her future.

For his part, Moss Gray sent flowers and candy and encouraged and reassured her when he visited. Still, Gloria cried often, wished herself dead (though she never conveyed that wish to anyone), ate very little, ignored her grooming, and hid behind sleep.

Then, inexplicably, almost a month after the surgery, Gloria woke one morning in her Haven Convalescent Center room with clear eyes, a strong voice, and a half-smile. After eating a sizable breakfast, she called Pat Marsh.

"Pat," Gloria said, "I'm feeling good today. Woke up feeling almost wonderful."

"It happens," Pat told her. "Maybe a near-equivalent of coming out of a coma. And to share another piece of good news, I'll tell you that I have it on good authority that two Manor apartments have

Sap and Green People

opened up, and barring the unforeseen, one will be ready for you when you're ready for it."

"Oh, it's my turning point day," Gloria squealed. "The turning point! Watch me, Pat, 'cause I'm finally, finally on my way!"

"Girls," Joan Cutler said as she addressed the five women sitting at the dinner table with her, "I signed up to go out Tuesday evening with the Haven Dinner-out Club, and the bus is leaving at 4:30. I'm also slated to push wheelchairs to and from a mass in the Chapel at 4:00 that day, I've belatedly realized. Can't do both, so would one of you push wheelchairs for me?"

"Gracious!" Mary Spritzer exclaimed. "I'm signed up with the Club and to push wheelchairs too. I'd almost forgotten! Good thing you brought the subject up."

"Mary," Elaine Bruce observed, "you can't 'almost forget' something. You either 'forget' or you 'remember'."

"Oh, you purist," Myra Kelly said. "At least she's volunteering for something, which is more than I can say for myself right now. So-o-o-o, I'll take the place of one of you."

"You be Joan," Elaine said to Myra, "and I'll be Mary. Man alive! We'll be an impressive pair of wheelchair-pushers, won't we?"

Sap and Green People

"Thanks," Joan said, "thanks a whole lot. You should report to the nurses' station, second floor north, the first station if you're coming from the north end of the hall. At about 3:30. Someone will tell you whom to get. You roll 'em into the chapel, stand or sit near 'em during the mass, then get 'em back to their rooms. If you need help, the aides are on the scene. Like most kinds of volunteering, not real pleasant but a good thing to do and something that makes you feel good after it's finished."

"I guess helping in the child care center would be pleasant and gratifying," Gail Russell suggested.

"Personally, I couldn't do that because I haven't had any children so know less about children than I do about...elephants," Mary Spritzer volunteered.

"I'd take children," Bertha Brinkman volunteered. "They're impulsive and unformed but more communicative and huggable."

"I'm not exactly nuts about children, but then, I'm not crazy about elephants either."

"I'll go with elephants. They could mess you up, I suppose. Squirt you and get your hair wet. Throw hay on your clothes. But you don't have to change their diapers."

"Really, this conversation is juvenile," and everyone laughed.

"Better than griping about how tasteless the carrots are, how dry the fish, how stingy the size of the cake servings."

"Or hearing about aches and pains. Incontinence."

"What's zat?"

"How big, how grand the house someone gave up to move here, complete with a thousand details."

"There is a lot of discussion about homes, but I'm somewhat sympathetic to love of home because doing and keeping up a house can be an artistic expression."

"Houses are a big part of some women's identity."

"Like jobs. Isn't it interesting to hear how important and successful people's careers were?"

"How extensively we've traveled."

"Successful their children."

"Talk about one-upmanship!"

"How we define ourselves."

Sap and Green People

"Don't forget about what wonderful marriages everyone had when how many—half?—were, statistically speaking, wanting?"

"Or worse, the pits."

"Mine was swell."

"Mine too."

"I'm glad for you both," Joan, who'd never married, said graciously.

"So am I," Mary said in an uncharacteristic tone of voice which everyone tried to interpret.

"Back to elephants, please," Bertha said. "Mary, you were the one who brought them into the conversation. I'm supposing you lived some place where there were elephants?"

"Well, yes," Mary said coyly, "though I never had one. Cats, dogs, a horse once, but never an elephant."

"And where was that, may I ask? That you lived with them?"

"You may," Mary granted without elaborating.

"Well, to persist," Bertha asked after a pause, "where did you live that there were elephants, Mary? You've piqued our curiosity."

"In India."

"I thought you'd say Africa because you told us you once lived in Africa."

"Elephants in India," and Mary raised her hand to summons a waitress. "A cup of decaffed coffee, please, and a two-dip chocolate sundae, vanilla ice cream."

"Going to tell us more about elephants and India?"

"No." Mary answered.

"Well," Myra said, "in that case, I'd like to say that I enjoy our conversations. They remind me of table talk at college: smart, clipped which made them fast, sassy and brassy. Big difference, though: We seldom talk about men and that's all we talked about in college, it being wartime and we being man-hungry."

"I like them too," Gail, the newcomer, confessed.

"Men?"

"No, our conversations," Gail laughed. "My bridge club in Chicago was a little like this. But you're more accomplished. Quicker and smoother."

"When I lived in Chicago, almost all the people I met were quick, smooth-talking, and 'cool', Mary

Sap and Green People

Spritzer volunteered, and her companions added Chicago to the list of places where she had lived.

"But, Joan and Mary, you and your friends were young then," Myra interjected, "and I bet they haven't held up as well as we have."

"You're right," Mary conceded, "because they were way older than I and are probably all dead now while we're very much alive."

"We beat Chicago, and that's hard to do!" Bertha insisted. "Hurrah for us!" a notion her friends seconded noisily and with a show of amicability.

"Better," Bill Davis told Marg who'd questioned him about his sore heal. "The heel's quite a lot better, but even at that, I'm tired of the dull, nagging pain."

"All the time?" Marg asked.

"No. Only when I'm walking, and then, only half of the time, meaning with every other step," and the two interrupted their daily walk, now abbreviated because of Bill's heel, to look over the waist-high, white plastic, picket fence surrounding the community garden which was so dear to the hearts of committed resident gardeners.

"Everyone's got tomatoes in his plot."

"Well, almost everyone," Marg answered, "'cause that one corner plot over there has only flowers in it."

"Lettuce. Peas. Pole-beans. Beets. Peppers. Couple kinds of lettuce. Swiss chard, I'll guess, since it looks like what Ruby gave us last week and called Swiss chard. Corn. That's about all I recognize, which is pretty damned good for a plant ignoramus," Bill said.

"You're not an ignoramus," Marg countered. "You're just stupid generally," and Bill bopped her playfully on the top of her head with his visor.

"I've heard there were more plots other years, that some gardeners have given up. Supposedly because the soil's really bad. Despite a lot of improving. Garden's where the builders dumped their trash. Rocks and stones, insulation scraps, lumber leavings, hunks of cement and cement scraps, who knows what else."

"We'll see what that little, 101-year-old-lady can get out of that soil, 'cause I'm telling you, she's one determined lady who's gardened since she was knee-high to a grasshopper, starting back in 'the old country', I hear. Hungary, I believe it was."

"Saw her out there one morning last week, a straw hat protecting her head, hoeing while her two daughters were down on their knees weeding industriously."

"Do you have to garden in the hot sun to live 'til you're 101?" Bill asked.

"If so," Marg answered, "let's go for ninety-nine," and when sweaty gardeners, as greasy as pieces of bacon, looked up from their labor, Bill and Marg waved.

After they'd walked on, Bill said to Marg, "You know, I'd rather be dead than have to garden again."

"Oh-h-h, Bill, you don't mean that."

"Not really. I'll restate my point: I'd rather have plantar fascia than have to garden."

"Well, you've been granted your choice," Marg responded as she took his hand and they crossed a parking lot, footbridge, and the band of woods which encircled three sides of the campus, she on knees swollen with arthritis, he on the toes of his fascia foot, on the ball of the other.

Sap and Green People

"What's this?" Molly Marks asked as she stooped to study the plates of hor d'oeuvres arranged on the oak table situated in the first-floor 'great room' of Apartment Building 709. "Smells yummy."

"Sausage bites," Sue Steele answered. "I brought those, and the crackers next to them are spread with crab, Barb's specialty. Mabe brought the bacon-wrapped water chestnuts. Quite obviously, those" and she nodded at a half-dozen bowls, plates, and platters "are the nuts, cheese, and goldfish crackers we can't do without."

Sue oversaw the 4:00 happy hours planned for residents of her Apartment Building on the first and third Monday afternoons of the month. Other happy hours were scheduled in The Manor and Recreation Center, and occasionally Building 709 residents attended those. Most, however, took advantage only of their own, in-house affairs, and Molly had been the first to arrive at the afternoon's soiree.

Happy hour was held in the west end of the room. At the sides of the room were bookcases set opposite each other, their shelves lined with items residents brought with them when they moved but were unable to find places for in their small apartments: glass vases, plastic flower arrangements, ceramics, figurines, and candle-holders, an eclectic assortment, not coordinated but, with a few exceptions, not exactly in conflict with each other either. Printed sofas were placed in front of the bookcases and facing each other, and at the side of each was a leather chair attended by a lamp table and lamp. A large, stone fireplace, the room's focal point, dominated the end of the room. 'Acceptable', 'dull', 'restrained', 'unimaginative', 'comfortable', 'homey': any one of the words would have characterized the area.

In the middle of the smaller, front half of the room, the east side, was the entryway, flanked by dwarfed trees based in ornate tubs. A deck of mailboxes lined one wall; a long table bearing magazines and newspapers, the other; and the round table presently bearing the hor d'oeuvres stood between the mailboxes and table. A half-dozen plants, some healthy and some not, sat hither and yon in both parts of the room.

Sap and Green People

The sixteen apartments in the building were home to twenty-three persons, seven men and sixteen women. Perhaps six had earned college degrees, though no one knew for sure or cared. Their ages ranged from 70 to over 100, a 101-year-old woman and her two daughters having recently moved into an apartment vacated by a beloved woman who'd died unexpectedly.

Hellos were exchanged as later arrivers joined early comers. Each set down any food and the drink he or she had brought, loaded a paper plate with food, picked up their beverage, and settled in for the one-hour gathering. Also in attendance was the Resident Pet, Taffy of Jack Russel lineage, who circled the room non-stop for most of that hour and was regarded as a bona fide member of the 'family'.

"Now that it's hot," one woman said to the persons seated near her, "the flowers on my deck are petering out," and she was given a plethora of container gardening information.

"They're scrappy little things," another woman commented in reference to the hummingbirds frequenting her hummingbird feeder, and a lengthy bird discussion followed.

"Every year, it's the same darned thing," Joe complained in his booming voice. "They say we'll have a winning team, and the team starts out fine, then nosedives," and a number of theories about how the Cardinals could win the World Series were advanced.

In one corner, recipes were parsed. In another, weedy Haven flower beds were deplored. Two men, whose voices were rising and faces reddening, expressed opinions about the forthcoming Presidential election until Kit Barnes, the ad hoc mayor of the building, called out, "I think we're all here so I'll ask our resident pastor, Milton Schultz, to lead us in prayer—or do whatever he's planned for us today." While Taffy continued circling, the residents became attentive to Milton.

Milton recited the One Hundredth Psalm by heart, not long in length but long enough to earn the respect of those who couldn't always remember their own telephone numbers. Then he raised a prayer which ended with a petition for everyone's good health. "But

Sap and Green People

with whatever happens, Father, grant us faith, strength, and patience for managing whatever comes our way. Amen.

Friends," Milton continued as he looked at the seasoned faces around him, "I've heard you voice so many regrets during recent days and weeks about our time of life, our elderliness, I'll call it, and I've also no doubt done the same.

We keep saying that we wish we were this, wish we were that. That we regret the way we feel, our lack of vigor and mobility. That we're worried about financial security. Embarrassed by wrinkles and blemishes. Very much regret hurting backs and aching knees and clumsy feet.

Perhaps, Dear People, listening to what pundits tell us will help. Coleridge, the long-ago, British poet wrote, 'I have often thought what a melancholy world this would be without children, and what an inhuman world without the aged.' Ralph Waldo Emerson, the American writer and philosopher, stated, 'We do not count a man's years until he has nothing else to count', meaning that life should not be over 'til it's over.

James Garfield, the twentieth President of the United States, said, 'If wrinkles must be written upon our brow, let them not be written upon our heart. The spirit should not grow old,' and Margaret Deland, an American regional writer, suggested that 'As soon as you feel too old to do a thing, do it.'

On top of those tributes and admonitions comes the Biblical promise in the Hundredth Psalm which I just cited: that the Lord's 'love and faithfulness will last forever'. Until we're eighty. Ninety. One hundred. Forever. And a modern translation of Psalm Ninety-two states that the righteous oldster shall 'bring forth fruit', meaning 'achieve' in old age, even in old age, because the elderly are 'ever full of sap and green'.

Think of that: We temper society. We're loved by a faithful, everlasting God. We're kept vital by the sap of life flowing through us, flowing through us still.

Take heart and rejoice. Rejoice even your agedness. Show forth your vitality and march on. And on. And on. For God's sake and your brother's sake and your own. Amen, amen."

Sap and Green People

"Thank you, Milton. There's nothing like having a live-in prayer-maker and -counselor, is there?"

"A coach."

"Right," Kit replied, which induced enthusiastic agreement.

"Moving from the sublime to the routine," Kit said, "are there concerns we should talk about?"

"Bugs. I hate to state in front of God and everyone here that I have roaches, but if I do, some of you probably do too," Mary Teller said.

"Everything known about roaches has been said a million times," Kit commented, "so there's no need to discuss the little devils again, I'm thinking. Instead, I'll just remind you to arrange for spraying if you have a problem. The guy comes every Thursday morning."

"Who do we call?"

"Housekeeping. Anything else?" Kit asked.

"Squeaky doors."

"Call maintenance."

"A good new trip was announced yesterday," Sue said, "a half-day boat ride on the Missouri River, commencing in St. Charles. I'm going and hope some of you do too."

Taffy snatched a bacon-wrapped water chestnuts off the low table which everyone regarded as 'cute', and her masters apologized, then scolded her soundly.

"Did they get the bats out of the belfry yet?" Alice asked.

"Seems so. Nobody working over there any more."

"Always wanted to live in a place where there were bats in the belfry," someone said, and everyone laughed.

"If there's nothing else, do you have anything from the Association meeting to pass along, Mr. Association President Bill?" Kit asked.

"Yes. 'Bout six of you were at the meeting," Bill Davis said as he looked around the circle, "so please excuse the repetition. A September picnic was announced, and you'll get fliers about it later. The lake will be drained and dredged again next summer. It'll look terrible and be messy, cause a lot of noise and be hard on pond life, but it has to be done. Our lawyer

Sap and Green People

is still working to keep the city from rolling back The Haven's tax exempt status. He's hopeful that it will not. The minutes of the meeting will be put in mailboxes, so read them, please, and attend the next meeting if you're free and so inclined."

"Pardon me, Bill, but there's a lot of confusion about how a resident gets moved from the independent living facilities to Assisting Living or Convalescent quarters, the process and costs," Jack Clausen said.

Taffy chomped and gulped as she ate a handful of pretzels given her, which amused everyone, prompted affectionate comments, and required that Kit struggle for several minutes to reestablish order.

"Having to move to what we regard as a 'lesser' quarters is in the back of all our minds. How we'll get moved if things get worse for us," Bill said, "and such. A meeting has already been called to review those procedures, and a flier on the bulletin board gives particulars, so many of you will want to attend. Also, following that meeting, we can tour the Assisted Living and Convalescent quarters, another reason for getting there."

"I'm going," Jay volunteered. "I'm expecting to kick off before Esther does, and I want to make sure she'll have a good place to go since she can't see well and needs help."

"The Haven will take good care of Esther, Jay," Kit told him, and those of us still here will see to that!" Jay nodded appreciatively.

"Guess that's all for this afternoon," Kit said. "I therefore adjourn the meeting. But notice that we've got," and he looked at his watch, "twenty-five minutes left for talking and eating before happy hour's officially over, so hang around. Stay green," and he nodded at Milton. "Thanks Milton, thanks for coming, and thanks to Sue and her helpers for another good spread."

A salad bar, creamy garden vegetable soup, roast beef, pork chow mein over rice, whipped potatoes, Harvard beets, Asian mix vegetables, homemade rolls, and strawberry pretzel dessert comprised the evening menu, and six residents left a little before 5:00 so they could ride the 5:00 bus to the Manor dining room. Kit and the others left a few minutes later, feeling communal, mellow, and almost full enough to either skip the dining room meal and settle for cereal or cheese and crackers in their own apartments.

Patricia Dick

In early August, when the temperature soared high enough to break weather bureau records, the sense of heat sent so many air-cooled Haven residents to the ice cream parlor that extra workers had to be recruited, additional supplies ordered, serving hours extended, and a security officer assigned to handle pedestrian and wheelchair traffic in the halls around the parlor.

Prepared and equipped to handle the onslaught and ready for another Tuesday opening, set for 1:30 instead of the usual 2:00 P.M., Grace Kuhn, volunteer manager, said to her helpers, "Anyone know anything about George?" When apparently no one did, Grace explained, "Because we'll be under siege this afternoon, I 'phoned all of you to make sure you'd be here, but I couldn't get George. Left a message but never heard from him. Anyone know if he's ill or maybe away?" When no one responded, she asked everyone to watch for or make inquiries about George, given the chance, then pushed open the serving windows to the waiting ice-cream eaters.

"A butter pecan sundae, please, with chocolate syrup and whipped cream," the first patron, a palsied

Sap and Green People

old man with clouded eyes and an ivory-handled cane, specified, and he grinned as he handed Grace a quarter to pay for the extras, syrup and whipped cream.

"Three double-dip strawberry cones," an aide ordered next. "We're beat from trying to keep people cool and happy. Need refreshment ourselves," the perspiring woman explained as she paid for the cones and handed two to her associates who were standing at the side of the hallway.

An attractive middle-aged women attending a wheelchair-bound, wisp of a woman said, "A chocolate malt for Mama, please, and a dish of yogurt for me."

"The usual," a walker-dependent, repeat-customer specified, and he secured what he was given in the basket attached to the handlebar of his walker before giving up his place in line. While service was efficient, the length of the line stayed the same because as many joined it as left it after being served.

Third in line was Gloria Fields, who'd transported herself by means of a motorized wheelchair and was smiling broadly to hide the strain of having navigated through a crowd while protecting her extended right leg.

Betty Mansfield was taking orders at the time, and she said, "You're Mrs. Fields, aren't you?"

"I am," Gloria replied.

"We've heard about you and hope you're doing well."

"Oh, I am," Gloria assured Betty. "My cast comes off next week, and after I finish therapy, I expect to move into a Manor apartment."

"Well, the best from all of us here," Grace said as she joined Betty at the serving counter.

"I want to remind you, though," she said with a smile, "that when you live in the Manor, you'll have to pay for your own ice cream."

"You don't think that would stop me from moving, do you?"

"Of course not," and "Not really!" Betty and Grace answered almost simultaneously.

"I'll be so happy to be in Independent Living that I'll not complain at being dropped from the dole," and

Sap and Green People

the security officer cleared a path so Gloria could return to her Assisted Living apartment.

Serving proceeded until closing time, and as her crew tidied up, Grace said, "Glad we're done. We're all tired, and we need to be out of the way so people can get to today's special mass in the Chapel," whose entrance was about thirty steps beyond the ice cream parlor.

Soon after Grace and the workers left, Elaine Bruce and Myra Kelly, volunteer replacements for Joan Cutler and Mary Spritzer who were otherwise committed, rounded the corner pushing two Chapel-bound wheelchairs. Inside, they placed the wheelchairs at the ends of two rows of pews, asked able-bodied persons seated nearby to keep watch over their charges, and left to collect two more women whom they parked at the ends of two other rows, as suggested by Joan and Mary who'd met with Elaine and Myra to drill them earlier in the day.

Seating themselves behind the four women, Elaine and Myra kept watch over them. When one suffered a coughing spell, both attended her until she ceased coughing and fell asleep. A second woman also slept through the entire mass, but gratifying to their caretakers, Woman #3 and Woman #4 remained alert and responded appropriately throughout the mass.

Because they'd seated themselves near the front, Elaine and Myra had to wait until almost everyone filed out of the Chapel before they could leave. Their way finally clear, awkwardly, ineptly, Elaine pushed one wheelchair and pulled another out into the hallway, and Myra followed, using the same push/pull technique recommended by Joan and Mary. Parking the chairs in front of the now-closed ice cream parlor, the two stepped aside to confer.

"Lord help us!" Elaine exclaimed. "Looking for these ladies' rooms may be like finding your car in a mall parking lot when you forgot to note where you parked."

"Yeh, only we're talking people rather than cars," a tense Myra answered.

"You're so right," Elaine agreed, and an audible sigh indicated the uncertainly she felt.

Sap and Green People

"Just between you and me," Myra confessed, "I was so nervous when we started out that I didn't register much of anything, certainly not where we picked up and should return the ladies!"

"I didn't do any better, so we may be in a fix," Elaine agreed. "Interesting: They don't seem the least bit worried," and she turned from Myra to address the women anyway, saying, "Ladies, we'll get you home. You can be sure of that."

"Does anyone live down this hall, the one ahead of us?" Myra asked. When no one answered, she turned the wheelchair she was pushing so it faced the opposite end of the same hall and posed a second question. "Anyone live down there?"

"Well," said one of the women, "I do," and only minutes later, Myra was wheeling the woman into her room and positioning the wheelchair so the woman could watch birds flitting in and out of the tree tops outside her window.

"Nothing to it," Myra said as she rejoined Elaine, and she rolled her eyes to cast doubt on what she'd just stated. "Down the hall we go, Ladies, and around the corner to…traverse another…lovely hall. Anyone live along here?"

"I think so," came a tiny declaration.

"Where?"

"That way," and the woman pointed with an unsteady forefinger.

"On the left or right side?" Elaine asked.

"I'll know when I see it," the woman whispered. "A kite picture is the door," and the procession proceeded uncertainly until the woman exclaimed, "There! There!" Deposited behind her kite-door, the woman's obliging roommate summoned an aide who helped the woman get situated.

In the hall once more, Elaine asked, "Where to, Ladies?" Neither of the two, yet-undelivered residents answered. Bending close to one, Elaine asked, "Can you tell me where you live?" Silence. When she then said, "I've forgotten your name. Will you tell me what it is again, please?" the woman stared at her with dark, blank eyes. A despairing Elaine then shook her head and looked to Myra for help.

Sap and Green People

Gently, Myra wakened the woman seated in the chair she was pushing. "And where's your room, Dear?" she asked. When she repeated the question, paraphrased it, but still got no answer, she told Elaine, "We'll have to get help. Find a nurses' station, I guess."

Retracing their steps, they arrived at the station situated just south of the ice cream parlor. "Do either of these ladies belong here?" Elaine asked an attendant in a voice that she hoped reflected efficiency.

"No," the attendant answered. "They're not ours, either one" and she smiled at Elaine and Myra's charges and asked how they were. Neither woman registered that she'd been addressed.

"Thanks anyway," Elaine told the attendant gamely. "We'll check on down the hall." Arriving at the last station on the floor, she approached an aide, "Do these ladies go here?"

"I'm new and don't know the patients. I'll get someone who does," and the woman entered an office and returned with a nurse who virtually exuded efficiency.

"Elsie," the nurse said to the woman who'd just awakened, "here you are. We were wondering when you'd get back. Was it a good mass?" and Elsie nodded. "This nice lady will take you to your room, and I'll come get you ready for supper in just a minute. Hungry?" Elsie nodded again. "Good 'cause we're having chicken tenders, and I know you like them."

"She wouldn't respond in any way to us," Elaine said plaintively. "Was no help at all. And just where is her room, please?"

"205."

Left with one delivery, Elsie and Myra reasoned that since they'd covered all second-floor corridors, one of them twice, the remaining charge must have been handed off to them when they'd stepped off the elevator to begin their tour of duty, that she must have been brought down from the third floor.

As the chair-pushers and pushee boarded the elevator, Elaine asked the woman, "Do you remember whether we go left or right when we get off the elevator?" No answer. Off the elevator, Elaine smiled

Sap and Green People

broadly at a nurse whom they met and said, "Hello, and here she is."

"There must be some mistake," the nurse answered. "She's not one of mine."

"Sorry. Our error," Elaine said. Further, at another station, she offered the woman to staff members there.

"Never saw her before," a smiling spokesperson stated.

"Damn!" Elaine exclaimed after she and Myra had advanced to a point where they wouldn't be heard.

"Naughty girl," Myra scolded.

Further along, they met another aide who couldn't help either because she was also new.

"Is everyone new?" Elaine asked crossly.

"About a half of us. We take good care of the residents, understand," the aide was quick to explain, "but we do come and go," and her giggle further irritated Elaine.

At a fourth point of inquiry, however, an exuberant aide identified the patient by clasping the woman to her gigantic bosom, issuing a laugh which resounded the length of the hall, and saying, "Carrie, it's 'bout time you got back. Another ten minutes and I'd have eaten your supper. You wouldn't have liked that, would you?"

"Thank heaven!" Myra said as she and Elaine headed for the elevator. "Wow! I'm telling you that pushing wheelchairs isn't all it's cracked up to be."

"Definitely not," her partner answered. "That was terrible. I'd sure do it differently another time."

"How so?"

"Bring a note pad. Write down names and room numbers. Glad you can't smell my armpits."

"Who said I can't?"

"What dummies we were!"

"Think word will get around about this?"

"No. No one perceived our confusion, I'm assuming. That we had a problem. So we're safe."

"This may happen often, what with using volunteers."

"Didn't do any harm. The ladies weren't frighted. We got them back okay."

"Let's not tell anyone," Myra suggested, and, to her credit, Elaine didn't tell anyone until the following evening at the dinner where the story was very much appreciated. Exceedingly well received.

The second forty-five minute, multi-media presentation Jack Clausen prepared for Haven residents featured the life and career of Mahalia Jackson. While his first work had taken him three months to complete, the second took only two and a half months, this due, at least in part, to his being more experienced and having enlarged his cadre of helpers to include Norbert Blair, the bank president turned computer lab organizer. Norbert's responsibilities included making purchases, keeping inventories and records, managing funds, arranging showings, and otherwise assisting Jack as required.

The operation was also better housed. Jack had managed to put together his first feature in one of his apartment bedrooms, small by any measure, which he modified to serve his purpose. He was, however, able to make the second in the seldom used residents' workshop located in the lower level of the Manor, as arranged with Harry Wright, which made production easier and the product better, Jack thought.

The arrangement wasn't totally satisfactory though, for while his computer and files remained in the

Sap and Green People

apartment, Jack's equipment (cameras, screens, splicers, recording paraphernalia, and such) was kept in the workshop where the filming was done, mandating that Jack trek back and forth between the apartment and the workshop a number of times most days.

"Another hour and we'll be playing to a full house," Rob Reynolds predicted as he checked plugs and sockets, switches, and speakers in the auditorium located under the Chapel where the second presentation was to take place.

"Probably not," Jack cautioned. "Don't be too optimistic."

Continuing the conversation while inspecting discs, tapes, microphones, and amplifiers, Bud Schultz, Jack's other technician, said, "We had sixty-eight the first time and our fame's spread, I know for a fact. So, I predict a hundred. Easy!"

"Think they'll be interested in Mahalia Jackson?" Jack asked dubiously. "I picked her because she was female and black, helped establish gospel music, and contributed substantially to her community and a number of other causes. Since she's black and not exactly a pop hero or present-day celebrity, we'll see if 'you should know' and 'good for you' will get people out."

"We could contact all the black groups in town, especially female black groups, and show the video to them for a nominal charge," Norbert, who'd joined the conversation, suggested. "They'd appreciate the subject and you could recoup your investment, Jack."

"No," Jack answered. "I'm standing on my resolve: no soliciting and no decisions based on money. We're talking about the twin sisters, enlightenment and entertainment, here. Look like the original six shows will be all I can afford, but I'll decide what to do when I have to. Then."

"What's the eats tonight?" Bud asked.

"Little tarts. Does that make them tartlets?" Norbert answered with a nervous chuckle.

"Pecan and other flavors. Also molasses cookies and dried fruit chips."

"Classy."

"Southern."

Sap and Green People

"Ethnic maybe."

Rob opened the door to look out into the hall leading to the auditorium. "Man, there's people out there already," he exclaimed. "How they gonna stand long enough for the doors to open? And a half-dozen wheelchairs lined up along the wall. Really!" he said when Jack looked to confirm Rob's appraisal. "No kiddin'!"

"If that's the case," Jack answered, "we'll have to open the doors early. Can't keep those people on their feet that long."

"See," Norbert said. "They're convinced, Jack, that this is worth coming to. That you've done the professional job you aspired to. I'm glad for you."

"Free eats brought them," Jack rebutted.

"It's more than that," Norbert replied. "After all, watching the tube in their pajamas would be easier. They've heard that what we've got is better than the tube, and they're amazed that one of us could do what you've done. Me too! No way would I have thought of doing this. Again, I sure do thank you for suggesting I work with you."

The outside door leading into a galley-kitchen running along the auditorium's east wall opened, and Harry Wright stepped in. "Gentlemen," he said by way of addressing the four men, "what are we going to do about the mature, some-impaired mob that's gathering out there? I started to come through the hall door, decided against plowing my way through the people, and used the side door. Couldn't believe my eyes. We shouldn't have more that 150 in the room because we have no attendants per se and because of the slow-walkers, wheelchair-bound, visually-impaired, and nearly-infirm who are in the group. For reasons of safety."

"Think we've really got a problem?"

"Oh, the joy of being so blessed!" Wright answered.

"Can't believe we'd have more than 150", Jack said, "but we were just saying that perhaps we should open the doors early."

"My thought exactly," Wright replied, and as soon as Rob and Bud moved their testing equipment out of the way, he opened the heavy doors, invited those who

Sap and Green People

were waiting to enter, and saw to their seating and wheelchair arrangement. "If there are too many," Wright told Jack when things settled down a bit," I'll issue rain checks for a second performance, if that would be okay."

"Of course," Jack assured him, "but frankly, Harry, I'm nervous. About the subject, now that attendance is not a worry. How it'll be received. Received and perceived."

"Why?"

"The Negro factor. A lot of the people of this generation, my generation, are prejudiced, and I don't know if I can make them accept and appreciate Mahalia, especially in the light of her close association with Martin Luther King who's…not exactly appreciated universally, if you know what I mean."

"The people who refuse to appreciate the woman won't come," Wright told Jack, "so it'll be fine."

And indeed it was. People clapped enthusiastically when the narration, depiction, and music were over and during the refreshment period, they flocked around Jack, Norbert, Bud, Rob, and Harry Wright to comment on Mahalia and express their appreciation for what they'd produced and would continue to produce. The audience had not outnumbered the available chairs and facilities, necessitating a follow-up performance, but people, especially those who'd missed the first presentation, said they wanted to see it and that night's showing again. Gratified, Jack promised a rerun after he'd completed and shown the rest of the series.

One of the last to work her way up to Jack was Gloria Fields who was using a walker and sporting a brace on her right leg.

"Hello there," Jack said. "I remember you from our meeting outdoors one fine day, and from our first show. How nice to see you again. Your status has changed, I see," and he looked down at Gloria's legs to indicate his meaning. "Weren't you in a wheelchair then?"

Being recognized always flustered Gloria. Because recognition made her realize that her disability was obvious. Distinguished her. That she might be a subject of conversation, that things were perhaps being said about her, and she wondered what those things were. She blushed and stammered as she tried to explain in the fewest words possible what had happened, and her voice faded away to the point where her words became almost inaudible by the time she finished talking.

"You are going through a difficult time," Jack responded sympathetically, and he questioned the wisdom of making reference to her condition, of having looked at her legs.

"Thank you," Gloria managed. "I enjoyed this so much, a beautiful thing. Informative," and she hurried, if 'hurried' could be said of her labored gait, so she could pass through the double doors while Harry Wright was still holding them open.

"Good night," Wright said, and Gloria replied, "That's what it was: a very good night."

Patricia Dick

Mary Spritzer, Elaine Bruce, Joan Cutler, Myra Kelly, and Eloise Brady sat on the patio of a new, neighborhood restaurant to talk, snack, and drink. Animated, wide-awake, and desirous of extending their evening after attending a play staged in a nearby performing arts theater, they sat with their chairs turned to the exterior wall of the restaurant and watched people drive by, file in, and come out of the restaurant.

"Nice place," Myra said.

"Didn't pay much attention to the inside, but it's nice here on the patio. Quiet. Breezy. Cool."

"But do we need another new restaurant?"

"Why not?"

"It's the free enterprise system, isn't it?"

"I loved *Into the Woods*. Great performance."

"Swell."

"Excellent."

"Heard it was…"

".. and it was."

"What'd it say?"

"Does a play always have to say something?"

"As far as I'm concerned it does."

"Me too."

"Have to have something to think about."

"Agreed."

"Said that everyone has to go into the woods at some time during the course of his life…"

"…and going into the woods is scary…"

"…because there's a lot of unknowns there."

"Nobody comes out the same…"

"…but we learn from having been there."

"Very, very good, Ladies. I believe we got…"

"…the message…"

"…and we should be proud of ourselves."

"How can we be sure we did?"

"By accepting our consensus."

"That decided, we can spend time remembering how bouncy and bubbly and musical and fun the play was," which marked the end of a second discussion.

"Lots of people out tonight."

"Because it's such a nice, fall, weekend night, I guess."

"Who'd want to stay in."

"Or go home if they're out."

"Unless they have something to bring them home, and we sure don't."

"You can say that again."

"Unless they have something to bring them home, and we sure don't."

"Silly," Myra said as she was bent forward by laughter, "we sound like my kids did when they were teenagers."

"Or younger."

"Miss the kids? Their interplay?"

"Not anymore," Myra answered. "I did for a long while but not now. I love it when the whole family gets together a couple of times a year and gets real crazy. Laughing and kidding and shouting back and forth, shouting because that's what we have to do to be heard. It's wonderful. But at my age, I like it quiet. Calm, peaceful, quiet."

"Me too. God, how I miss George, but still, I like the quiet."

"Likewise."

Sap and Green People

"I don't even understand half of what the kids are talking and laughing about anyway."

"Or know half of the personalities and songs and books they mention."

"They're too frank for me."

"I know what you mean. There's not anything they don't talk about. Nothing's sacred, personal, or private."

"Amen."

"Being together must be animated, though," Mary said. "Convivial and…invigorating. Having no family at all, I'm thinking I might welcome family craziness. Even too-frank talk."

"Let's get some more fried veggie appetizers. The first round wasn't enough."

"Two scant bites each."

"Boy, we were stingy. Need more drinks too. Having wine this time, Joan, or another coffee?" Myra asked as she signaled the waiter.

"I'll stick to coffee and be the designated driver," Joan answered.

"But we came in Eloise's car."

"I'll continue drinking," Eloise volunteered, "and let Joan drive."

"Think you can handle that big, ole' thing?" Elaine asked.

"Try me," Joan said, and the women sat quietly as they looked out at the night until their young, exceedingly handsome waiter returned.

"A hunk," Joan said as he walked away with their orders.

"Yep."

"Looks like my grandson Stanley," Myra said.

"Does anyone name a kid 'Stanley' anymore?"

"Not to question the judgment of Stanley's parents, Myra, but I hope our waiter isn't named that."

"You've hurt my feelings with your comments about my Stanley," Myra complained, and her friends giggled, then halfway apologized.

"Thank you, Young Man," Joan said when the waiter returned. "By chance, is your name Stanley?"

"No, Ma'm, it's not," the hunk answered. "It's Brett."

"Glad it's not Stanley," Joan said, and Brett nodded, pivoted on the ball of his foot, and left them to their repartee.

"Brett!" Myra said, her voice scornful. "That's worse than Stanley."

"Myra," Mary said, "you're tipsy."

"Who cares?" Myra answered.

"Not me."

"Me either."

"I'm going to order yet another bottle of wine. To make sure we're all tipsy."

"We'll shorten our lives," Mary warned, her lips formed in a grin.

"Oh, I hope so," Myra answered.

"Speaking for myself, I hope I don't have to live forever."

"Me too."

"For how many more years?"

"Ask me tomorrow."

"Late tomorrow."

"I said the same thing ten years ago," Mary told her friends.

"How old were you then?" Joan asked.

No reply.

"Where were you living at the time, Mary?"

"Ten years ago? In Hong Kong."

"Jesus!" Eloise said at the mention of another foreign stay.

"Live there long?"

"Only a month."

"Is a month 'living there'?"

"Sure, if I'm there long enough to completely unpack my suitcases and use the hotplate, I'm living there."

"In how many of the places already cited did you live for that short a time?"

"Several. Can't remember exactly, as a matter of fact," Mary stated.

"Where else not mentioned to date have you lived, even for only a month?"

"Johannesburg."

"The one in Africa?"

"How many are there?"

"Quick! Who's got the list with her? Add Hong Kong and Johannesburg! Get 'em down."

"We'll remember."

"Not after all the wine."

"Joan will. She's not drinking. She'll remember."

"Testing, Girls, testing. What were those places?" Joan quizzed. When no one bothered to answer, she said, "Never mind. I'll remember," which wasn't funny in the least but provoked peals of laughter.

"Ladies," Mary said.

"'Girls' is better."

"Girls, I'll tell you what. When I'm dying, on my deathbed, I'll tell you about my background and where I've lived, as many places as I can remember, and why I've lived in so many of them."

"Is that a promise?" Elaine asked.

"It is," Mary answered.

"What if we go first?"

"Yeh, how would we know then?"

"Any idea when you'll be on your deathbed, Mary?" Elaine said. "I want to make plans to be there."

"You can't plan that."

"Why not?"

"'Cause we have no way of knowing what your drinking and other bad habits will do to you."

"Let's cut them all out 'cause I sure as hell want to hear what Mary's going to tell us."

"Bad language. Shame on you."

"That's what happens when a person has a good time," Myra answered with a toothy grin. "If you think her language is bad, you should have heard my husband's."

"Wow!" Elaine answered. "You had a profane life?"

"Profane and connubial one."

"Let's not get into connubial!"

"I don't know connubial. Only conventional."

"Convex."

"Crass."

"Crazy."

"Read in the paper about the man in Atlanta who's advertising for an over-70-years-old wife?"

"Any woman that old knows better."

Sap and Green People

"Oh, I don't know," Eloise interjected.

"That's why I don't read the paper much any more. Junk and international problems which we can't solve. That's what the paper is nowadays."

"And health."

"National obsession, health."

"And still nearly everyone's grossly overweight."

"Feeling guilty about it but still pigging out."

"That really bothers us, doesn't it?"

"We keep talking about it!"

And so it went: back and forth, round and round, intimately, nonsensically, irreverently, the conversation continued. Until ten minutes before the restaurant was to close, at which time, with the exception of Joan, the women stood up on dottery legs. Helping each other, they maneuvered the six steps which took them down to the street, crossed to the parking lot, located and climbed into Eloise's car, and, at Joan's insistence, buckled their seat belts.

"You're going to have headaches in the morning and be ashamed of yourselves," Joan scolded.

"Not me," one answered.

"Nor I," said another.

Nothing from Mary who was sound asleep, her head pillowed by Elaine's obliging shoulder.

Sap and Green People

The Davises and Grahams sat in the Grahams' third-floor Manor apartment, looking through the open deck doors at what lay below. At the Haven's lake and the fountain jetting from its center, intended to keep the lake from scumming over. The cement dam over which the water cascaded and the graveled streambed it followed from there. The stones and boulders piled along the stream to keep the banks from washing away.

A winding, black-topped path followed the north bank of the lake and stream, curving right, then left, again, again, representing an imposed spontaneity. Beyond the path, a strip of thick woods framed the lake with shades of green.

"How are your neighbors, the elderly couple without family and so unwell they couldn't take care of themselves but wouldn't admit it?" Marg asked the Grahams.

"We asked the chaplain to call on them," Georgia answered. "He got social service people involved, and they got the help they needed. The husband finally died two weeks ago."

"She'll not be far behind," Henry added with a doleful shake of his head.

"We have two cancer patients in our building," Bill said, "plus a serious heart problem and a bigtime case of angina. But right now, they're doing okay."

"Look at the Queen Ann's Lace at the north side of the stream, to our right," Marg said, and she pointed to the tall, elegant weed-plant. "When it was in bloom, my grandma had vases, Mason jars mostly, everywhere in her house, or so it seemed to me then. And I picked blooms in fields near the condo where we lived until we moved here. I'd always come home from picking covered with bites, wouldn't I, Bill?" and Bill nodded. "One time, I swear I had no less that fifty chigger bites around my middle."

"Why'd you pick weeds?" an incredulous Henry asked.

"So I could dry them and make wreaths out of them."

"Dry them in the oven?" Georgia asked.

"No. Used a square of chicken wire with the Queen Anne's Lace. Let the stems hang down through the wire and spread the blossoms out on top. Worked fine.

When you look out in front of you, you see nature," Marg went on to say as she swept the horizon with her hand. "When we look out, we see most of the Manor, the sides of the other two Apartment Buildings like ours, part of the Assisted Living complex, and the top of the old convent and church. Your view is 'country'. Ours makes me think of a European village, especially when the church bells ring."

"The two faces of the Haven at Oak Hill," Georgia said.

"Speakin' of country, this place is a far cry the scrappy little Tennessee farm where I came from," Henry said. "We lived with my grandma and unmarried aunt. My mother, who was always sickly, died when I was eight, and my father, a bricklayer, died of T.B. two years later, leavin' Grandma and the aunt to raise us four boys. After Grandma died, there was only Aunt Jenny."

"Good childhood?" Marg asked.

"The only one I ever knew," Henry answered. "Our house had an outhouse, the school too. Wore overalls and went barefoot to school most of the year."

"Not because he didn't have shoes," Georgia interjected.

"'Cause I didn't want to wear 'em. Except for one kid whose father owned a company and made him wear shoes, none of us kids did. Went to a one-room grade school for a few years, then moved to a three-roomer. Went into town for high school. Started workin' at a drugstore as soon as I was old enough to work. Was named by my class as the most likely to succeed, I'll have you know."

"Good for you. Bill started delivering newspapers when he was eleven," Marg volunteered. "I got my first job when I was fourteen. In a grocery store. Made fifteen cents an hour, which was a lot better than the ten cents I got for babysitting."

"Our reasons for working were sure different from why our grandkids work now," Bill interjected. "Their pocket money goes for $50.00 concert tickets, designer clothes, cars, CD's, limo transportation, if they use their own money at all."

"Them's 'wants' rather than 'needs' as far as I'm concerned," Henry said.

"Our wants were so simple."

"Everyone was poor then," Georgia said. "Some poorer than others. My family was okay because my grandfather acquired a number of acres of farmland. I don't know how: a land grant, I've always presumed. He had enough to plat farms for his sons, which is why we lived where we did: out by Grandpa. I rode the bus to school, and eighteen days after I graduated, I went into the Cadet Nurse Program so I could help with the war effort and get my training free."

Her listeners knew what 'war effort' she meant and to which war she was referring, for their youths had also been cut short by World War II, adulthood having been forced upon them at the time of their eighteenth birthdays or graduations, the time when a young man was inducted into military service, a young woman into the work force if she didn't go to college, and most did not.

"Our daughter and her husband vacationed in Europe with their children when the kids were twelve, fourteen, and sixteen," Bill said. "They'd already been to Hawaii twice. A grandson started taking glider-flying lessons when he was fourteen, powered-flying lessons when he was sixteen. Our granddaughter was on her third horse by the time she was fourteen and quit riding. True, those kids aren't typical of all kids, but lots of youngsters fare well materially, in contrast to us 'Depression Babies'."

"Our youngest grandchild had gone on cruises twice with his parents and to Mexico once before he celebrated his tenth birthday," Marg continued. "The grandchildren are great and we're not criticizing them or their parents. We're just contrasting what they have and are able to do with what we had and did."

"Is it for the better?"

"Who knows."

"Time will tell, I guess."

"Richer in terms of things and experiences certainly."

"Lackin' in other respects, maybe."

"The first time we drove past our daughter's second house which was still being built," Marg said, "I gulped. Literally gulped! Couldn't believe one of our kids could have a house like that at that point in her life. And the family's in an even bigger house now."

"August Busch, the beer man, had our younger doctor-son and his wife and three other doctor-couples flown to Florida on a Busch jet for a fancy weekend because one those doctors, an associate of our son, did successful heart surgery on a Busch," Henry said.

"Make you jealous, what your sons have?" Bill asked Henry.

"No," Henry answered after he thought a minute, for he'd never really considered the matter before.

"Neither are we," Bill stated, "but I believe that some of our generation are."

"Ask them and they'd deny it, but listen to them," Marg said. "They criticize their kids by saying things like, 'My son-in-law's got to have everything. The very best. His kids, too.' Or, 'My grandkids had to have $75.00 sandals this summer. What's the matter with $20.00, sale sandals?'"

"Aren't those just observations?"

"Or bragging? People have always bragged about their families."

"Maybe."

"Maybe jealousy's the wrong word," Bill allowed. "Maybe some of our generation just begrudge their kids having what they did not."

"Life is more complex now, and people are driven in ways we weren't."

"Young people feel they have to achieve a really high standard of living."

"And arrange 'comfortable' retirements, comfortable meanin' "indulgement" to my way of thinkin'.

"They feel they have to work too hard, but we worked hard, didn't we, Henry? Fighting a war, then putting in sixty-, seventy-, and sometimes eighty-hour weeks without compensation for overtime or the frequent flyers' points we had to turn back to our company."

Sap and Green People

"In our case, Georgia and I moved nineteen times for that company."

"Here's an example of things being different," Marg said. "Our granddaughter visited us when we were vacationing in Florida one time, when she was fourteen, and she didn't bring enough underwear with her. We meant to buy some but didn't get around to it, and when I realized that she might be suffering from the shortage, I told her that since we didn't have a washing machine in the place we were renting, maybe she could wash a few things out by hand to tide her over. 'How do you do that?' she asked. I described the procedure, and she said, 'Yuk!' and wrinkled up her nose. 'I'd never do that!'"

"Poor baby," Georgia said. "Seems like the gap between generations gets bigger and bigger which calls for a lot of love and understanding," and as the Davises and Grahams watched the sun drop in a pink, western sky, a pair of low-flying Canadian geese honked their intention to land on the Haven lake. Descending, they unfolded their legs, spread their webbed feet, dug their heels into the water's surface, and skied to the far end of the lake.

"What a sight," Henry said. "Reminds you that some things go on forever. Without changin' a bit."

"And thank goodness for that."

"Thank goodness for sure."

Sap and Green People

A sick, pained, weary Marg Davis studied the inside of her closed eyelids as she lay in her hospital bed. Her leg throbbed, back pounded, head ached, and the port sited in a vein in the back of her hand to facilitate infusions stung and smarted. All in all, her body registered red, flaming red, and she'd wondered if her eyelids were also red.

Their undersides were not. Black, olive, and gray, all swirled, blended, and whirled together, with a little black dot appearing on and off in the middle of the right lid.

Could the black dot open into The Black Hole of the Universe, she wondered? Be an access to that Big Wonder? Clearing her head with a shake, she scolded herself for the absurd notion and clawed her way back to reality.

Relax, she admonished herself. Stay grounded. Focused. Rational.

Marg had left her apartment in the Haven three days earlier to undergo knee replacement surgery. She'd had her right knee replaced eight years earlier, and either the first operation had gone better than the second or she'd edited its memory because when anyone talked to her about replacement in those intervening years, she'd recommend proceeding. Stated that the operation wasn't bad. Even called it 'a piece of cake'.

Man alive, Marg thought, if those people had surgery, I hope they fared better than I. Should I try to find them? Warn them? Stop them if it's not late? Only, I can't remember who they were. Absolutely can't.

Oh, the complications I've suffered, she lamented. None life-threatening, but oh, the big, throbbing hematoma had swollen her leg so it looked as substantial as the trunk of a tree. Pain, big-time pain that prompted her to gulp down pain pills, all she was offered. Chew them. Chug them down! Only, she was allergic to them, the hospital people finally declared. Hence the nausea. Might never be able to eat again.

I'll include nausea in the list of the tribulations I'll share when I discuss my second implantation, she planned. Cite nausea but not tell about the gagging

Sap and Green People

and heaving and throwing up, for who'd want to hear about that? When she was better and had an audience, what she'd do was cite the tribulations and tell the "Tuesday Night Hallucination" story, so outrageous, so rare, so funny.

I was wakened at 1:15 in the morning, she'd say. On a Tuesday morning actually. By a couple in the next room who were having a terrible fight. Banging against the walls, throwing things, hitting each other over the head with furniture. Hollering and yelling to beat the band. Saying terrible things. Like, "I'll kill you, you bastard." "See you in hell." And worse, things I wouldn't repeat for anything. Terrible profanities. Obscenities. Heard them clearly. On and on the fight went.

I kept mum for as long as I could, but finally, thinking the people were going to hurt each other terribly, I called the nurses' station. Nurses' because I didn't know Security's number. Told about the fight, whomever I talked to thanked me, and a couple of minutes later a nurse came into my room.

"What's your name?" the nurse asked, which sort of cued me that something was wrong. I was able to cite my full name, I'm happy to report, but then she said, "Do you know where you are?" which confused me. So I looked around and said that I was either in a hospital or in a hotel, probably a hotel.

"What's happening," the nurse explained, "is you're hallucinating. Suffering a reaction to something, probably to your painkiller which contains morphine. There's no couple next door. Only an old man who doesn't speak a word of English."

That surprised me, Marg decided she'd say, because I'd distinctly heard the voices. Also heard someone leave the room, the woman whom I'd heard yelling, I'd presumed.

"That was me," the nurse said. "Talking in a loud voice because the old gentleman in the room was very hard of hearing. I came to your room right away, after having been told about your call."

I'm telling you, is how Marg planned to end her story, what the nurse said was hard for me to fathom because the whole thing was so real. But I'll tell you

Sap and Green People

that I surely didn't take any more of those painkillers. Took another sort but continued to have hallucinations for almost a week. One, several times repeated, had our bedroom ceiling overgrown with vegetation which hung down as far as my fingertips. Hallucinations finally went away. After the morphine was out of my system, I guess.

Practicing the Tuesday Morning Hallucination diverted Marg's attention from her intense pain. Only for a few minutes. So in an attempt to alleviate it, she redistributed her weight. Flexed her back. Her shoulder and leg muscles. But it persisted.

Wham, wham, wham, it went. Transmitted from sawed-through bones and cut-through nerve endings. Zing! Zap! Flashed through her torso, neck, head. Tingle, pow!

The musical phrase "O-h-h, Sweet J-e-e-sus" kept playing in Marg's mind. From a song she'd known long ago, she presumed. A hymn or camp song. 1960s lamentation? Oh-h-h, Sweet J-e-e-sus, G-G-G-F-F-E. Oh-h-h-h, Sweet Jesus, G-G-G-F-F-E. Over and over. From deep in the bowels of her mind.

Sweet Jesus, Marg prayed, get me through this. Stand beside me, here by my bed. Take my hand. At least 'til my darling Bill comes, Jesus. Please, Jesus, please! At least until then.

Sap and Green People

In his 'previous life', Norbert Blair had been committed and content as president of his hometown bank for almost four decades. He'd willingly accepted his responsibilities—with one exception: having to wear a starched shirt, sober tie, and navy, brown, or charcoal suit to work every day, from the first day on the job until the day he carried home the last box of personal possessions he'd retrieved from his office following his retirement.

In reaction to that wear-suits imperative, henceforth Norbert wore knit shirts and shorts most days of the year. 'Walking shorts', he called them, whether they were longish or short, whether he did any walking in them or not.

The shorts were of all fabrics: chino, denim, corduroy, broadcloth, seersucker, and nylon, anything except jersey which, modest man that he was, Norbert regarded as being too body-conforming. Color-wise, he favored navy, light blue, forest green, khaki, black, brown, and summer white.

Norbert wore shorts in his apartment, in the computer lab, around campus, in the neighborhood as he ran errands and tended to personal business. When the temperature dropped to, say, forty degrees, he'd top off his shorts with a sweatshirt or sweater, add a jacket if required.

As might be expected, Norbert did not wear shorts to church, funerals, and weddings, and he certainly did not to the few 'dress occasions' he attended. Otherwise, though, it was shorts and casual shirts for Norbert Blair.

Relative to the legs Norbert exposed in the course of his shorts-wearing, perhaps surprising in light of his age, Norbert's legs were quite presentable: slim, shapely, straight though short, and as hairy as the legs of an ape which is acceptable, it seems, even admirable, in the case of human males.

Norbert's idiosyncratic shorts-wearing bothered some persons when he wore them to dinner in the Manor dining room, to the point where several diners (women) called for a dress code at a Residents' Association meeting. After lengthy, animated discussion, however, a plurality voted against such a rule. Fortunately for everyone, the complainers

Sap and Green People

accepted their defeat and Norbert was magnanimous in his victory.

Jack Clausen and a shorts-clad Norbert were sitting on folding chairs in their workroom one Monday morning, drinking coffee and rejoicing that they'd finished moving the last of Jack's documentary-making supplies and equipment from his apartment to the Manor, a chore accomplished during the last two days of the previous week.

"Time to get going on the next one," Jack told his friend. "George Orwell. I expect we'll be introducing Orwell to many of our audience, and my thinking is that we need to place him in time and country, establish him as a visionary, and help our audience appreciate Orwell's opposition to totalitarianism and his commitment to social justice."

"You could have aimed simpler, Man," Norbert suggested with a grin. "Chronicled Shirley Temple movies, Bill Clinton's affairs, or stock market crashes. But I'm glad you didn't."

"Treating 'visionary' won't be hard," Jack continued. "Jesus and Voltaire and Thomas Jefferson and umpteen historic figures were visionaries. We'll use their examples and quotes and the definitions we find or work out to make that point. But say the word 'totalitarianism' and most people think only of 'Communism'. We'll have to broaden their 'totalitarianism' conception. 'Social justice' is doable."

"Orwell's *Animal Farm* is easy reading," Norbert said. "I remember when my kids had to read it, and I think junior high students are still assigned the book."

"So I've been told. But a lot of people take the book literally. Don't understand symbolism. May reject the book because they presume it's an animal story."

"Or a child's book."

"Needs to be interpreted broadly. Applied to contemporary society."

"We've got our work cut out for us, and that's swell because we welcome challenges, don't we?" Norbert said while stifling a yawn.

"Know what?" Jack asked. "All I can think about this morning is the good response we got to the Mahalia Jackson production."

"It was swell, simply swell."

"The best comment came from that pretty little woman," Jack said. "You know who I mean? The one with the walker and cast on her leg? Did you notice her?" and Norbert nodded. "'Beautiful and informative', she said of the show. Or something like that. Wasn't that great?"

"Stroke victim, apparently. Obviously 'senior' but surprising pretty," Norbert answered.

"Appreciated what she said and keep thinking of her," Jack said, and reading the scrutiny on Norbert's face, he hastily added, "Once or twice, Buster, only a couple of times, and of what she said. Her words."

"Struck me funny," Norbert explained, and that seemingly took care of Jack's comment.

"Aw shoot," Jack admitted, "I'm not up to this today. Told you what I was planning, and that's all I feel like doing. Ever have those days?" and Norbert nodded vigorously. "Let's go somewhere. Do something."

"Movie?"

"Yeh! Don't know when I've been to one of those!"

"An imbecilic 'action film'?"

"Not!"

"Sentimental, 'coming of age' thing?"

"Wouldn't like that. Don't think I was ever that young. Came of age."

"Eddie Murphy's on."

"Heck no!"

"'Cause he's black?"

"You know better than that," and Jack laughed at what Norbert knew was a ridiculous question.

"Something foreign?"

"If something's showing. We can get the newspaper and see. If nothing's good, we'll do a museum or the Garden."

"My shorts clean enough?" and Norbert stepped to the door, opened it to a flood of morning sunlight that made both men blink, and looked down at his midregion. "Good enough," he declared. "I can usually get two, three days out of this pair, and today's number two."

"How tacky," Jack kidded. "We'll get back on track tomorrow. Bob and Bud are coming in the afternoon. That'll get us going. Have to be sharp and enthusiastic for them."

"Also energetic. That's why we need to take it easy today. So we can generate a store of energy," and between them, they managed to pull the coffee pot plug, close and lock the door, and walk over to the garage where Jack's car was parked.

Boarding it, a vintage Mercury, they found that the car was as lacking in enthusiasm and energy as they, a thing which they readily understood and consequently did not hold against the antiquated machine.

Robert Hudson turned his stretch limo off the busy street and onto a broad pedestrian pathway which took his gleaming white Cadillac over the crest of a hill and a hundred yards further into the city park. Turning onto the grassy hillside, he swung the limo around so it pointed towards the street, parking its left wheels on the grass, its right on the shoulder of the path, a place where his passengers could off-load easily and safely, the limo would not obstruct pedestrian traffic, and it was positioned to move up the pathway when his passengers chose to leave the Sunday evening band concert, whether it was finished or not.

Robert pushed away from the steering column, opened the door with his left hand, turned to address his passengers, and said, "Ladies, I'll leave the air-conditioning running while I get your chairs set up, and then I'll return for you. It'll only take a few minutes, so please relax and make yourselves comfortable."

"Thank you," Essie Brinkman, the organizer of the outing replied.

"And remember that there's ice water in the decanters. Thermo cups," and with that, Robert got out and shut the door behind him quietly but with unmistakable vigor.

"You had a very good idea, coming here," Mary Spritzer told Essie, "and we thank you for implementing it."

"Not original with me," Essie responded. "My husband, two grandchildren, and I came once, maybe twenty years ago, when the children were little, and we saw a bunch of typical, old ladies seated in webbed, aluminum chairs. Remember those? Listening to a concert while their driver leaned against the side of a limo, smoked cigarettes, and whiled time away. The grandchildren thought the women comical, seated as they were like crows on a fence, but I thought them clever. Admirable, what with their determination to get out and enjoy a park concert on a summer evening.

And here I am, an old lady myself, spending a Sunday evening with a bunch of quaint, 'older ladies'. Dear me," she said wistfully. "I know where dear Harry went, but where'd all those years go?"

"Don't be morbid, Dear."

"We may be oldish like those women but we're not comical."

"And certainly not quaint either."

"Heavens forbid!"

"That Robert's pretty cool," Joan Cutler commented after an awkward moment of silence. "Turn you on, Mary?"

"Nothing turns me on these days," Mary Spritzer answered quietly.

"You do look a little puny," a concerned Joan remarked. "Seems to me that your curls are even a little limp," an humorous effort on Joan's part to enliven Mary who appeared uncharacteristically listless and passive.

"That's wasn't a nice thing to say," Gail Russell, the newest member of the group, said.

"I thought it discerning," Mary countered, "because I'm not quite my usual self," which initiated expressions of concern.

"And by the way, Gail, we've never aimed at being 'nice'," Eloise Brady said.

"In your case, nothing could be truer," Essie responded, and everyone tittered.

Robert opened the left back door of the limo, bowed slightly, and announced, "Ladies, the chairs are ready. If you please…," and he helped the women out, one at a time, and assisted each to one of the chairs he'd securely situated on a ledge sculpted by time or design into the side of the long hill. The hill capped the acreage and formed a natural amphitheater where a featured band had performed for a number of summers. When he'd seated everyone, his beneficiaries expressed their appreciation by applauding, which attracted the attention of persons sitting nearby. Rather than minding, Robert and the women appreciated the recognition, and they waved and mouthed greetings and thank-yous.

"And now," Robert said, "I'll get the coolers out and take your beverage orders, the beverages having been specified by none other than Miss Essie."

"Wine?"

"Of course," Essie assured the asker.

"I'm taking too many pills to drink wine."

"Won't kill you."

"It might."

"Good way to go."

"Nice cause of, place and evening for it."

"But think of the commotion it'd make. Disturb all these people. Detract from the concert."

"Rather die in my own bed anyway."

"Who wouldn't?"

"That's about all I pray for anymore: being able to die in my bed."

"Selfish. You could pray that I die in mine."

"Play the numbers and you know someone's got to be shot in a place other than her bed."

"Strangle on a meat ball in our dining room or restaurant."

"Be run over."

"Dropped by a heart attack."

"Done in by cancer."

"You ladies are something," a laughing Robert interjected as he finished matching everyone to the beverage of her choice. "Snacks? Peanuts? Popcorn? Pretzels?"

"Plain or coated pretzels?"

"Yogurt-covered. East on the tummy."

"'Bout the only thing that is," Elaine grumbled. "Hate to think what peanuts and popcorn would do to my…"

"Stomach?"

"Guts?"

"Colon!" Elaine said.

"Might clear it out."

"Too bad the others girls couldn't come," Myra Kelly said to change the subject.

"Well, we said 'nine', the 'first nine to sign up'. Maybe we can bring two limos another year."

"To one concert early in the season, then to another 'cause I could go for two."

"In another year, we might not need two limos. There may be fewer of us by then."

"My, aren't we gloomy tonight."

"What are we hoping for?" Mary asked. "That we'll require two vehicles to transport our numbers or that we've been whittled down so we can get by with one?"

Made somewhat uneasy by rapid repartee seemingly turned sour, Robert interrupted by exclaiming, "Ladies, ladies! What a night for a concert. Hear them testing the amplification equipment? See the band members taking their places in the bandstand? They'll begin tuning their instruments soon, and it won't be long before they start playing. Here are your programs," and he handed one to each woman. "'An all-American concert', it says. 'Cause it's Labor Day Sunday. 'American composers and American favorites'. While I serve you again, look around. At the families, spread out on the spots they've claimed. At the children, all kinds, many over on the playground equipment," and he pointed to the play area. "They'll run between their families and the playground, their folks can watch from where they're seated, and when it's dark, they'll call the children over. Couples sprawled out on blankets. Dogs. Notice all the dogs? I'm telling you that there are lots of dogs in South St. Louis, lots, and they most certainly are lovers of park concerts, every single one. Ted Drewes ice cream stand down by the stage. I'll get ice cream for anyone who wants me to. Just call or wave. And I have bug spray. Anyone?"

Sap and Green People

"Got spray."

"Thanks anyway."

"Too greasy. Never wear it."

"Smelly."

"I always just take my chances."

"Well then," the obliging shepherd concluded, "have a good time, and I'll just be ten steps or so away. By the limo and at your command," and the women curtailed their conversation to look around as Robert had suggested.

They looked until the National Anthem was introduced by the Mistress of Ceremonies over the public address system and they had to stand, which entailed straining, genteel groaning, and the assistance of Robert Hudson who also helped them reseat themselves and picked up the things they'd dropped during the standing-up, sitting-down process.

"It'll be a half-hour 'til intermission," Robert reported as he returned to the side of the limo and commenced dusting the car, its headlights, its windows.

"Enterprising," one of the women commented.

"Think we'll get to dust him?"

"Probably an ordinance against it."

"Sh-h-h-h-h!" Mary Spritzer hissed, for the band was playing its first rendition, a portion of ***The Grand Canyon Suite.*** Mary's admonition had silenced her friends down, and they listened to the late-August band concert which Essie had planned and they'd subscribed to, their thinking being that a Labor Day concert would top off their list of summer entertainments, in fact a rather short listing.

Sap and Green People

Early one morning, having resisted his shorts-wearing compulsion, Norbert Blair put on a yellow knit shirt and creased khaki trousers and readied himself for making a day-long visit to his hometown, Smithton, Missouri. Battling warring emotions, anticipation and dread, his stomach so knotted that he couldn't partake of his usual, substantial breakfast, Norbert gulped down black coffee and departed for the place where he'd been born, schooled, and married; where he'd lived with a wife he'd adored and two children he'd worshiped; which he'd cherished but foresworn when he moved to the Haven at Oak Hill.

Arriving in Smithton at 9:45 following an easy drive, Norbert first drove past his previous home, an all-brick, '60s ranch house which he found well maintained and still surrounded with autumnal mounds of yellow, burgundy, and bronze chrysanthemums, mums he'd planted and replaced and nurtured for years.

Norbert was unsettled at the sight of his former home, but he reminded himself that leaf-raking would soon begin, raking which entailed the filling of well over a hundred yard-waste bags usually. The thought of raking and finding his plantings flourishing kept Norbert from feeling too melancholy; finding that his garden had become a bark-covered play area containing new swings, slides, and jungle bars damped down his nostalgia; and the fine appearance of his home and its neighborhood made his inspection less painful that he'd anticipated.

Having passed the initial test, Norbert drove on to the cemetery where his wife was buried. Pulling his newfangled, put-it-together-on-the-spot, narrow-gauge pipe lawn chair out of his car trunk, he assembled it and sat facing the marker which designated the hallowed ground where Mary Louise rested.

Norbert sat there for an hour. He sat and he cried as he reminisced. He started out subvocalizing what he told Mary Louise, but wanting to hear what he was saying so he could measure the truth of his words and plumb their meaning, he switched to speaking aloud. Softly, lovingly, haltingly, he talked to Mary Louise, talked and talked.

Sap and Green People

He told his beloved how their shared home now looked, and he also told her about how the Haven grounds and buildings and adjacent neighborhoods looked. About his apartment building. How he'd furnished his apartment. Whom he'd met. Who Jack Clausen was and how he and Jack had become close friends. How their children and grandchildren, recent visitors to his St. Louis quarters, were doing. What hopes he had, what concerns. And again, he described the awful, awful agony he'd suffered when Mary Louise had left him, agony that had eaten away at his "heart and gut" and nearly driven him out of his mind. That with time, the agony that was diminishing.

To prove that it was, Norbert moved on to recite frustrating and amusing things that had happened to him, the sort of thing he'd have told Mary Louise during their dinner each evening. All the time sensing Mary Louise's love and regard, he attested again to the depth of his love and how much he missed her and bid her adieu. Following that, Norbert dismantled his chair, returned it to the car's trunk, and strolled through the family plot where others of Mary Louise's family had been interred, speaking briefly and affectionately to each member whom he'd had the privilege of knowing. (His own family's plot was located in another town which he would visit on another occasion, he'd decided before setting out that morning.)

Over a century ago, a member of Mary Louise's family, he'd forgotten which one, had staked out the family burial field. Intent upon seeing to it that deceased persons would be shaded from hot summer sun, the founding personage had planted maple trees along its north and west ends, and as Norbert left the cemetery, when the sun stood high in a cloudless sky, he smiled at the sure knowledge that the planter had achieved his lofty purpose.

It had been almost a year since Norbert had returned to Smithton, his long absence due to the fact that the first visit had been so painful that he'd not been able to drive past his former home or visit Mary Lou's grave. He had met two friends for coffee, which he managed without becoming unduly emotional, but

Sap and Green People

following that, he'd turned tail and sped back to St. Louis.

When he'd dressed this morning, however, Norbert had felt deep in his heart that today's visit would go differently, and as he drove past where his children had been schooled, the family had worshiped, and he'd engaged in fiscal dealings, he felt almost elated because his Smithton visit was going so well.

Norbert parked in front of one of the three cafes on Main Street where he and his men friends gathered on Saturday mornings. Bounding out of his car and reminding himself not to bother with locking it (surely things hadn't changed that much in Smithton!), he walked to the first of the three, Elmer's; opened its wide front door; stepped into the noisy, smokey, revitalized brick building, furnished as it had been with heavy oak tables and scarred oak chairs; paused; and looked around.

"By god!" Elmer Longstreet, the proprietor, sang out from behind the cash register. "Would you look at who's here!" and greetings rang out. Thundered, actually. Also the sound of chairs being pushed back from a table at the far end of the room where his friends traditionally sat.

Those men surged to where Norbert was, hugged him, slapped his back, and swept him back to where they'd left their breakfasts, with Norbert waving right and left to others in the room, calling out names, and shaking the hands of those who flocked over to him.

For over an hour, Norbert and his buddies updated each other, sometimes with two or three persons speaking at a time and Norbert's head swivelling as he struggled to get what they were saying. Looking at his watch, he finally felt compelled to say, "Fellows, maybe I better get on up the street. To catch the guys who're hanging out at Emma Mae's. Not going to stay in town long, and I want to see as many of you old buzzards as I can."

"We'll go with you," Burt Adams said, and he and the others seated at the table slapped down tips for the waitress who'd been so dutifully serving them. They paid Elmer as they passed him by, then traipsed up the street to Emma Mae's, with Norbert in the lead.

Sap and Green People

Before entering, Norbert stopped the exuberant group and said, "Surely you guys don't expect me to pick up the tab just 'cause I'm from out of town and leading the parade, do you?"

"Hell no," someone answered. "You ain't got the bank to bleed anymore, so we know better 'n 'at."

"How's about you getting a table while I go on to the Cozy Cafe," Norbert proposed. "Settle in there, and I'll bring anyone in Emma Mac's who's free to join us back with me," and off he went.

Close to tears at seeing more friends and knowing that others were waiting back in Emma's, Norbert stammered to his Cozy friends, "You fellows, you guys, you're the best. So glad to be here with you. I've met a lot of new people and they're swell, but they aren't long-time, if you know what I mean."

"They will be," John Chase assured him. "Give 'em time," and three Cozy friends and Norbert left the restaurant and walked back to Emma Mae's where the number waiting for his return had swelled considerably.

There followed a thoroughly spontaneous, noisy, comfortable, good time. Until Norbert said, "If I don't let you guys go, your wives will be mad at me. Tell them all hello. Kiss 'em: that's what you ought to do to wives," which induced a number of protestations and considerable laughter. "Be good to them, Fellows," a serious Norbert added, "cause you're lucky to have them," which changed the tone of things and brought tears to the eyes of several of his friends.

"Get back sooner next time, will you?" Harry Walton said.

"Let us know when you're coming, and we'll get up a bar-b-que," another suggested.

"The girls will like to see you too."

"They think the world of you, you old Son-of-a-gun, you."

"You know, some of Mary Louise's friends are alone now like you," someone said, "and they'd like to see you. Know how you're doing.'

"Would help them," Maurice Edwards, the town's Methodist pastor, said. "You'd be helping everyone by returning, so, get back, Buddy. Soon."

Sap and Green People

"Will do, and meantime, come see me. Surely some of you hicks get to St. Louie at one time or another, and I have a studio couch I lend. Make you eggs for breakfast."

"That big, dirty, scary city?"

"Well, know that you have a standing invitation if any of you are ever brave enough to get my way. 'N tell anyone else who'd be interested that I'm well and doing fine," Norbert said. "Love you all, every one of you," he uttered, the sort of thing he'd not have said previously, his friends couldn't help thinking.

Norbert mulled over his visit while listening to St. Louis' classical music station on his way home, and he turned off Laclede Drive and into the Haven at the a little after 5:00. As he approached his apartment building, he spied the figure of a man, not in uniform, climbing up the embankment bordering the lake and the stream which feed into it, something he'd never seen anyone other than uniformed maintenance people do. Drawing abreast to the figure, he determined that the man was George Steiner.

Stopping, Norbert rolled down his window and called, "Want a ride?"

"Too muddy," George answered.

Though George was indeed muddied, Norbert replied, "Come on! Do my staid Oldsmobile good to get mucked up a bit." George wiped the seat of his pants, stomped as much mud off his feet as he could, rubbed his hands together, and climbed aboard. "Besides," Norbert said, "how else am I going to learn what you've been doing in the ditch?"

"Followed the creek up two, three blocks. Lookin' at stuff in it. Alongside."

"Done that before?"

"Yup."

"Often?"

"Ever once in a while. I'd go farther up but I'm afraid someone will see me 'n call the police. Not sure it's all right."

"Don't know either," Norbert said, "but why? Why do you do that?"

"Explorin'. Gotta explore."

"What do you find?"

Sap and Green People

"Rocks. Minnows in season. Birds, lots of them. Squirrels. Four coons in a bunch once. Trash, mostly trash, though. Some of it worth picking over. Rock formations in the banks. Missouri's sure got a lot 'a rock."

"Too bad about the trash."

"Yes. If it rains heavy, the rain washes things out of people's yards and into the ditch. Toys. Tools sometimes. Stuff like that. 'N people dump things into the stream to get rid of them. Like grass clippings and dead bushes they dig up. Limbs. Even oil from their cars!" George said indignantly. Passionately.

"Maybe there'll be less oil over time," Norbert suggested, "now that it's becoming harder to change the oil in one's own car."

"Hope so," George answered. "Everything gets washed 'n throwed down into our poor lake. Lowest point around."

"I understand the lake's only a few feet deep."

"Yup. At its deepest point."

"That's too bad," Norbert ventured. "Have to keep digging it out."

Patricia Dick

"Can't because it's lined with rock. Know that?"

"No," Norbert answered as he stopped in front of the Manor to let George out. "Thanks for telling me about the lake and dumps. Take it easy, George," and as he pulled away from the curb to drive on to his own building, Norbert found himself thinking that all people should have a passion. To keep life charged up, like George's obviously was. Their minds active. Bodies as age-resistant as possible. Personalities from becoming tedious. Themselves from turning into couch potatoes, the most demeaning designation of all, Norbert believed, one implying a shriveled up, non-thinking, indulgent, passive individual. A couch potato: the absolutely last thing a person should let himself become. An honest-to-gosh couch potato, the lowest form of human life on earth.

Sap and Green People

Marg Davis was "coming along", as she told the many persons who inquired about her recovery from knee surgery. By that she meant that the non-nauseating pain pills ("take 1 every 4 hours") relieved her pain, and her non-addictive sleeping pills ("take 1 at bedtime, repeating if required") helped her sleep. Her stool softener ("take 2 hours before or 2 hours after the intake of prescribed medicines") was doing what it was designed to do, and she presumed that the anti-depressant ("take once daily") was, as explained by her doctor, relaxing her wounded leg muscles and bones so they'd heal more readily. Moreover, her multiple vitamins ("take with food if upsetting to the stomach") and iron ("don't take within 1 hour before or 2 hours after taking antacids, eggs, whole grain breads, cereal, milk or milk products, coffee, or tea") were making her stronger, she felt sure, though not as rapidly as she'd hoped.

In other regards, the hematomic swelling that made her leg elephantine was going down, and she no longer had to wear the brace that protected and immobilized her implanted knee. She'd traded a walker for a cane and been instructed by her physical therapist as to how to go up steps ("good leg first, then the bad leg and cane") and down them ("bad leg and cane, then the good one"). She had trouble remembering which was which until the therapist reminded her that stepping down probably felt like hell, a truism if there ever was one.

Marg no longer required a home nurse, and her home physical therapist had turned her over to for-real physical therapists, the big, fit, merciless persons who subjected compromised bodies to pain-inducing procedures rendered in dark, cavernous, intimidating rehabilitation centers.

And so it was that while she lacked stamina, still hurt, and her leg seesawed between being more, then less, then more swollen, Marg was able to say, "I'm coming along, and thank you for asking."

Being confined by Marg's disability, the Davises frequently sat on their deck, in the afternoons and evenings usually because the summer sun beat down on the east-facing, deck earlier in the day.

Sap and Green People

On one pleasant evening, a half-hour short of dusk, seated in their small, round-backed, wrought iron, ice cream parlor chairs, Marg said, "Too bad we scared the birds away again by coming out."

"Yes," Bill answered, "but they didn't go far," and he pointed to where the dove-pair was hunkered down on the roof of the apartment next to theirs, perhaps thirty feet away. "We won't hurt you, pretty birds," Bill called softly. "Don't you know that by now?" and with his tongue and lips, he made the 'whoo-oo-oo' whistle-sound he'd heard his father make long ago when his father raised and trained racing pigeons in the family's back yard.

Earlier, for a dozen days, Bill and Marg had watched the doves check out second-story decks, flitting back and forth between porch furniture, planted containers, nooks and corners, deck floors.

"They're in the process of selecting a nest site," Bill had explained to Marg, and having finally made a choice, the doves settled in a planter mounted on one side of the Davises' deck railing, between the struggling clumps of dianthus and candytuft Marg had planted at either end of that planter. On a little patch of sun-baked soil in the planter's middle.

Doves are notoriously casual about nest-building, as proved by the fact that all the soon-to-be parents did to establish a 'home' was hollow out an oval indentation in the soil, one large enough to host eggs and one attending parent.

That pleasant evening, as Marg and Bill watched the doves, they, in turn, eyed Bill and Marg from the nearby roof to which they'd fled. "The smaller dove, the female, keeps flying and landing closer, then closer to us," Bill reported to Marg whose back was turned to the birds and nest. "Closer," he whispered a few minutes later. "Came closer." Then, "Ver-r-ry near. On the roof over the building's entryway just beyond us." To encourage the dove's progression, Bill whoo-oo-ooed repeatedly, and he and Marg sat motionless.

Minutes later, Bill exclaimed softly, "She's behind you, Marg, and in the nest."

"Wants you to whoo-oo some more," Marg said softly, and she and he talked back and forth as they

Sap and Green People

watched the comings and going of cars and walkers in the streets and on the sidewalks below them.

"Marg, look," Bill virtually hissed. "Slowly, slowly, turn and look."

Turning in her chair, Marg saw the female standing above the nest and looking down into it. Verifying, apparently, that she'd just produced a single, white egg. The fact confirmed, the dove lowered herself into an egg-covering position.

"I watched her in the nest as we talked," Bill told Marg, "and I finally decided that she was giving birth. Her back feathers were standing up about forty-five degrees, I'd say, and she was quivering all over. Straining, I suppose. So, Mrs. Davis, we're now foster parents to an egg."

"Oh my gosh," Marg said, one of her pet expressions. "How…wondrous, simply wondrous!"

"She had to come back to the nest," Bill speculated, "threatening as our presence was, because though she didn't understand what was to happen probably, she knew she had to get back."

Marg leaned across the small, glass-topped table, bent forward towards her husband, and took his hand.

"Bill," she said earnestly, "this is significant, really significant! Tremendously significant to me!"

"How so?" Bill asked.

"Because it's a reminder that everything has its time. The dove waited, then did what she had to do, and I'm waiting, doing what I have to do, and my time will also come, the time of my recovery, my healing. Maybe that's maudlin, and I know we hate maudlin, but that's what I'm thinking, and it encourages me. Immensely!" and the Davises turned to look at the nest in time to see the mother bird go through the birthing process again, the process Bill had described just minutes earlier.

"Oh my gosh," Marg exclaimed again, again softly. "Another bird-child! Wondrous! Hoorah, hoorah, hoorah!

Sap and Green People

Like a bronchial cough, summer dragged on and on. Through September and into October, a long, drawn-out scourge with short-lived periods of relief tucked in ever so often. During those relief periods, when the temperature moderated, humidity dropped, and wind moved the air, people said to each other, "This is more like it." But then, things heated up, and the cycle played through all over again.

Jack Clausen got himself outdoors during one of those relief-periods, on a temperate, relaxed, revitalizing day when the feel of autumn was almost discernible. Beds of passionless vinca had been replaced with perky, cushy chrysanthemums, he noticed; limp petunias, poor things who'd given birth to bloom over and over during a five-month period, with a new kind of pansy that was supposed to survive the winter. The autumn sun was kinder than the relentless, summertime one.

Jack had spent his summer hermetically sealed in university libraries and his bedroom-study, researching and writing the script for his third production. If not there, he'd been locked in the Manor-basement workroom with his helpers, Norbert, Rob, and Bud, fitting film, music, and script together, intense, exacting, confining work performed in dark, dank quarters. The three weren't working that day, so Jack, uninspired and unproductive himself, took to the outdoors to do whatever he could find out there worth doing.

I'll go for a walk, he decided. Haven't gone on one for maybe…three years. Despite that record, when he passed another walker as he crossed the streets in front of his apartment building, he called, "Hello-o," jauntily and gave the impression that he was committed to what he was doing, that walking was a regular part of his regime.

Continuing east, he passed the grotto, an arch made of the kind of pocked stone which covers a substantial part of Missouri's surface, with a stone Jesus-figure figure at its center. Ten feet beyond stood a weathered, splintery, two-person, wooden swing, suspended from equally weathered, inverted-v supports. KEEP YOUR BOTTOM COVERED should be posted on that thing, Jack mused, and he recalled

Sap and Green People

the time he'd slid down a wood teeter-totter when he was ten years old, got an inch-long sliver in one buttock, and had it removed by a doctor while he lay unclothed on the dining room table, in full sight of God and the relatives who had gathered around him.

Oh, the mortification, he thought, but oh, the joy of back then. Of being surrounded by his parents, grandparents, and distant cousins of his mother's who'd long since gone to their 'eternal resting places'. Back then, before he was alone, always alone. Before he'd become a 'man' and left home to embark upon a journey which had proven to be totally solitary.

Beyond the swing, Jack stood poised at the top of a long decline leading to the campus' pond-sized lake. Conceding that he was out of condition, he muttered "Ye gods" when he eyed the descent. Cautiously, he started downward, with his toes pointed out and flattened against the soles of his shoes for braking purposes, his front shin and thigh muscles stretched lengthwise, those in the backs of his legs shortened up. "Ye gods," was what he uttered at the bottom of the hill as he turned left to circle the lake.

"Hello-o-o-o," Bill Davis called from the gazebo that projected out into the lake. "Didn't know you were a walker."

Tempted to insist that of course he was (for didn't everyone walk"), Jack answered, "Well, only for the last ten minutes actually, and perhaps never again."

"Oh, come on," Bill joshed as Jack joined Bill and Marg. "Everyone should walk. You're an informed man and must know that."

"Oh, I do, I do, but how many 'must-do things' can be expected of a fellow?" Jack asked.

"Quite a few, seems like," Bill answered, and Marg nodded her assent.

"Hear there are muskrats in the lake," Jack said.

"Last year, two and a baby made three," Marg answered, "but we've seen only one this summer. Back in the spring, actually, and the people whose Patio Homes back up to the lake," and she pointed her index finger to indicate to which Homes she was referring, "say they haven't seen any for some time."

"May be victims of the lake's silting up," Bill said.

Sap and Green People

"Well, keep me posted. About the muskrats and the silt," Jack said facitiously, and he continued to circle the lake.

What'd Bill mean, he wondered as he trod on, 'victims of the lake's silting up'? That the muskrats had drowned in the muck? Moved because the lake was too shallow for swimming and concealment? Had to go elsewhere for some other reason? Should have asked, he told himself, because I like knowing things, yes I do, and he spotted two little blue herons and one white heron and three egrets (these he knew from having spent time in Florida), plus two Canadian geese swimming with what he presumed were their offspring in tow.

Further along, the paved path gave way to a bark-covered trail that took him into a woods. "Primitive," he exclaimed after his pant legs had been caught on low-hanging branches a half-dozen times. Fallen trees, rotting stumps, knotted vines whose origins were unknown, and the rustlings made by creatures in the underbrush designated the woods 'ominous', to his way of thinking.

Tired of turning his ankles, lurching from one side of the uneven path to the other, having to use his hands to push aside wide-ranging branches, becoming aware that he was miserable, Jack resorted to pawing and beating his way out of the woods by breaking through the tangle. Stepping out onto well-tended lawn, he returned to a segment of the same level sidewalk he'd followed when starting the walk at the front of his apartment building. Rounding a corner, Jack saw that he was approaching two women seated on a bench, with their walkers parked in front of them.

"Good afternoon, Ladies," he said as he drew near, and immediately he realized that one was the pretty, twisted-faced woman whom he'd met and who'd attended his first two presentations.

Both women responded cordially to Jack's salutation, and he found himself lost, totally lost, for words, a thing that almost never happened to him.

When he failed to get beyond his salutation, the woman whom he hadn't seen before asked, "Do you like walking in the woods?"

Sap and Green People

"Actually, I think it's abominable," he answered so seriously that his listeners burst out laughing. "You could trip on the path. Get strangled by vines and branches. Bitten by bugs. Infected with poison ivy. Attacked by squirrels and whatever was popping, crackling, and snapping back in that murky mass. Enough to scare a man out of his wits. Why, a person could get killed in there! I'll never walk in a woods again," Jack stated. "Never!"

"Too bad," the pretty, crippled woman said after she finished laughing, "because we were going to ask the next person who came out of the woods to walk through it with us."

"You got the wron-n-ng man," Jack responded.

"Why don't you sit for a minute," the stranger-woman suggested. "Keep us company while we wait for someone else to come along. You look like you need to rest for a spell anyway."

"Good idea," Jack answered, "but before I sit, let me introduce myself. I'm Jack Clausen. I live right there. In 709."

"I'm Gloria Fields, and I'm moving from Assisted Living into the Manor very soon."

"Gloria Fields," Jack repeated slowly, savoring the name and the look of the woman but trying to appear as though he were working to commit her name to his memory. "Glad to hear about your move."

"And I'm Jenny Wentworth. I live in Assisted Living."

"Jenny Wentworth. Happy to know both of you," he said as he struggled to keep himself from looking at Gloria, for what he wanted to do was stare at her. Study her face. Determine what made her so appealing. Appraise her state of health. "How long have you lived in the Haven?" he asked Jenny, a means for keeping himself from staring at Gloria.

"Three and a half years."

"And you, Gloria?"

"Fourteen months," she answered.

"That's about the length of time I've been here. It's a good place to be," Jack stated.

"A lucky place," Gloria stated carefully so as to totally control the constriction compromising the one side of her mouth. "Beautiful campus. Excellent accommodations."

"Expert, kind caretakers," Jenny added.

"Agreeable, interesting, diversified group of residents," Jack said, and he allowed himself to look intently at Gloria. "As you said, Gloria, it's a lucky, lucky place, and we're most fortunate to be here."

Patricia Dick

"Lotta bad news today," Marg Davis said to Bill as they seated themselves on their deck in the early evening. "Bad news on the Haven campus," and as evening slowly eased daylight into oblivion, she commenced relaying the unsettling reports she'd garnered while Bill had been occupied with responsibilities and recreations.

"Mid-morning, I watched Bill Martin supporting his frail little wife, shadow thin, her shoulders bent and bowed, as they took their walk. Past our building and the Manor, around the bend and Recreation Center corner, and to the patio homes street, I'm supposing, 'til they came to their own place. Almost every day, they try to regain her health—or hang on to what's left of it. And about two hours later, when I saw Clara in the garage, she said she had reason to believe that Bill wouldn't have his wife much longer. So sad."

"How many times on a given day," Bill asked, "do you say 'so sad'?"

Regarding the question as rhetorical, Marg continued her report. "You know that old, old couple who eat just before the dinner line shuts down, the big, really deaf, goofy guy?"

"The one who almost knocked Meg down as he pushed his wife's wheelchair through the dining room the other night?

"That one. Well, his wife fell while he was trying to get her out of her wheelchair last evening, Clara also said. Broke her hip and maybe her leg. Going to be operated on early tomorrow morning.

And Jenny McClure's son took Jenny's car away from her."

"How'd he do that?"

"Showed up at her door unannounced and just out-and-out told her that he'd come for the car because he couldn't arrange insurance for it anymore."

"How old is she?"

"Ninety-four. She's really angry and doesn't believe the insurance bit and told him so. But he wouldn't back down."

"Probably a good thing but obviously Jenny doesn't think so," and intending to counter the bad news Marg was sharing, Bill said, "That cheerful, accommodating little woman who serves up salads in the dining room?" Marg nodded. "She's had her husband in the Nursing Home here and told me when I dipped ice cream this afternoon that he's doing remarkably well. Getting out next week. Able to go home."

"According to Maggie whom I talked to in the hall, Pete," Marg continued without missing a beat, "our own Pete, right downstairs, was told by his doctor yesterday that after being in remission for almost two years, his cancer is now active again."

"Sho-o-o-o-t," said Bill. "How many more stories did you hear today? Might as well turn on the news. No worse than what's around here, though on a broader scale of course, like national and international."

"Two more," an unrelenting Marg replied. "Only two. We didn't know her well, but Charlotte Kline, who planned excursions and activities for the Haven until she retired recently? She found she has breast cancer. Ruined all the plans she and her husband had made.

Sap and Green People

'N that lady who was struck and killed when she jumped in front of traffic last week?"

"Last one, Marg. This, already started, is the last thing I'll listen to. Hear any more and I'll be weeping and howling and gnashing my teeth."

"Well, she'd suffered from depression for over thirty years, Jenny said, so guess her suicide was no surprise. Hope she's finally at peace."

"Between seven and eight hundred people live here, Marg, old people, and that makes for lots of changes and news, much of it unfortunate. That's inevitable, and all we can do is sympathize and get on with our lives. Help if we can, of course, then get on. Focus on other things because tales of woe aren't what we're about."

"I know, but they're so sad."

"There it is again: 'so sad'. Let's change the subject, shall we? How's your knee?"

"Hasn't swelled much today. It's tired tonight but not hurting. Just signaling that it's been through a lot. People are beginning to forget to ask me about it," and Marg laughed.

"You're losing your celebrity status. How're the birds?"

"One was back while you were at the ice cream parlor. Hung out on the deck for a while, waiting to see if the others would show up, seemed like. Sweet how the mother was back yesterday afternoon, cooing to call the now-grown babies back."

"All our hypothesizing about bird behavior may have been wrong, Marg. Like our notion that the three birds on the deck last evening were the mother and babies who'd nested with us and had returned to spend the night together in the old nest. That the absent bird was the father who proved to be just another no-show, dead-beat dad after all. We might have been wrong, but the making up bird stories was healthier than getting bogged down in 'so sad' tales. Old people have to guard against depression. Heed the state of their mental health, especially the ones who have had depression tendencies previously. Another argument for living in a community like ours.

And speaking of birds, look at what they've done to the deck. I thought 'poop deck' was a naval term,

Sap and Green People

but now I know that a poop deck is what resident doves make of a deck floor."

"I've gotta lug the planter where they nested outside, dump it, and scrub the thing all up," Marg said. "It's really unsightly and unsanitary. Having baby birds is work."

"The big question is when are we going to be free of them."

"Not yet, Bill. They're sweet. Interesting."

"Soon, Lady, soon. They're either going to have to find a new home or submit to toilet training. I'll give them two more days. Then, watch out 'cause Heap Big Chief, me, is going to take over."

"Oh, I forgot: Georgia's brother died. In Tennessee. Likewise, Mary Lee's sister."

"Marg…!"

"Okay, okay. You're the best thing that ever happened to me, Bill, and what'll I do if I lose you?"

"Well," Bill answered, "what would I do if I lost you? Totally retreat, probably. Listen to nature television programs and World War II documentaries all day long."

"But you don't worry about the future. You're not afraid of it."

"I might be if I dwelled upon it, but I don't. All I'll say, and I've said it before, is that we're good together. A great combination. I help you, you say, and you keep me going, and we've been happy and successful by our own, humble standards. Turned out three great kids. Been richly blessed. And when something happens to one of us, with the help of family, friends, and God, the other will stumble on. Alone but on."

"That's how it'll be, I guess," Marg conceded.

"That's all it can be, and that's enough."

"How sad," Marg said. "The awful pain of being alive. Wasn't there a movie with a similar title?"

"Yeh. Good flick. I'll tell you what," Bill said, "let's go inside, get our nightclothes on, watch the evening news if it's not too horrid, then pile into bed and forget everything you heard this morning, everything Clara and Maggie and who-else told you. Put our arms around each other and rejoice in our…happiness and good fortune."

Sap and Green People

And thus ended another day for the Davises who did precisely what Bill had suggested.

Jack Clausen, the 73-three year old, forever-single, no-nonsense leader of the Great Discussions group and organizer of a documentary company, appeared to be undergoing something of a metamorphosis. Jack wasn't aware of the transformation, but his associates were beginning to make comments regarding the changes they'd seen in him.

"A couple of times he's kidded with us. Been almost silly."

"More human."

"He was sitting in a chair, smiling and relaxed, when I came in the other morning. Not all stiff and hot to get started."

"The other night, he expressed concern about some people instead of worrying about what was happening with the international monetary system," Bruce Moffitt, a friend of Jack's, told George Steiner who had absolutely no idea what 'monetary systems' were or what Moffitt was inferring about Jack.

"I've seen him smile, laugh, and scratch his butt in public!" Bud Walsh, one of Jack's technicians, said to Rob Rymer, Jack's other technical.

Sap and Green People

"He's wearing cotton pants instead of…"

"Trousers?"

"…trousers every day. How come, I wonder."

"Forgets things. Lost his train of thought twice Tuesday when I was talking with him. Never knew him to do that before."

People saw changes, but they weren't speculating as to their cause, and even if they had, they'd have missed the mark because they didn't know that pretty, handicapped Gloria Fields was playing with Jack's head, so to speak. Causing him to change, even err occasionally. Indeed, Jack Clausen was smitten, but even he hadn't as yet realized that such was the case.

The smittening first evidenced itself when Jack woke one morning, turned from his back to his side, looked out the bedroom window, and for no reason at all, found himself saying aloud, "Gloria Fields." So surprised was he that he repeated Gloria's name three more times, and saying the name brought Gloria's face to mind. Further surprised by that, he blinked his eyes, sat up, then perched on the edge of the bed and shook his head.

Fed, showered, shaven, and, for no reason discernable to him at the time, attired in definitely-casual clothing instead of the more formal clothes he'd usually wore, Jack had walked from his apartment to the back of the Manor where he entered the east-most door and then entered the documentary company office.

Rob had greeted him with, "Heh, Man."

"Likewise," Bud said as he looked up from reading the Orwell notes Jack had gathered during the previous few days.

"You're a little bit not-punctual today, aren't you?" But Bud received no answer because without having said so much as a word, Jack had immediately disappeared.

Jack had disappeared to see if a truck he thought he'd heard was coming up or down the street running behind the Manor. Finding none, he returned to the office.

"Where'd you go, Man?" a puzzled had Rob asked.

"Out in back," Jack answered vaguely.

"Lost something?"

"No, no," Jack replied. "Just wanted to see if there was a moving van out there."

"A moving van?"

"When I first came in, see, it occurred to me that anyone moving into The Manor had to off-load back there."

"Someone you know moving in?"

"No," Jack insisted. "The moving van thing just popped into my head. Don't strange notions ever pop into yours?"

"No," Rob said. "Never. They pop into Bud's head but not into mine."

"Well, I'll try to keep it from happening again," Jack said jovially, and without willing its appearance, Gloria's face appeared before him again. Right in the center of his field of vision!

In the days since that morning, Bud and Rob had watched for repetitions of such behavior. They'd thought of asking Norbert if he'd seen Jack check the street or otherwise act bizarrely. Thinking that asking would be out of line, they'd not followed through, deciding instead to be on the alert for themselves.

November had blasted October right off the calendar, and several weeks later, on a chilly, fall morning, Bud, Rob, and Jack arrived at the office almost simultaneously. Once inside the damp, cold room, they lit a space heater and huddled around it.

"Hard to get the place warm on days like these," Jack said as he held his hands up to the heater. "I wonder if something's delayed Norbert."

"Maybe he ran into a train," Rob suggested cheerfully.

"Fell out of an airplane," Bud said.

"Drowned?" Jack added. "He'll be along, but before we go ahead, I'll see if he's coming up the street," and with that, he left the office as he'd done previously.

"Bingo!" Bud exclaimed and Rob grinned.

"See any vans or Norb?" Bud asked when Jack returned.

"Neither," Jack answered defensively. "So, back to Orwell," and the three left their heat-source to sit around a beaten-up, conference table. "You guys, please, should determine which Orwell books have been made into movies. Get hold of the movies, whatever they are, and familiarize yourself with them. Like you did prior to the making of the other two documentaries. So you'll know where to go for information and clips.

Norb and I have come up with three buzz words, 'visionary', 'anti-totalitarian', and 'social reformer', and we're working with them. Still need more biography and anecdotes."

"Hello, hello," chirped Norbert as he joined the three men.

"Short pants," Bud observed, "even today?"

"No coat?" Jack asked.

"Sweater," Norbert answered. "Sweater was enough."

"Black shorts yet, black with a brown shirt!" Rob said after Norbert shed the sweater.

"What creativity! What imagination!"

"Even the cows don't put black and brown together," Jack kidded, and he, Bud, and Rob enjoyed a round of laughter at Norbert's expense.

"Seems to me," Norbert said in his own defense, "that I've seen black cows with brown spots and ears, or vise versa."

"Whatever," Jack said, "but let's get started."

"Where we at?" Rob asked.

"I just told the boys…"

"Men!"

"…what we're presently focused on 'visionary', 'anti-totalitarian', and 'social reformer'. That we're checking those, looking for more info, still reading. About to start the writing. And I asked them to find Orwell movies. Newsreels. From there, they'll get what they need, for which I'll pay them well." Everyone laughed. "And while we're talking money, as you know, I've bankrolled our operation up to now. Everything: equipment, supplies, fees, wages, and so forth. I don't pay Norb 'cause he's volunteering…"

"No, Man, no, you're not getting me for free!" Bud protested.

"Me either," Rob added.

"Just fooling," Bud explained. "We knew that wasn't what you were saying."

Sap and Green People

"What I was trying to say is that it's time Norb and I talked about my paying him because I want him to do more in the immediate future if he can commit the time. The truth is that while I'm not in danger of being wiped out, of losing my '95 Mercury or anything awful like that, I do plan to ask Mr. Bank President here, Mr. Norbert Blair, to set up a non-profit company. Have him work out a budget and talk with the Haven people about some sort of financial assistance, probably not much. Look for other donors. May be some right here in the Haven.

And the time has come, Gentleman, for me to follow up on his Norb's suggestion that we show our documentaries to other groups for a charge. Truthfully, I can't afford to continue as I have much longer. I'm sure you appreciate that," and as Jack looked at his little band of helpers and read the loyalty and concern written on their faces, he was so moved that he wanted to express the appreciation and affection he felt, but he could not. "So, get out of here, Pups. Off to the film companies and libraries and the computer, but before you go, want donuts? Got four right here," and he retrieved a sack from a desk drawer.

Bud and Rod responded by complaining that Jack had been stingy, that he'd purchased too few donuts, and they announced what would be, in their opinion, a fair, logical donut acquisition and distribution henceforth: "Two or three each for the Pups, one or one-and-a- half each for the Old Guys."

"You're a sweetheart, Jackie," Bud called as he crammed his gear in his backpack and slung it over on his shoulder. "Only, I sure don't understand what that moving van stuff's all about and can't help wondering if you're going a little soft in the head on us."

Sap and Green People

Henry Graham woke in fine fettle on Wednesday morning. Having showered after watching the 10:00 news the night before, he had no cause to shower again, usually part of his morning routine, enabling him to proceed in a more leisurely manner than usually.

Henry dressed, affixed his volunteer's badge on his volunteer's shirt, ate breakfast, and brushed his teeth, in just that order. Thanks to an electronic contrivance which compensated somewhat for his macular deficiency, he scanned the headlines in the newspaper, pecked Georgia on her cheek, picked up a wheelchair at a nursing station, and set out to fetch Doris Temple, the first wheelchair-bound person whom he was to transport to the doctor's that morning.

"Mornin' Doris," an exuberant Henry called at Doris' door.

"Go 'way," Doris answered.

"It's Henry, Doris, your wheelchair wheeler."

"Don't want any."

"Good, because I don't have anything. Nothin' but an empty wheelchair. I've come to put you in that chair and take you to the podiatrist who wants to beautify your feet. You'd like that, wouldn't you, Doris? Havin' beautiful, soft feet and toenails?

"Don't want any."

"You've already told me that."

"Go away."

"Can't 'til you get in the chair and I get you to the foot doctor who's waitin' for you."

Henry followed up his attempt at persuasion by rapping persistently on Doris' door. When the rapping proved ineffective, he pounded on it.

"No one's here," Doris responded.

"You are, Doris Temple, and it's you I want. I'm Henry Graham, your wheelchair man, ready to take you to the foot doctor."

Silence.

"Dor-is-s."

Silence. Henry knocked again.

Silence.

"She'll be comin' round the mountain when she comes," Henry sang. Not loudly, of course, for he and Doris had already generated quite enough commotion.

Sap and Green People

"She'll be..." and the door inched opened. "Top o' the mornin', Dear," Henry said as he shouldered his way into Doris' room. "Hop in, Girlie, and off we go."

At the doctor's office, however, Henry's luck and charm played out, for Doris refused to leave the chair he'd had to coax her to get into in the first place.

"Please come, Mrs. Temple," the doctor's nurse implored, and the doctor himself finally stepped into the reception room and invited Doris to cooperate.

"I don't understand," Henry said to Doris as she let the doctor take her hand and lead her forward. "Usually, we're the best of friends. Work together. But today you were Doris, The Draggin' Dragonlady. I'll forgive you, however, and come get you later," and he returned to the elevator with the empty wheelchair.

Henry exited at the fourth floor, crossed the bridge which linked the building he was in to another, and knocked at room 408 in Assisted Living where he was to pick up Innis Standley, a retired physicist, Henry had just learned. It being the third Wednesday of the month, Innis was to visit the barber.

"How are you, My Man?" Henry asked.

"Fair," Innis answered glumly. "Just fair."

"Why the 'just fair', Sir?"

"I can't find Bonnie this morning. She's gone off somewhere."

"Well, let's get your hair cut, and then we'll see if we can locate your wife," and Henry situated an uncertain Innis in his wheelchair and headed for the elevator.

"Don't want to get on," Innis insisted in reference to the elevator.

"How else, short of jumpin' out the window, can we get you down to the barber?"

"Want to find Bonnie."

"I know, I know," Henry sympathized. "I'm sorry about Bonnie. But let's get that haircut. It's your haircut day."

"Bonnie," Innis insisted as the elevator announced its presence with a resounding 'ding'. "She in the barbershop?" he asked.

"We'll see," Henry answered.

"Barbershop's up and you went down," Innis observed when they commenced descending.

Sap and Green People

"Barbershop's down."

"Up. You're trying to fool me."

"No I'm not," Henry said in his most sincere voice. "You're my friend, and your son asked me to get you to the barber."

John, the barber, was ready for Innis when Henry delivered him.

"Sorry we're a bit late," Henry told John. "Got held up tendin' my last charge."

"No problem," John replied. "All cleaned up from shearing Bobby O'Donald so I've time to tell Innis how sorry I am that he lost his wife," and John and Henry settled Innis in the big, black, cushy barber's chair.

"Been gone a month, I guess it is," Innis said. "Miss her, but I'll get by. My son said he'd see that I did," and Henry retreated to the elevator which inched him up to the second floor.

In the second-floor Convalescent facility, the point where the least-able lived and were attended, Henry claimed Mildred Turner who was totally compliant until they approached the elevator.

"Want to ride!" Mildred insisted.

"We stay on this floor, Pretty Lady," Henry explained. "Not ridin' up, down, or sideways. We stay on the second floor for physical therapy. At the end of this hall."

"Damn you," Mildred grumbled.

"Now, now," Henry scolded. "Is that the way to talk to your favorite fellow?"

"Damn you," Mildred repeated, and as if preparing to climb out of the wheelchair, she lifted her body several inches off its seat by bracing her elbows on the chair's arms.

"If you'll sit down," Henry proposed, "I'll make a bargain with you." Mildred sat. "We'll take an elevator ride on the way back to your room, after your therapy. That be okay?" Mildred answered with nonsensical, guttural noises while settling back into the wheelchair.

When Henry took Milton Stokes from the second to the first floor, also to see the podiatrist, Milton wanted off immediately. He wanted off so badly that he sputtered and yelled as the elevator moved down to

Sap and Green People

where he and Henry were going, and in the podiatrist's office, he refused to get out of the wheelchair. In fact, he didn't until the nurse and Henry virtually pulled him out, which required considerable effort since Milton outweighed the total of what Henry and the nurse weighed, they hurriedly figured, by approximately thirty pounds.

Mildred enjoyed a short elevator ride on the way back to her room. Saying he'd wait for Bonnie to come get him, Innis resisted return until Henry and Barber John persuaded him to entrust himself to Henry's care. Milton continued sputtering and occasionally yelling until staff members got him into his bed, and since Henry had no other right-then assignments, he sat at Milton's bedside, held Milton's hand, and visited with him quietly for nearly a half hour before returning to his own apartment.

"Georgia," he called as he stepped through its door, "look at the little moon pictures on the calendar for me, will you please? See if today's the day before a full moon. Bet a dollar it is!"

"You're right" Georgia reported. "How'd you know?"

"By the way my patients behaved today. Knew it had to be the day before a full moon. Happened twice before, makin' three times altogether. They did everythin' they weren't supposed to do, includin' yellin', tuggin', and holdin' on. And almost nothin' they should have done, like gettin' in the wheelchair and getting out when they were supposed to get out. Wanted on the elevator when we weren't going to use the elevator. Wanted off at the wrong floors. To stay on it forever. Wouldn't go where they had to; wouldn't return to where they'd come from. Holy cow! I could have used two helpers today. The day before a full moon! Whadda you know? Really strange."

Henry Graham was no ignoramus. An experienced, educated man who'd graduated from engineering school, he had helped design and test sophisticated military and civilian aircraft, the best in the world. Been involved in their manufacture as well. While that background, his training and work-experience, might have discouraged him from believing that the moon influenced human behavior, his volunteer experience persuaded him otherwise, and he fervently hoped that he'd never again be scheduled for duty on the next day-before-a-full-moon.

Patricia Dick

Bill Davis had banished the doves. He'd banished them by watching for them through the deck door and two living room windows, bursting out when they landed on the deck, and flailing his arms while yelling, "Scat or you're dead meat," or "Out of here, you feathered, deck-pooper, you," or "Don't even think of it!"

Bill was most certainly not an animal or bird hater. Not by any means. After all, he'd been the caring owner of a dog, three cats, a series of birds (which either died because of disease or in the mouths of family cats), and a series of replacement pets. He also had genuine regard for his grandpets, numbering seven at the time. No, Bill, The Dove-chaser, had assumed a new persona in the interest of driving away the four-member dove family because he was a practical man, his own man, one not willingly 'used' by anyone or anything. Certainly not by birds whose survival was not dependent upon their occupying his deck.

"Bill," Marg complained during the driving-away period. "People can hear you yelling those terrible threats at the poor birds, and they'll think you're nuts."

"I don't care if they do," he'd retorted. "Besides, since we've now lived here for three years under the same roof as our neighbors, they already know I'm eccentric, eccentric rather than nuts, and they figure that I've finally wised up to the necessity of doing what they probably had to do to their own resident birds before we moved in."

"I can't help feeling guilty when I think about how warmly we welcomed the birds. I cooed and talked to them. Called them 'Sweetie'. Even stroked the mother's head," and she moved her extended, right index finger back and forth to illustrate how she'd caressed the bird. "And now you're acting like a pit viper."

"What's a pit viper, Marg?"

"I don't know. Scaly? Fangy? Poisonous?"

"That's me, all right. You fully understand what I am."

"You're out of sorts."

"Not really."

"Bored?"

"No."

"Too much of me?"

"No. Really! Unless you talk too much, which isn't often, I'm never that."

Marg laughed. "Want to go to a movie?"

"No. Already checked. Nothing really good is showing."

"You could get back to your genealogy stuff."

"That's what I've been doing. Can't sit at the computer any longer. My eyes are tired. Positively bugging out."

"Go get coffee and a donut?"

"You looked at my waistline lately?"

"Haven't been to the Rec Center for a couple of days…"

"That's what I should do."

"Alone or with me?"

"How's your waistline?"

"I'll go with you," and the Davises traded the heavy khaki pants, shirts, and sweaters they'd donned that morning for sweat suits which were conducive to exercising.

Sap and Green People

Bundled against the cold, Bill and Marg walked a portion of the street running behind the Manor and Jack Clausen's office, down a hill, alongside the lake, beside the slow-moving stream, and to the Recreation Center, now a little more than two years old, the latest-built campus facility.

"Right knee up…, down. Left knee up…, down. Right…, left," Bill and Marg heard Janet Tabor, the manager of the Rec Center, call directives as she oversaw the water exercise class. Statuesque in any of her spandex swimsuits, Janet's dark, curly hair and sharp, blue eyes made her look more nearly Irish than German, her claimed heritage.

"And now, Boys and Girls," Bill and Marg heard Janet say, "jumping jacks," which prompted a series of heartfelt complaints.

Hanging up their outerwear in the workout room, the Davises signed in and turned on television so as to divert their attention from what they'd be doing. Bill pulled on half-fingered, leather glovelets and seated himself on the gargantuan Weight Master while Marg picked up free weights and assumed weight-lifting posture. Out...in, they breathed as Bill pulled down and Marg thrust her arms out. Down and out, then back. Down, out, back. Down, out, back. Seven more times.

Changing to the next set of exercises, their arms went up...down, up...down. Ten of another thing while watching world news which afforded no pleasure either. Stretches, ten times altogether, and then they rested and drank from the fountain.

Ten of this, rest. Ten of that, rest.

More, more, and after a half-hour of working out, they took long drinks before pulling on their jackets, saying hello to people whom they passed in the hallway, waving goodbye to Janet, and walking back to their apartment, the cooling-down part of their routine.

"Glad we did that," Bill said as he unlocked the door.

"Always hate to do it but am glad I did."

"Of how many things is that true?"

"Is or has been?"

"Both, like going to the dentist."

Sap and Green People

"Chaperoning the kids' parties and dances."

"Having to put our cats 'to sleep'."

"I believe people say 'put down' nowadays."

"Either's an euphemism."

"Well, I'm telling you that ours 'went to sleep'."

"Absolutely!"

"Wearing tri-focals."

"Getting flu shots."

"Referring to ourselves as 'elderly'."

"There's no way to be glad about that. I say 'older' which is a lot more acceptable."

"Leaving our condo to move here."

"We can truthfully say, can't we, that we're glad we did?" Bill asked.

"Yeah," Marg answered. "I tell people that coming here was a winner. It took me awhile, but I could swear to that now."

"Good girl," Bill replied, "and how's about cookies and milk once we get home?"

"You mean diet soda, don't you? Dr. Pepper, Pepsi, or Coke."

"Yeh," Bill said. "Make that ice water."

"George Orwell," Jack Clausen said, "the subject of our third presentation, was born in India in 1903, at a time when, as the old saying went, 'The sun never sets on the British Empire'," and at that point, Norbert took over.

"After graduating from Eton, an institution designed to turn out young imperialists…"

"…one presumes," Jack interjected to underscore the importance of objectivity.

"Point well-taken," Norbert conceded. "After graduating from Eton, he went to Burma to serve with the Indian Imperial police." The two men had collected enough data to commence verbalizing and writing down the Orwell script, and that's what they were doing in their Manor-basement office.

"Following that," Jack continued, "having decided to become a writer, Orwell lived in dire poverty in London and Paris while writing about the homeless and poor and what he considered to be the evils of imperialism. Orwell then went to Spain to fight for three years against Spain's king and the imperialism that he and others believed the king represented.

Sap and Green People

There, historians tell us, he used his skills to write excellent reports about the struggle to overthrow the monarchy.

Back in England again, while working in the coal mines, Orwell continued to struggle to establish himself as a writer.

And here's the statement I really want to establish somewhere, Norb," Jack told his friend and helper, "one place or another: 'By that time, he was dead-set against tyranny, governmental and social tyranny and even the tyranny one person exerts over another.' That okay?"

"Good. Excellent," Norbert answered enthusiastically. "Maybe repeat the statement even. It makes a fellow think. Should anyway. Not just about governments but also about how he treats other people, one-on-one. Good, good point."

Before the discussion continued, however, Jack was distracted by what sounded like a truck negotiating the street behind the office. "Excuse me," he said to Norbert. "Keep on thinking or reading and I'll be right back. Got to investigate something," and he threw open the door to check on the truck so he could determine if Gloria Fields was being moved into the Manor that morning. Where, as far as he was concerned, Gloria would be more...visible, accessible, and where he'd get to see her shiny hair, a perfect frame for her pretty face and very-alive, blue eyes. High cheekbones; small, straight nose; ever-present half-smile. Trim, bent body, thin legs, and small feet which were shod more stylishly than the feet of the other female Haven residents who either wore shoes outdated by as much as a decade or designed for male athletes.

How could he have made these observations about Gloria during only three, brief encounters, his rational self asked. He, who'd had such limited, fleeting contact with women. Traditionally ignored them. Disdained them because of their reticent or aggressive natures, for they were one or the other, he'd always believed. Because their voices were loud, too high, shrill. Eyes evasive and furtive. Mouths capricious. Bodies, too full, non-linear.

Sap and Green People

Clearly, he mused while looking for the truck, he'd been too negative about women and had assigned positives to Gloria he could not have observed. Subjectively assigned them, and the best way to check their validity was to spend time with Gloria so he could get rid of preposterous notions he'd built up in her favor.

In truth, ever since Gloria had told him about her move, he'd been checking for trucks at the back and front of the Manor and also in front of Assisted Living quarters where Gloria had been living. In addition, he'd haunted the Manor's dining room where she'd take her lunch or dinner each day. He'd not found her there, but he reasoned that she might have already moved in and be avoiding the dining room out of shyness. Be nibbling in her room until she became at least somewhat acquainted, which would be a shame since she needed to form friendships. With the right sort of women, certainly: those not too old, mentally limited, overly talkative, self-centered, or embittered. Friendships with men too, the right kind of men.

The truck Jack had heard was a grocery truck whose driver was idling his motor while waiting for clearance to pull up to a loading dock. Should have known, he told himself, for it's about now that food trucks arrive every morning.

A disappointed Jack returned to face a puzzled Norbert who asked, "What was that all about?"

"A grocery truck."

"You're expecting groceries?"

"I thought it might be a moving van."

"A moving van?"

"Norb," Jack said in a voice so uncharacteristic, so tight and unnatural, that it grabbed Norbert's attention immediately, "I have to tell someone something because it's about driving me crazy and you're my best friend, if I may call you that."

"Absolutely," Norbert answered earnestly. "We've become close, for which I'm glad, and I thank you again for inviting me to work with you. What's on your mind?"

Haltingly and with embarrassment, Jack confessed to his obsession with Gloria. In a voice that dropped

Sap and Green People

away several times. Became so intense at one point that he leaped from his chair, paced the room, and waved his arms. When finished, thoroughly spent, he sat back down, ran his fingers through his gray hair, wiped his brow with a handkerchief, and waited for Norbert's comment.

"Jack," Norbert said sympathetically, "I think what you're feeling is great. Healthy. Very human. Wonderful, even. A little delayed," and both men laughed, "but normal and swell. Don't feel embarrassed.

Remember the word 'twitterpated'? From some musical, I believe it was? Well, that's what you are, and there's nothing wrong with twitterpation." Jack laughed at his friend's pronouncement.

"My only concern," Norbert continued, "is that you don't have much basis, I'll say, for your affectionate regard, if that's the right term. I'd hate to see you disappointed or hurt. So, for goodness sake, instead of watching for trucks, get going! There's no time to waste!"

"How?" Jack virtually demanded. "I don't have the slightest notion of how to proceed."

"Seems like that should be obvious," Norbert answered. "Especially to a smart, resourceful guy like you. Call Gloria where she was living. If you're told that she's moved, ask where you can get her and call her there. That's hard to figure out?"

"What'll I say?"

"Well, don't tell her that up to now, you've disliked women, and don't tell her that you've been chasing vans like a frenzied puppy. Tell her you called to see how things were going, particularly the move. If she hasn't moved, ask if you can help her. If she has, ask if you can visit her because you'd like to become better acquainted. Carry on from there, but either way, don't for heaven's sake hang up until you've make a specific arrangement."

"Oh thank you, thank you," Jack effused. "Thank you so much."

"Wasn't anything. Glad you talked to me. Anytime, okay?

Sap and Green People

"And say, did you bring donuts this morning or was it my turn? It says in the Good Book that man doesn't live by bread alone, you know, meaning that even a twitterpated guy like you needs nourishment, especially at a time like this."

On Friday mornings, when Henry Graham called for the wheelchair-bound women whom he pushed to the beauty shop, he occasionally had to wake his charges up. More often, he had to wait for them, and in several instances, he'd had to help them finish dressing. Henry also returned them to their rooms, which is what he was doing in the case of Alice Brown.

"You're sure lookin' pretty," he said as he and Alice took the elevator up two floors and then to Alice's room. "Think those girls in the shop could do the same for me?

Alice turned her head to look a long look at Henry. "You haven't got any hair. Nothing to work with."

"I was afraid you'd say that," Henry answered. "Know why I shave? So my face will match my head."

Alice responded with a feeble laugh. "You're funny, Henry."

"I try to be funny since I can't be pretty. But tell me, Alice, what's happenin' in your neck of the woods?"

Sap and Green People

"A cleaning lady stole a ring from a lady's apartment."

"Darlin'," Henry countered gently, "whoever told you that story was either wrong or fibbin'. Cleanin' ladies don't take things at the Haven. The bosses make sure that they don't."

"How come the ring's gone then?"

"Maybe the lady misplaced it. Maybe she'd had a ring taken a long time ago and mixed up times in her mind. Maybe she gave it away and forgot that she had. Maybe the person who told you got the story wrong. Rest assured: no cleanin' lady around here's takin' things. Too big a risk for her."

"A lady down the hall went to the hospital," Alice went on to say. "Very sick, I hear."

"Who was that?"

"Mary something. The ambulance came for her but she wouldn't let them put her on a stretcher. Made them take her arms and walk her out."

"Plucky lady, I guess. Or foolish," and then he asked, "Know her last name?"

"Can't remember. White hair."

"Everybody's got white hair here," Henry said, "if they're lucky enough to have hair at all."

"Thin. Real thin," and with finesse, Henry wheeled Alice's wheelchair into the elevator, turned it to face forward, and initiated the elevator's ever-so-slow descent. "She has AIDS," Alice went on to say.

"No!" Henry answered.

"How do you know she doesn't?" Alice demanded rather than insisted.

"Well," Henry answered emphatically, "if she has AIDS, she'd have gotten it way, way long ago, when she was young, and have died before she got this old and moved here. Also," he told Alice though he wasn't sure what he was about to claim was true, "AIDS-people eventually get covered with blotches and sores, all over, face and everythin', and if it's the woman I'm thinkin' of, Mary Spritzer, whom I know, a lovely lady, she's lookin' just fine. Saw her a couple of days ago and no sign of sores on her. Someone gave you the wrong information, Dear." Henry had added the term of endearment to placate Alice who might be getting her hackles up, having just been contradicted a second time. "Shame on that person. Passin' on wrong information. Knowin' the story's not true, we won't pass it along, either one of us, will we?"

When the elevator stopped and he pushed the wheelchair out into the hallway, Alice dismissed him with, "Thank you."

"Wait a minute, wait a minute," Henry answered. "You're not home yet. Your place is way down at end of the hall."

"It is? If you tell me a couple more times, pretty soon I'll know where I live."

"Well, shall I leave you here or take you on?" Henry joked, and he smiled broadly.

"Here's fine. That's my room," and Alice pointed to the door across from where they were standing. "I can get in by myself. Come see me anytime, Henry. Anytime at all."

"Alice, you may have lived in that room there once," Henry said lightly, "but not anymore," and he delivered Alice to where she belonged.

On his way back to the beauty shop, Henry met Jake Gabble in the elevator, Jake who, even equipped with two hearing aids, was as deaf as a fence post.

"How're things?" Henry asked in what he thought was a loud-enough voice.

"What!" Jake yelled. "Remember, my hearing aids are German and you're speaking English so you're hard to understand. Where you going?"

"To the beauty parlor to take some woman back to her place," Henry shouted.

"You know, Henry, you're a volunteer which is a good thing 'cause if you work for nothin', you'll never be out of work."

"True," Henry shouted back.

"You're a gentleman and a scholar," Jake said. "What else is the matter with you?"

Though Jake had said the same things to Henry a dozen times, Henry threw his head back and laughed as if he'd never heard them before. "Nothin' else, Old Man."

Resident services were undergoing change at the Haven. "They're in a flux," Henry had told the

Sap and Green People

Davises when he and Georgia had dined with them Tuesday evening. "While Thursday beauty shop hours for women remain the same, 8:30 until 12:00 noon, Tuesday's hours have been altered, switched with the men's, all very confusin' to its patrons and us wheelchair-pushers.

The new beauty shop schedule isn't workin'," Henry had also said, "and to make things worse, other services have yet to be changed because, for one thing, the part-time, woman-dermatologist is pregnant and goin' to be a full-time mother after her baby's born so a new dermatologist has to be found.

Also, the ophthalmologist is bein' replaced by an optometrist whose schedule hasn't yet been determined, and as if all that's not enough, the podiatrist's Thursday morning slot has to be expanded because he needs more time to treat all the 'emergencies' comin' his way, meaning all the sore toes, achin' heels, and fallen arches. Got that?

On the plus side, however, the internist has a new assistant who's workin' out well, better than the previous one who, people said, was incompetent, rude, and 'a whippersnapper,' to use Roy Smith's words.

"I'm tellin' you," Henry concluded, "things are so confusin' that Georgia has to point me in the right direction to get me where I gotta go. I just hope I don't take some poor urology patient to a psychologist who'll hype him all up with energizin' pills which might worsen his condition."

Arriving back at the beauty parlor and spying a woman who appeared to be ready for return, Henry put his hand on the woman's arm. "Ready to go?" he asked.

"Let go of me," the woman screeched, and she shook his hand off. "Get away! Get away."

"Excuse me," Henry pled. Stepping back several feet, he asked, "Are you ready to go back to your room now, Madam? I'm Henry Graham, and I push women down from their rooms and then back. That's my volunteer job. What I'm doing here."

"I'm done," the woman said in a more conciliatory voice, "but not ready to go. I want to sit for awhile. Listen to everyone talking."

Sap and Green People

"Certainly," Henry said politely. "I'll help someone else and check back to see if you're ready after that."

In the course of delivering his next charge, Henry overtook a man in the hall whom he'd taken to the dentist earlier in the week.

"How are you?" Henry asked in reference to two extractions the man was to have undergone.

"Great," the man answered, "only I feel like hell."

Twenty minutes later, the woman whom he'd angered in the beauty parlor with his too-direct approach, agreed to let Henry take her back to her room. Deciding that silence would be his best approach, Henry refrained from talking during the return.

"Stop!" the woman ordered at a point near the end of their shared journey. "Here comes my doctor."

The doctor drew abreast and paused to ask about the woman's health. As he turned to move on, the woman said, "My son's an engineer. I guess, Doctor, you weren't smart enough to be an engineer."

"No," the doctor answered, "but Henry is. He's an engineer."

"Who's Henry?" she asked.

"The man pushing you. Right there."

Looking back at Henry, the woman asked, "If you're an engineer, what are you doing pushing wheelchairs?"

Henry was busy most days with his own exercising program, pushing wheelchairs, serving on and chairing committees, running errands for himself and others, and observing what went on. He kept himself busy which was a good thing because he'd been forced to give up golfing, using the computer, reading, and, for the most part, driving because of his macular condition. The involvement also challenged him and left him feeling contributory. It also made him one of the best known, most respected, and most popular persons on the Haven campus, high compliments indeed.

Sap and Green People

Jean Turner, a long-time resident of the Haven at Oak Hill, ran the traffic signal at the intersection in front of the Haven's entrance. She collided with an oncoming van which was simply gigantic in size, and Jean was injured grievously, her Ford Escort demolished. Morgan Smith, a lifelong diabetic, had to have both legs amputated, a procedure sorely taxing to his fragile system, and his survival was in question. The Edward Strongs sold their Arizona vacation home to finance a six-month trip around the world on a freighter, and Geri Greenman's son won $1,000,000 on a television quiz show. Antithetical stories illustrating 'bad' and 'good' fortune pique people's interest, especially if age and circumstance have narrowed their own lives.

The stories about Jean, Morgan, the Strongs, and Geri's son were not the #1 topic of conversation on the Haven campus, however. The #1 topic was the romance between Jack Clausen and Gloria Field. The couple was seen together almost daily, and they appeared to be thoroughly enamored with each other, which no one questioned or resented for, after all, who could begrudge a lifelong bachelor and beleaguered widow companionship and joy?

Jack was able to follow Norbert Blair's advice that he become proactive in terms of courting Gloria, and on that same day that Norbert made the suggestion, Jack spotted Gloria eating supper in the dining room. He consequently zipped through the serving line without showing any judgement whatsoever regarding his food choices and advanced to where Gloria was sitting with four women at the window-end of the dining room.

"Hello, hello," he exclaimed brashly in a too-loud voice. "May I sit with you ladies?" and he pulled out the lone chair left at the table before they were able to respond. "I presume you saved this for me?" and he laughed self-consciously. Clumsily he transferred what was on his tray to the table, smiled a fool's smile, deposited the tray on a tray rack, plunked himself down in the chair, and looked at the female faces around him which registered curiosity to out-and-out astonishment.

Sap and Green People

"Gloria and I have met, and I saw her sitting here, and I figured I'd take the opportunity to get a little better acquainted with her," he said by way of explaining his intrusion. "I'm looking forward to that and also to meeting you ladies, of course."

"Of course," one of the women echoed sardonically.

"When did you move and how did the move go, Gloria?" Jack asked.

Unprepared for Jack's appearance and puzzled by behavior contrasting so sharply with how he'd conducted himself previously, Gloria answered elliptically with, "Wednesday and very well."

Gloria's brevity was not lost to Jack, but resolutely, he plunged ahead. "My thanks to all of you for allowing me to join you," and the women murmured one thing or another, nodded, and focused on their food and eating. Silence prevailed for some minutes.

Eager to further his acquaintance with Gloria, Jack emitted a rush of unpunctuated words about the weather and the view from the window and that night's menu, a rush ending with, "I don't know all of you or only by sight so if you don't mind I'll proceed by telling you that I'm Jack Clausen and I live in the middle apartment building over there and please tell me about yourselves." When no one responded immediately, Jack followed up his initial utterance by saying, "I really don't want to intrude upon your conversation, Ladies, so please continue with what you were discussing because I like listening to lady-talk, really I do," and several of the women snickered at the improbability of what he'd just said.

One of them finally spoke. "What do the ladies you like listening to talk about?" she asked.

"Recipes." Jack answered. "Grandchildren."

"Both, in all probability, though not all women have grandchildren."

"True but they all have recipes, don't they? At least I presume that they do."

"Tell me, do you favor recipe-talk over grandchildren-talk?" Jack was asked. By which woman, he had no idea, for he'd turned to eating and had trained his eyes on his plate as a means of coming to terms with his embarrassment at having presented himself so unfavorably.

"Actually, either's okay. Men are likely to discuss sports," he stated in a more profound tone than his statement warranted.

"That has to be true."

"Which sports?"

"Baseball. Hockey. College teams. The football Cardinals," Jack stated.

"You mean the Rams, don't you? The football Rams?"

"Of course," Gloria interjected helpfully. "Can you believe that I went to all the games long years ago, was a season ticket holder, but still I, myself, forget, even now after what must be a decade, to call the new team 'The Rams'," and with her remark, the women commenced talking about sports figures who'd come from St. Louis or played on St. Louis teams.

The next topic of conversation was travel, a subject with which Jack was better versed. He contributed intelligently to the discussion, and during the course of the conversation, he identified London and Vienna as favorite overseas destinations.

"Vienna's my favorite too," Gloria spoke up to say, and the subject of travel took Jack and his eating companions all over the world.

As the women finished eating, one by one they excused themselves, and several went so far as to suggest that the six eat together another time. While Jack had relaxed and come to terms with his embarrassment and put forth a 'better face' by the end of the meal, he doubted if he should take the invitation seriously.

"Absolutely," Gloria assured him when he expressed that doubt, and forever female, she teased him coyly with, "That is, if you'd like to."

During the meal, Gloria had come to realize that Jack was interested in her. The fact so surprised and pleased her that it flushed her cheeks and curtailed her appetite. Pushing away a half-plate of food and conversing with Jack while he ate a sundae he'd ordered and drank several cups of coffee, the two exchanged 'basic information' about themselves.

Sap and Green People

It was Gloria who noticed that the waiters and waitresses had cleared the tables around them and were setting them for the next meal, that the dining room was nearly empty.

"We should be going," she told Jack.

"I know, I know," he responded. "I'll walk you to your place."

"My place is right above us," and she pointed to the ceiling. "Overhead. On the next floor up."

"Oh," Jack said with obvious disappointment. "We never got to talk about your move, and I still have questions to ask. How you like the Manor. If you've found the people congenial. Made some friends. Lots of other things."

"Another time," Gloria thought to say.

"Tomorrow. Tomorrow morning?" Jack suggested even though he knew full well that Norbert, Bud, and Rob were scheduled to meet with him at 9:00. "We could go for a short walk. I know you walk," and he smiled at the memory of meeting her the day he'd ventured into the woods.

"I can't think of a reason not to," Gloria answered, and they worked out walking details. "So, we're set then, aren't we?" she asked while smiling the smile Jack thought simply dazzling.

Jack stood, pulled Gloria's chair out from under the table, took her right arm (the one having sensitivity), and escorted her as far as the elevator. "We could sit in the lobby and talk," he suggested, but Gloria declined that invitation.

"I really am quite tired," she explained while not revealing that what had sapped her vitality was Jack's improbable appearance and the sweet, sobering realization that he was in pursuit of her.

"Well," countered a Jack who was desperate to insure a continuing association, "after we walk tomorrow morning, I can help you. Unpack or move boxes or carry out trash." The latter sounding indelicate, so he added, "if you have any trash. Or run errands. I'd be glad to drive you anywhere. Even to…Chicago, if you need to go there," at which they both laughed.

"We'll see," Gloria answered.

"Thanks for spending the evening with me," Jack stammered.

"It was only an hour."

"Really? Well, thanks for the hour," and without reason, they laughed again.

"We've had a pleasant dinner hour, haven't we?" Gloria asked.

"Yes, yes we have, but I'm sorry I made such a fool of myself. My appearance at your table. Forcing myself upon you. I hope I didn't embarrass you in front of your friends. If so, please forgive me."

"No apology necessary," Gloria assured him, "You were fun, and now I'll say goodnight." As she extended her finger to press the elevator button, what she found was that Jack had already placed his finger on it, and the fingers touched.

"Ou-u," Jack said without intending to, an exact expression of how Gloria had reacted to the touch as well, and she flashed another Gloria-smile.

Jean Turner's injuries mandated that she move into Assisted Living. Morgan Smith died a few weeks after his surgery, and his well-attended funeral was held in the Haven's Chapel. The Edward Strongs finished their six-month, around-the-world, ocean voyage without being subjected to the accidents and illnesses that their friends and family had projected. And, saying that the Haven was 'home' and its services 'far more than simply adequate', Geri Greenmann refused her millionaire son's offer to move her to the most luxurious seniors' complex in the whole, metropolitan St. Louis area. All were matters of interest and concern, but the most talked-about goings-on was the blooming and blossoming of Jack Clausen and Gloria Field's relationship which was monitored closely by just about everyone who knew or knew of them.

"Did you think that depressing?" Elaine Bruce asked her companions as they left one of the Manor's meeting rooms. She was referring to the 'wellness' lecture that she and they had just attended, one regarding mental depression.

"No," Joan Cutler answered, "not depressing, and it was more informative than some of the talks in the series."

"Seemed to me," Moira Sheer said, "that the speaker tried so hard to make the point that genetic heritage and body chemistry contribute heavily to depression that she let too many ninnies, who just won't shape up and ship out, off the hook."

"I don't agree with you," Ruth Roberts countered. "I think that because so many people believe that depression is 'self-induced' or 'self-sustained', to use the speaker's words, she felt compelled to overstate her point so we'd recognize the body chemistry factor."

"Speaking for myself, I'm ready to forget about the subject for the time being."

"So, what'll we do? Where'll we go?" Joan Cutler asked.

"Too early for dinner."

"Too cold to sit out on benches."

"The ice cream parlor's not open today.

"We could get a car out and go to the mall."

"Naw-w-w," said Essie Brinkman. "Not enough time to get organized and there and back before supper."

"So, let's sit in the library 'til dinner."

"I keep telling you that it's 'supper'."

"Call it what you will," Moira said, and she and her four friends took the elevator up two floors. There, they turned right and arrived at the pleasant, well-furnished, light and airy library, replete with donated fiction, non-fiction, and reference books, plus the magazines and newspapers subscribed to by Management.

"We'll sit around the newspaper table," Essie Brinkman said, "and I'll get copies of the *Wall Street Journal* for each of us. We'll hold them as if we're reading but talk instead, and if people come in, they'll ask, 'You an investment club?'"

"What'll we say then?"

Sap and Green People

"Oh, something," and Ruth pulled another chair from across the room and pushed it up to the elongated table while Elaine turned on the lamps strategically placed at its two ends.

"Don't need the lamps."

"Do too."

"Certainly we do if we want to look like investors."

"Investors are always flooded with light?"

"Absolutely."

"Two are too bright."

"One on then, one off."

"East one off."

"No, west one."

"They're north and south."

"Who cares. Turn one off."

"The first thing to talk about," Joan stated, "is Mary…"

"…who doesn't look well…"

"…and said she was going away…"

"…for a short period of time."

"Had some business to attend to."

"Gosh, I'm worried about her."

"We all are."

"So thin…

"…but still so lovely."

"Haven't seen her since Friday."

"At dinner."

"Last meal she ate with us," Gail said.

"I was there that night, and she didn't eat much at all."

"Not enough to fill a bird."

"Smiling and gracious nonetheless."

"Beauteous," Moira said.

"Exactly right—beauteous."

"Lovely word. The right choice in Mary's case."

"In her black faille with the high, velvet-bound neck, she looked like someone out of an eighteenth century painting."

"Two tables of us that night, and she ate at one and had dessert at the other, as if she wanted to visit with everyone."

"Or as if she'd not be with us much longer."

"I had the same thought. Gave me the shivers."

"The Last Supper."

Sap and Green People

"God bless her."

"Does that mean God should help her stay or lead her away?"

"Certainly it hasn't come to the latter!"

"Turn pages, Girls. The elevator's dinging, meaning someone's coming," and with their eyes trained on their papers, the women waited. No one appeared.

"Three sets of encyclopedias over there," Joan finally said. "Wonder how old they are."

"Everything's computers now."

"But you know, history doesn't change, and a person can still use encyclopedias to look up history things."

The elevator dinged again, the women waited, and Gloria Field came through the door. Startled at finding the grouping, she stopped dead in her tracks.

"Good afternoon," she said. "You surprised me because usually there's no one around."

"Don't let us stop you from doing what you came to do," Elaine answered so sweetly that she almost sounded sarcastic.

"You're new here, aren't you?" Ruth Roberts asked. "We've seen you around but haven't met you," and she introduced herself and her companions to Gloria.

Gloria talked with the women briefly, mostly about how happy she was to be living in the Manor, then explained, "I've come to look up Lady Bird Johnson. Some friends have been discussing her, and I need to know more so I can contribute to their conversation."

"We were just talking about encyclopedias," Essie said, "saying that even in the Computer Age, they're still useful when it comes to researching historical subjects."

"Only, not exactly with those words," and everyone laughed while Gloria smiled politely.

"I'll let you continue what you're doing," Gloria said. "I'm glad to meet you and look forward to seeing you again," and assisted by her cane, she moved across the room to where encyclopedias were shelved, putting the women in the unexpected position of having to return to papers they'd not intended to read.

Sap and Green People

Gloria pulled out several volumes, apparently scanned them, and wrote notes on a tablet she took from her purse. She seemed not to write extensively, for, to the women's relief, she returned the books after a relatively few minutes. "Goodbye," she called as she left.

"Heard she's sweet."

"Sweet, and we saw that she's pretty, even up close."

"Very."

"Suppose she has any idea how many people know who she is and that she's going with that super-duper Jack Clausen?"

"Nope."

"If I'd known Jack was up for grabs, I'd have worked him over myself."

"How do you 'work' someone 'over'?"

"You took my words too literally. I didn't actually mean anything special. Have no idea what the expression infers."

"If something, I've totally forgotten."

"Personally, I never knew. My hubby, God bless his dear, departed soul, may have worked me over, to use your expression. If so, thank goodness, for if he hadn't courted me, my life would have been quite a different story."

"A better or worse one?"

"Far worse because he was a wonderful guy."

"Think they'll get married?"

"No."

"Think they engage in…?"

"Naughty! Naughty!"

"Shame on you for speculating."

"None of our business, anyway."

"They're just keeping company."

"I'd wager a dollar that they will marry."

"Bring your dollars to supper, ladies, and we'll set up a pool."

The gauntlet having been thrown down and the hour having advanced, the friends folded their newspapers, placed them on the periodical rack, turned off the single lamp, repositioned their chairs, and left the library to tidy themselves before meeting again at precisely 5:30, the time they always assembled for supper (dinner) in the Manor dining room.

"Lastly came winter, clothed all in frieze'," Marti Morton cited softly as some of 'The Girls', as they'd come to call themselves, huddled over coffee following dinner in the Manor dining room. They'd scooted their chairs close together at one side of the table so they could look out the window at the snowy winter scene.

"Nice quote, Marti," Joan Cutler said. "What's it from?"

"Spencer's *The Faerie Queen.*"

"What's the next line?"

"Can't remember. I came from Wisconsin where we had a Winter Festival every year. High school girls, all draped in white, recited those words and for my soul, I can't remember what came next. Can't remember the other passages they recited or sang and danced to either. On a wooden stage built in the middle of the town square. That's all I remember, the one line, and I'm mad at myself that I can't come up with more."

"The snow's bringing back memories to me, too," Gail Campbell said.

"What of?" Bertha Brinkman asked.

"You mean 'of what', don't you? With the preposition first?" Essie Brinkman asked her sister-in-law.

"I didn't know we were talking about prepositions. I thought we were talking about snow."

"Of what do you have memories, Gail? Snow memories?"

"I lived in Michigan when I was a child, and when a lake froze over, we'd build a big fire on its shore. Skaters would gather, and round and round the edges of the lake they'd go, with non-skaters playing in the snow and sitting around the fire. At some point, everyone roasted weinies and marshmallows. Sang camp songs and Christmas carols.

We skied on the hills and dunes, too," Gail continued. "Pretty much used one-size-fits-all skis. Not knowing that the correct length was critical to skiing success, we just traded whatever we had back and forth. No ski boots, poles, lifts either. Unlovely, bulky, woolen snowsuits if we were lucky, overalls or heavy pants pulled over long underwear if we weren't. Kept us warm until our clothing soaked up the wet.

I look at beautiful people pictured in sleek, beautiful snow clothing these days, with all their up-to-date equipment, and I want to say to them, 'Well, we could have done well too if we'd had all that stuff. Lucky you!'"

"You draw a pretty, happy picture."

"We were happy, but skating or skiing was cold."

"Winter came too soon this year," Bertha noted. "Crept up on us."

"Reminds me that I've seen many, many first snowfalls. Lived through many, many winters."

"Many Christmases!"

Except where campus lights illuminated portions of streets, walkways, and attending stretches of lawn, at 5:45, darkness prevailed already, and someone asked, "How'd it get so dark so soon?"

"How'd it get December!"

"How'd I get to be 81?" Moira Sheer, who'd recently celebrated a birthday, mused.

"You don't look that," Myra assured her.

"Feel like it some days. Yesterday, for example, I hurt all over. Back. Hip. Legs and knees. 'N my neck. Shoulder. Arm, my right arm. Fingers. You name it."

"That's the way it goes, doesn't it?"

"To our credit, we don't complain much around here."

"Here are all these old people, suffering sometimes like we do, and we don't hear a lot of discussion about bodily pain."

"Really don't."

"Most of us are pretty valiant, when it comes right down to it."

"Those of us who 'have a life,' as the expression goes," and the women returned to their study of the accumulating snow.

"We didn't have snow or lake-skating or hill-skiing where I grew up," Marti said which broke the silence. "Sometimes it was cold, but not too bad. Even so, I never liked winter."

"Me either."

"Who does?"

"Winter's...winter. Comes, leaves, and people sigh their relief when it's over."

"But, Girls, winter brings Christmas, and everyone likes Christmas."

"Not everyone."

"People who are alone or have no families probably don't."

"Or come from what are now called dysfunctional families."

"Most are these days."

"The holidays used to be so joyous when the children were little and we were strong and able, weren't they?"

"And busy."

"I entertained a lot and really regret that I can't much anymore."

"Hate not being able to shop for gifts like I used to."

"Don't like having to give money to the kids and grandkids."

"What's money mean to them?"

"I give gift certificates."

Sap and Green People

"This is a dumb conversation, Ladies," Bertha said, "a downer, and even though we don't like winter and Christmas isn't what it used to be, we can make a nice—hate the word!—Christmas together if we choose."

"Have a little gift exchange. Late at night around the tree in the lobby when everyone else, we hope, is in bed."

"Go out for a festive holiday meal."

"Catch a Haven bus to a seasonal concert. Busses go to several."

"Help each other shop for family members, if required. 'Cause we're still good for an occasional venturing into the stores, you better believe!"

"If it's short and we wear sloppy shoes."

"We could hire Robert—the park concert Robert?—to take us around to see Christmas lights."

"Go to church together, here on campus or to one of the churches we belong to…"

"…but don't attend as much as we once did."

"And, we can watch out for people around here who don't have anyone."

"Include them somehow."

"Collect toys for poor children."

"From who?"

"Whom!" Essie said.

"Tell me: did you used to be an English teacher?"

"Girls," Gail Russell said, "in somewhat less than," and she lifted her wrist so she could look at her watch, "seventeen minutes, we've gone from being nostalgic to being…cheerful, know that? Good for us."

"Snow's coming down again," Eloise said. "Heavy."

"Pure and glistening under the lights."

"Things are pretty much okay with all of us," Joan said philosophically. "Except for our concern about Mary. We're not even sure what's the matter with her."

"Heart, you think?"

"Cancer?"

"Research is saying over and over that secondary prayer is beneficial."

"'Secondary prayer' is praying for someone else, I presume."

Sap and Green People

"Contributes to recovery supposedly."

"Then we should pray for Mary."

"Now!"

"Why not," Joan Cutler agreed, and without hesitation, she extended a hand in either direction and prayed that Mary's health improve, that Haven residents be blessed, and that 'The Girls' find ways to contribute to the Christmas happiness of others. And as the friends dropped hands and readied themselves to leave the dining room, they felt certain that theirs would indeed be a happy, memorable Christmas, in spite of their…seniority.

Because 'prognosticators' (the term Bill Davis frequently used when alluding to weathermen) had warned that up to six more inches of snow might fall during the night, Bill bounded out of bed the next morning to check their estimate, a dramatic departure from his usual negative reaction to getting up. After peering through Venetian blind slats in the bedroom, he called, "They were right, Marg! Six inches of snow! Probably more! Come look."

"Must I?" Marg grumped.

"Yes!" Bill answered as he strode into the living room to pull open the deck door and get an unobstructed view of the snow which was cast gray by morning's dim light. What he saw was tire-tracked snow on streets. Blanketing snow bowing tree limbs. Burdensome snow breaking down shrubbery. Snow carpeting lawns and thatching building roofs.

Throwing off the covers and settling on her back, Marg executed two quick sets of leg lifts and as many quad stretches, parts of the 'knee replacement regime' her orthopedist urged her to honor the rest of her life. She could have waited to do them, of course, but by delaying her appearance in the living room for a few minutes, she was asserting herself in the face of Bill's command, and she felt assertion was necessary from time to time, a component necessary to a good marital relationship. The exercises finished, she joined Bill in front of the opened door.

"Thermometer reads nine degrees," he told her.

"Remember that huge snow we had the first winter we lived in our ranch house?" Marg asked. "None of the other houses was finished so we had the neighborhood to ourselves. No traffic. You tied the kids' sled to the back of the car, put them on it, and drove round and round the block."

"Had a full foot of snow then, if I remember correctly," and he and Marg moved to the kitchen and commenced preparing breakfast.

"Or the Thanksgiving, way before that, when it was supercold and snowy, and you drove 18-month-old Dave up to my parents in Michigan because I was pregnant with Susan, in the hospital, and too sick to care for him?"

"And the drive up on Christmas Eve to retrieve him?" Bill asked. "Everything white under a cold moon...,"

"...and we listened to Christmas carols on the radio all the way, the whole ten hours it took then."

"The time when it was bitter cold and the furnace went out on a Friday so we all huddled around the fireplace, ate and slept there, until Monday when someone came to fix it? That was actually a fun time."

"How 'bout that night, December 23, a few years ago when we took the grandkids downtown for pizza and a carriage ride we'd booked, only the horse and carriage never arrived and we darned near froze before we realized we'd been stood up? Great evening anyway."

"Enough remember-whens," Bill insisted. "Don't want to get melancholy. As I always say, a little nostalgia goes a long way," and he and Marg sat down to their breakfast of oatmeal, juice, toast, and vitamin pills.

Sap and Green People

When finished, as they moved to the sofa to drink their coffee and read the morning's paper, Bill looked out the deck door again.

"Marg," he exclaimed, "there's something wrong down there," and he nodded towards the north end of their street. "A couple of cars blocking off the street, two parked emergency vehicles, guys milling around."

"Oh gosh!" Marg exclaimed as she joined him, then "Oh my gosh!" again. "Would you look at that?" After watching the goings-on for some minutes, Marg persuaded Bill to finish his coffee before going to investigate what was going on, which she knew he'd do.

Having finished it and hastily perusing the paper, Bill returned to the door.

"More guys are arriving," he reported. "Booted up and dressed in heavy parkas. A few residents talking to them. I'm going to get some clothes on and see what's up."

"Think you should?"

"I don't know why not. This is my street too," Bill insisted. "Can't imagine what could be the matter," and minutes later, outfitted in clothing Marg hadn't known he'd hung onto and looking as if he were headed for the tundra, Bill passed through the living room while Marg continued to look out.

"I'll be back soon," he promised.

Unable to concentrate on the paper, Marg showered, and the severity of the weather factored 'heavy' and 'warm' into her criteria for choosing the clothing she'd put on. As she was blow-drying her hair, Bill reentered the apartment.

"Marg," he told her in a voice that quivered either from concern or the cold or both, "you're never going to believe this, but old George Steiner's gone."

"Gone? What do you mean?" Marg asked.

"Disappeared. No one knows where. Been gone three, maybe four days, they think. Remember people saying that George sometimes followed the creek up from the lake? Went west and north? 'Explored it,' Norbert Blair said George told him once. Well, those booted guys in the street down there are deputies, and that's what they're going to do: follow the creek and look for George. 'Cause he's gone. Absolutely gone."

"Oh my gosh!" Marg exclaimed again.

"Marg, do you realize how many times a day you say, 'Oh my gosh'?"

"Is that so awful?" Marg retorted. "Never dreamed it was so bothersome. I'll spit the words right out," and she went through the motions of spitting on the floor and rubbing what she'd spit into the carpet with the toe of her shoe.

"Heh!" Bill insisted, "I was observing, not complaining. Didn't intend to criticize you. You're overreacting. I bet I say, 'What's that?' a dozen times a day 'cause I'm not a good listener and even with my hearing aids, I only hear part of what you say."

"'Dozens' of times?" Marg snapped. "More like dozens and dozens, Buster."

"I'm Bill, not Buster," Bill said in an attempt to lighten the tone of their conversation. "Buster was one of my other guys," and Bill could see her shoulders relax.

"Getting back to George, his disappearance is simply terrible. In weather like this."

"His daughter-in-law's down there now with her two sons." he told Marg "College-aged, maybe a little older. Good-looking, all three. Very upset. Concerned."

"Think the daughter and grandsons are going upstream too?"

"That's what they're talking about now: who should go."

"You read about things like this in the paper, but here? In the Haven?"

"Doesn't represent neglect on anyone's part. They keep saying that down there, our Security guy, John, the others who were watching with me. It could very well happen because if a person's in Independent Living and deteriorating but still situated there, he's still responsible for himself and no one's charged with watching him."

"Going to be a long day for the searchers and his family, whether they go along or not."

"It could be traumatic for them if they're with the search party when he's found."

"Yeh 'cause he might not have withstood the exposure well enough to be in good condition."

"Actually, he wouldn't have been out long enough to deteriorate, if that's what you mean, but he could be quite dead."

"Maybe we shouldn't be too pessimistic. He could have found somewhere safe and warm."

"Like some all-night, greasy spoon."

"Or in a farmhouse where he'd been given shelter."

"Hiding in a john somewhere."

"He could be in a little town. At a motel. Probably took some money."

"Be right here in St. Louis. In a motel or with the Street People under some bridge."

"Or in the History Museum where he used to volunteer."

"But," Bill said, "it looks pretty grim. Too bad!"

"Bill, do you know how may times a day you've come to say, 'Too bad'?"

"Yeah? I guess you're right. Forgive me. Not sure I can change at this point in my life, but I'll try. Good old George. Funny, loveable guy. Too, too bad," and Bill shed his heavy jacket, dropped down on the sofa, pulled off his wet boots, resumed reading the paper which he'd looked at in such cursory fashion earlier, and repeated, "Too, too bad."

Sap and Green People

"Good afternoon," Gail Russell said to Carol Clark, secretary to Harry Wright, the administrator of the Haven. "I'm Gail Russell. I believe it was you who called several hours ago and asked that I pick up a letter from Mr. Wright."

"It was, and thank you for coming," Mrs. Clark answered as she rose from her computer. "One minute, please. I know Mr. Wright is expecting you," and she knocked and entered the administrator's office which opened off her own.

Dressed typically in a charcoal gray suit, white shirt, and dated necktie, Mr. Wright appeared and invited Gail to follow him into his office. Thanking her for meeting with him and seeing that she was comfortably seated, Wright sat down behind his desk and said, "I suppose you wondered what in the world this was all about."

"Yes," Gail confessed. "I thought maybe I was going to be evicted."

"No, no. Should you be?" Harry answered, and his question and amused smile eased Gail's anxiety somewhat. "Nothing like that, though what I have to tell you is distressing, I'm sorry to say.

Mrs. Russell, Mary Spritzer died this morning," and he paused so Gail could take in what he had said.

"Oh dear," Gail said. "So fast. Such a surprise. We weren't expecting this."

"At the time Mary went to a hospice facility" Wright explained, "she gave me a letter which I was to give you, only you, when I was notified of her death. I was to explain, Mary said, that she'd given the matter considerable thought and come to the conclusion that you were 'the perfect instrument' for telling her friends about her past life. That's how she described you, a compliment, certainly."

"Thank you."

"After you read the letter, I will run copies off and have you distribute them to" and he read the names from a list he took out of his suit breast pocket, "Eloise Brady, Bertha Brinkman, Essie Brinkman, Elaine Bruce, Claire Campbell, Joan Cutler, Myra Kelly, Marti Morton, Ruth Roberts, Moira Sheer, and Rhonda

Stevens. In alphabetical order, you'll notice," which made Gail smile.

"I'll be glad to do that," Gail told Mr. Wright.

"Do you wish to read the letter now or take it back to your apartment, which would be more private? In the latter case, you could stop back at your convenience so I could make the copies or have them made."

"I'll read it now," Gail replied. "I want to get the letter's content to the others as soon as possible."

"I'll leave you alone then for a few minutes," and to afford Gail privacy but not give the appearance that he was abandoning her, Wright stepped out of his office but left its door open part way.

My dear friends, the letter, carefully written with black ink, read, *I address you as 'dear friends' because in truth, I have never had a circle of friends whom I've appreciated and cared for as much as I have you. Your friendships have meant a great deal to me.*

Patricia Dick

Some time ago, I more or less promised that when I was on my deathbed, I would tell you more about my life. At that time, because I wasn't sure whether I was serious about that 'promise' or not, I hoped you would regard it as something said in jest, and I think you did.

As things have turned out, I am dying, for I'm suffering an advanced case of cancer which I have decided not to resist. I checked myself into a hospice facility rather than into the Convalescent Center at the Haven or a hospital, and apparently I have only a few weeks to live. Please know that I am comfortable, well cared for, and determined to write the 'disclosure' I alluded to and now wish to make, which follows.

I was born in New York City to what is now called a 'single mother', a more charitable designation than the one assigned to unmarried mothers at that time. My father was a wealthy, well-known man who loved my mother but could not marry her. He also made evident that he loved me very much as well by supporting

Mother and me to a degree that allowed me to grow up blessed with material advantages.

I attended a private girls' school and college, and my clever, beautiful mother and I were very close. I had handsome, moneyed beaus who professed to love me dearly. They did not, however, ask me to marry them because my background was socially unacceptable in the social circles they represented. Fortunately, the fact that they didn't ask me to marry did not grieve me: I never cared deeply for any of them and had decided that I'd never marry anyone, a decision I won't try to explain.

My New York friends were an eclectic bunch, casually associated, busy studying and working in some instances, seeing and doing, experiencing and experimenting. In the course of things, I met an acclaimed black saxophone player eleven years my senior who performed up and down the East Coast. He fell in love with me, I with him. Extremely talented, intelligent, independent, big and beautiful physically, Jason charmed Mother as he'd charmed me. She understood my feelings for Jason and accepted him after making clear what she felt would be the problems and adjustments we'd face if we perpetuated our relationship, which she thought would be even more difficult than her own. I did commit myself to the relationship: I became Jason's 'wife' though we never married.

Jason found more acceptance and opportunity abroad than in the United States, so we went where he was touted and rewarded monetarily. Mother traveled with us more often than not, and the three of us traversed the world. What a fine time we had!

Mother died in Rome. Of what we were never sure but most likely some pancreatic condition which couldn't be diagnosed back then. As per her instructions, she was cremated, and we scattered her ashes on the waters of the Mediterranean.

Sap and Green People

Two years later, I gave birth to a beautiful baby girl in Manila. The child, Anna, died several months after her birth due to a heart defect.

Life went on for Jason and me, a life I would not have traded, had I been offered the world. Jason died when he was sixty-one, the acclaimed musician and world citizen he'd wanted to be, a happy man. I scattered his ashes on the Caspian Sea.

Thereafter, I visited some of the places where we'd been and some of our friends, served as a companion or personal secretary to several women, and studied in places of my choice until I returned to Missouri.

Why Missouri? (None of you ever asked.) Because Mother was from just south of Kansas City and she and I had spent happy vacations at points around the state. For no dramatic reason, I nixed Kansas City and chose St. Louis as the place of my final residence. Because it is in the middle of the country, I reasoned, also because it had what I regarded as a fascinating history. Too, when I visited the Haven at Oak Hill, I sensed that it harbored good things and good people, a judgement which time substantiated.

For your satisfaction, I could list all the places where I've lived during the course of my adult life, the thing we sparred about (and wasn't it fun?), but how important are they? What is important is that I have lived a full, rich life, so complete that I do not choose to take the measures required to extend it; that I have loved living with you and being your friend; that I care enough about you that I'm willing to tell you about my early years.

Some weeks ago now, Mr. Wright gave me the name of a lawyer who will see that my estate is taken care of and that my money given to the philanthropic organizations I have named. I've specified that my body be cremated, my ashes scattered on the Mississippi, no service be held.

Goodbye, dear friends. Thank you for what we've shared. I fervently hope that for the rest of your lives, you will bless each other with your affection, as you blessed me.

Your friend,

Mary Spritzer

Gail had wiped her eyes and pulled herself up tall in her chair by the time Harry Wright returned.

"Are you okay?" he asked in a solicitous voice. Assured that she was, he left the office a second time. "Is there anything I can do for you and the others?" he asked as he handed Gail copies of Mary's letter and Gail rose to leave.

"Nothing I can think of."

"If something comes to mind, please let me know, and you can all be assured that Miss Spritzer's wishes will be painstakingly carried out."

"I am sure of that, Sir. Thank you," and she returned to her apartment to decide how best to inform

The Girls about their friend's death and how she'd preface the distribution of copies of the letter.

"Help me, Lord," she prayed as she spread herself out on her bed to rest briefly. "Help me proceed in the right way. And thank you for Mary who, in the short time I knew her, profoundly enriched my life."

Sap and Green People

Preparing their fourth, multi-media presentation was certainly easier than preparing the first three. By the fourth time around, Jack Clausen, Norbert Blair, Bud Walsh, and Rob Rymer had clearly established a division of responsibilities; each man had become proficient in his area; all were more knowledgeable regarding available community resources; and they'd moved into a comfortable and productive working relationship.

That wasn't all the men had achieved. Their productions had become so popular that beginning with the George Orwell presentation, the third, they'd had to schedule two showings to accommodate Haven audiences. Other groups heard about the documentaries and wanted to see them, so Norbert arranged showings elsewhere and trained volunteers to help put them on. Finances were in good shape, thanks to the income derived from the elsewhere-showings and three grants Norbert received.

Several factors still had to be worked around, however: how to accommodate the men's personal schedules; how to reconcile their opinions; how to allow for differing degrees of involvement; and how to insure that no one forgot to bring donuts when it was his time to do so. There was also the matter of Gloria Fields.

Seldom could Jack work for an extended period of time without bringing Gloria to the workroom with him. "It'll take about four hours to do that," the men would agree during a planning session, "then, four or five more hours the following day."

"I'm not sure I'll be free for intervals that long," Jack would say.

"Shall we work without you?" one of the men might ask.

"I'd rather avoid that," Jack would answer.

"We do have production schedules and completion deadlines to meet," Norbert would remind Jack, "ones you always help work out."

"You're right. Of course you're right," Jack would agree. "I'll make arrangements to be there," and he'd show up with Gloria who'd look self-conscious and unsure of her welcome.

Sap and Green People

The men admired and liked Gloria: There was no question about that. Nor was there any question regarding their respect and fondness for Jack: none whatsoever. And they approved of Jack and Gloria's romance: totally. The problem was that Gloria's presence required adjustments on their part.

For instance, they felt impelled to clean up the office and keep it clean and picked up. They had to upgrade the overhead lighting so Gloria could read while they worked. Provide a comfortable chair for her. Stock napkins, paper towels, and plastic tablewear for use when they ate in the office. Scour the surface of the tiny serving table they ate on, also the coffee pot and cups. Keep the 'ladies' room' hall free of obstructions. Up the donut count. Refrain from belching and using inappropriate language. What Gloria's presence meant was that they had to adapt their domain and modify their conduct to accommodate a lady who was both refined and handicapped.

On the other hand, Gloria accommodated them in a number of ways. She kept out of their way. Was as quiet as a mouse. Most often, did the straightening up and dish-washing. Provided more than her share of donuts, plus snacks, veggies, fruits, sandwiches, and cookies. Made constructive suggests when invited to do so. Helped research. (She was very capable in this regard, having been an English major in college). Critiqued. Listened to personal problems. Cheered the men on when things failed to go as anticipated.

Some two months after Gloria had commenced accompanying Jack to the studio, after the men had completed what they'd planned to do and she and they were drinking coffee, for no reason other than to stoke the conversation, Norbert asked, "Tell me, Jack, if you're the director and producer of Tall Tree Technics," the name the men had given their organization, "I'm the business manager, and Rob and Bud are the technical staff, what is Gloria?"

"My soon-to-be-wife," Jack answered and a grin spread across his face.

"You son of a gun!" Norbert whooped as he leaped out of his chair, dashed to where his friend was

Sap and Green People

standing, and threw his arms around him. "You son of a gun," he repeated. "Congratulations!"

He moved then over to Gloria, who'd hidden her face in her hands, and congratulated her also and as heartily. Dropping down to his knees in front of her when she failed to respond, he gently pulled her hands away from her face, and said in a voice intense with feeling, "Gloria, I'm so happy for Jack and you, but why the hidden face?"

"I'm embarrassed," Gloria answered in a barely audible voice.

"Embarrassed? Why in the world would you be embarrassed?" Norbert asked.

"Because," came the answer finally, "I'm unworthy of Jack," and she began to weep.

"Unworthy? Who said so?" Norbert demanded.

"I did. Over and over. But Jack wouldn't listen. Wouldn't take no for an answer."

"Of course not and thank goodness," Norbert insisted. "Of course he wouldn't because he shouldn't. And you know why? Because he loves you and he knows you're wrong. He's the one who's not worthy of you!" which made Gloria laugh in spite of herself. Jack, Rob, and Bud were at her side by this time, and Jack pulled her to her feet.

"This is as good a time as any," Jack said, "to ask you, Norbert, Rob and Bud, if you'll witness our wedding for us. Be our witnesses? Sign the license? I know nothing about weddings, never having been a party of one before or even attended very many, but I hear weddings require witnesses, and we'd like you to witness for us. Won't cost you a thing."

"We're being married in the campus chapel," Gloria explained. "By the chaplain. There will be only the minister and the five of us, though possibly three women-friends of mine from here, a nurse and the two women who rescued me when I had my fall, will be there too. I haven't decided whether to invite them or not."

And that's how one cool Thursday morning ended for the five-person, Tall Trees Technics company, a morning none of them would forget for the rest of their lives.

Sap and Green People

During a restless night, Elaine Bruce had run Mary Spritzer's story through her mind, over and over again. The marvelous story interested her, and it inspired her to work out a telling of her own story. Hers was not as unusual nor poignant as Mary's, but it was worthy of its telling, she decided, and by the time daylight was streaking the eastern sky, she was hoping that all men and women would ultimately come up with distillations of their lives, distillations that would sustain and comfort them as they faced their deaths.

As she dressed the following morning, it occurred to Elaine that The Girls should scatter Mary's ashes on the Mississippi, for there was no one else, neither family or friends, to carry out Mary's wish. Suspending her dressing, Elaine called Gail Russell.

"Gail, did Mr. Wright say who was going to do the scattering of Mary's ashes?" she asked.

"No," Gail answered, "and I was so shocked by his news that I didn't give the ashes a thought."

"I'm thinking," Gail explained, "that we, we 'Girls' should take care of them, and afterwards, do something 'nice' together, a Mary kind of thing, in

Mary's memory and honor. Something cultural. Like going to the Symphony or a stage play or a concert at the Cathedral. That would finish things out nicely," Gail commented enthusiastically.

"How appropriate."

While Gail and Elaine talked further, under the same roof and two floors lower, Gloria Fields and Jack Clausen were discussing how best to rearrange Gloria's apartment so it would accommodate Jack's things, also matters relative to their forthcoming marriage.

"We see Moss Gray, who's been a great help to me,…"

"…at 3:00 tomorrow afternoon," Jack said. "I have that down in my date book. About merging our fiances."

"Already," Gloria laughed, "we're finishing each others' sentences…"

"…and reading each other's minds."

"You'll like Moss. An honest, helpful lawyer whom I'd bet my life on."

Sap and Green People

"No one will ask you to do that," Jack said, and Gloria laughed. Not being particularly humorous herself and having lived a life totally devoid of humorous influences, Gloria laughed at many of the things Jack said, whether they were worthy of laughter or not. "I'll arrange to have my things moved…when?" Four or five days before the wedding?" Gloria nodded. "That'll give us time to get things whittled down and settled before the big day," Jack stated, and "I'll arrange to sleep in one of the Manor's guest rooms 'til then."

"I'll get one of the charities to pick up what we're discarding. Some mid-afternoon, after you've moved in and we're sure of what we can use," Gloria offered.

"I may set some things aside for the employees to buy and give the money to the Haven's benevolent fund. I'm still thinking about how that might work."

"Oh, isn't this fun?" Gloria said, and she put her arms around Jack's neck.

"Strenuous, that's what it is and will be, but I'm just not going to let you get too tired," Jack said as he kissed Gloria lightly on the lips.

"And we'll…"

"No more 'we'll', 'then', and 'have to' this morning," Jack said. "That's all the planning for now. A few things at a time: that's how we're going to take it.

I want to be a good husband to you, Gloria," a serious Jack continued, "but as I've told you, I don't know a thing about being one. Haven't been around a married couple since I left home when I was eighteen, and my parents were not good models because they weren't loving. I honestly can't remember them ever showing affection. Touching, holding hands, kissing. Smiling intimately. I've nothing to emulate. And, as you know, I've never known a woman…in the Biblical sense."

"Hush," Gloria said, and she planted a hand over Jack's mouth. "Don't trouble yourself. Don't worry. Like you yourself said, a few things at a time.

I was a different woman when I was married, Jack. Lived a different life. I've chosen to forget all that, so we'll be starting out as equals. Learn together. Teach each other," and they clung to each other, at 9:30 in the morning, on the sofa in Gloria's living room, prompted by a budding passion they were discovering, a solid basis for the intimacies they were soon to share.

A floor above, on the Manor's second floor in another living room, George Steiner's daughter-in-law, Lauren Steiner, sat slumped and crying in her father-in-law's easy chair while her sons, Grant and Luther, stood over her. The three had met with Harry Wright late yesterday and heard a report that George's body had been recovered forty-seven miles north and a little west of the city of St. Charles.

"Under a cluster of young cedars where he'd apparently taken shelter," a policeman had stated.

"On the 'Great River Trail' which follows the Missouri River," a second officer further explained. "Based on what you and others have told us and our examination of Mr. Steiner's apartment, we've come to the conclusion that Mr. Steiner probably set out to follow the Lewis and Clark route."

"He was wearing heavy clothing and boots, and carried a backpack containing additional articles of clothing," the first policemen read from a list he held

Patricia Dick

in his hand, "two flannel shirts, a set of underwear, and an extra pair of gloves, those rolled up tightly and secured in inside pockets. He also had a can of Sterno, matches, four candy bars, two packages of dry soup, and two small cans of beans in outer pockets.

In a leather pouch which he wore around his neck, he carried a tiny compass, copy of Lewis and Clark's map showing how they'd returned from the West, his name and yours written on a folded note card, and $300 in bills plus change."

"We've placed the backpack and pouch in this bag," and second officer said as he handed the things to Grant.

"How he got to where he was is still a mystery," Harry Wright had stated. "The police have asked the public to report information which might answer our questions—conversations with him, sightings, rides he'd been given, those sorts of things. We're just glad that someone discovered his body before more time had gone by."

"Mr. Steiner," one of the policemen continued, "planned his excursion, as indicated by the heavy clothing which he was wearing, the items he put in his backpack, and particularly the map. He didn't just wander away. He planned but was not prudent in regards to when he started his exploration, I'll call it, four, possibly five, days ago. While we're not thinking foul play," he concluded, "we have ordered an autopsy."

The meeting over, Lauren, Luther, and Grant had returned to their home for the night, then returned to George's apartment a short time ago.

"Does having the autopsy bother you, Mom?" Grant asked.

"No," she answered. "What does bother me is his freezing to death."

"Mom, they didn't say that he froze," Luther said. "They said he'd been 'exposed to the weather'."

"I know they did, but he had to have frozen, the weather being what it is, and that's so awful. His being cold and alone. I feel just terrible about it," and she continued weeping.

"I don't feel neglectful," she said a few minutes later. "We saw him almost every weekend, and I called a couple of times a week, though often he wasn't at home. If he wasn't, I'd leave a message, but he seldom called back. Didn't the last time either. He'd tell me not worry over him, not to fuss, but oh how I wish I'd worried and fussed one more time!"

"He knew we loved him, Mom."

"He was always talking about how good we were to him," Luther reminded his mother.

"Maybe I should have just put my foot down. Told him he had to move to Assisting Living where he'd have been secure," Lauren said.

"I wouldn't have wanted to be around when you told him that!"

"You wouldn't have won and he'd have been terribly angry and hurt!"

"You'd have dehumanized him by taking away his right to choose," said Grant who was studying psychology. "You were showing him respect, Mom."

"Oh, I wish your dad were alive. I miss him so," and Lauren returned to her sobbing while Luther patted her shoulder, Grant held her hand, and the brothers cried their own tears.

Sap and Green People

"Mom," Luther said in a voice that registered discovery, "think about how clean the place is. Everything's picked up," and he circled the apartment with a sweep of his arm. "Not the usual, gosh-awful mess."

"You're right," Grant exclaimed. "No dirty dishes," and he opened the refrigerator, "No spoiled food. The fridge's been emptied out," and Lauren could hear him opening the refrigerator storage drawers. "One onion. Otherwise nothing."

"There's his checkbook. Set out on his desk," Luther observed. "Balanced," he added after flipping through its pages. "Bedroom and bath nearly spotless," he called after checking them.

"He put everything in order, Mom!" Grant declared. "Maybe figured he'd never get back."

"Maybe didn't want to."

"Probably got the biggest darned kick out of slipping away undetected."

"And think how excited he must have been when he started walking the Lewis and Clark Trail."

"So dear, such a rascal," Lauren said, and she smiled at the likelihood that what her sons were assuming was true and at the memory of her father-in-law. "See if there are any tea bags or ice cubes around here, would you please?. Something to sip. Something to drink," and she relaxed and settled against the back of her father-in-law's favorite chair.

Sap and Green People

As they'd done so many times since they'd moved into the Haven at Oak Hill seniors' complex some years earlier, Bill and Marg Davis and Henry and Georgia Graham were chatting and trading news in the Graham's apartment. She'd gone to her ophthalmologist, Marg reported, and he'd told her again that her macular vision had not degenerated further, very good news indeed, and when the Grahams asked about Bill's health, he said that though poky and creaky and gimpy, he was his usual "wonnerful self".

Georgia, steady, balanced, and practical, stated that at the moment, her arthritic knees weren't hurting too badly, her other physical concerns minimal, and though Henry hadn't pushed wheelchairs for three or four years, he continued visiting residents and helping in the campus clinic and otherwise make himself helpful.

The two couples expressed pride over the facts that their children were well, still married, and comfortably housed. The Grahams' doctor-sons were exceedingly busy, the Davises' son feeling more rewarded now that he was in a 'service' occupation rather than in sales.

Patricia Dick

The daughters and daughters-in-law were working, volunteering, and managing their households well. As for the grandchildren, those in high school and college were doing fine, and the older ones, in grad school or out of college altogether, were responsible adults who lived in a world markedly different from the post-World War II world that had confronted their grandparents.

As for the Haven, the black couple who'd moved into a patio home had added to a too-small resident minority, which was good for everyone, the friends agreed. Bruce Moffitt, the scholarly president of the Haven West's Residents Association when the Davises moved in, had recently died, likewise Essie Brinkman who'd been unable to adjust to her sister-in-law's death a year earlier. Jack and Gloria Clausen were aging gracefully in each other's loving company, and Norbert Blair had married a woman whom he met when sharing a documentary with residents of another seniors' community.

Because national and world affairs had become more depressing than interesting to the two couples, they gave topics of that ilk short shrift in the course of the conversation.

"The national debt?"

"Can't worry about it any longer," Bill said, and he shrugged his shoulders.

"The mess in Washington…"

"…stays a mess."

"Yet other countries seek to emulate our form of government, which makes some kind of a statement."

"Global disease is gettin' more attention."

"Seems like."

"Change in China and India, which we studied a couple of times in our discussion group, is coming about."

"Time 'll tell."

"Well, whatever changes, our lake and the stream are constants."

"Ducks keep flyin' in and out."

"Racoons still live in the woods and sewer system. Saw a couple the other night."

"New residents keep the complex filled up," and having touched on those and other matters in the span of an hour and a half, the four bid each other affectionate goodnights, and the Davises set out for their apartment.

"Henry mentioned the lake and birds and racoons," Bill said as he shortened his step and Marg lengthened hers, "but he might well have also pointed out that, except for the time when bats got into the belfry, during the whole while we've lived here, the clock has rung on the hour, no matter what."

"The seasons keep cycling, and I'm glad of that because I'm ready for spring."

"Moon keeps coming up and going down," Bill added, and Marg tugged at Bill's arm to stop him so they could pause to drink in the night.

In the east, a yellow moon shone through gossamer clouds which frenetic winds skipped across the sky. By turn, they ruffled Marg's hair, then plastered it and her clothing to her body.

"March wind in April," Bill commented, and Marg remembered an evening shared during the first spring of their courtship, back in the 1940's, when they'd stood in a park located near their college.

Sap and Green People

There, on the banks of a mill stream, with their arms wrapped around each other and their bodies pressed close, with darkness granting them cover, they'd listened to frogs herald the coming of spring and to their hearts pound wildly.

"Am I rushing you too fast?" Bill, then twenty-four and removed from military service by a year, had asked.

"No," twenty year old Marg had answered. Two years later, they married.

How sweet to remember, Marg thought. How important that spring, the spring when we fell in love.

In bed for the night, with their bodies chastely covered by a worn-smooth sheet, an aged Bill and Marg turned to each other and kissed. They kissed and they murmured. Stroked and held each other. Sensed smiles they'd not seen, heard words not spoken.

When Bill's grip relaxed and his breathing became heavy and regular, Marg rolled to her right side, her go-to-sleep side. Thus cued, a sleeping Bill did likewise, and Marg closed the gap between them by easing her back against Bill's chest and stomach.

Reflexively, Bill placed his left arm across her shoulder and closed his fingers around her breast. Had Marg been the first to fall asleep, Bill would have initiated the procedure, and thus they would have slept until one of them prompted a turning, several being required during the night in deference to their arthritis.

As she waited for sleep to ferry her away, Marg listened for traffic noises, few because the Haven was set back from the street. She also listened to water surge through pipes, an indication that a toilet had been flushed by another person who was also awake. She listened to the Venetian blind being lifted by the wind as it puffed through the open window, then tunked back in place when the wind tuckered out. To the soft, fleshy sound of Bill's breathing. And sometimes, only sometimes, she'd hear The Hum, an evasive, muted, night-time sound, mid-scale and reedy.

She'd listened for The Hum in other places. In the woods, church sanctuaries, libraries, hotels, other rooms in her apartment. When the nose of her car split the wind, its engine whirred, and its tires sang its own song. At the ocean and Lake Michigan. Mornings, afternoons, and evenings. She'd even had Bill listen with her. He'd strained to hear but couldn't, even with his hearing aids turned up. Indeed, only she heard The Hum. In the night when she was in her own bed. When conditions were just right, though she'd not been able to determine what those conditions were.

At first, Marg thought The Hum was the combined heartbeat of the persons living in her building. Then, The Sound of Life. The Common Consciousness. Collective Vitality. Commonality. George Bernard Shaw's Great Life Spirit, a notion that had always intrigued her. The Voice of God or the Holy Spirit. Whatever it was, having declared its source unknowable, she welcomed it, for it reassured her.

And, Dear God, how the elderly needed reassuring! They with their thinned hair, dimmed sight, and diminished hearing. Lumpy, sagging flesh. Blotchy, tissue-thin skin. Clogged arteries and porous bones. Blood clots and aneurysms. Varicose veins and fallen arches. Erratic stomachs. Minds which don't sense, think, remember. They who are lonely, disregarded. Hold them close, God. All of them.

She, herself, had been blessed with (how should she order them?) Bill's love and the love of her children, other family members, and friends. With having a good place to live. Good health and aptly prescribed medications. An educated and essentially sound mind. Faith and perspective. But others had not fared as well, and she felt compassion for them.

Be with us all and protect us, Marg prayed fervently. And when you can't protect or spare us, sustain us. Everyone. Everywhere.

And, Marg continued her prayer, though I know it's selfish of me to ask, God, please let Bill and me stay vital, stay green, to the ends of our lives. To the very, very ends.

ABOUT THE AUTHOR

Patricia Dick taught English and literature in several school systems, and during that time, she published articles in educational journals and was named a participant in the Missouri Writing Project based at the University of Missouri-Columbia.

As co-owner of a tour company, the author next wrote promotional travel literature until she decided to devote herself to her first love, writing fiction. In 2001, she was granted residency at the Ragdale Foundation artists' community in Lake Forest, Illinois where she edited *Sap and Green People*. She is presently editing a second novel and a series of short stories.

Mrs. Dick grew up in Michigan and now resides in Missouri. She lives in St. Louis with her husband, a "stone's throw" from her three children and their families.